FOUND OBJECTS

UNEXPECTED MAGIC – BOOK 1

CHRISTINE POPE

FOUND OBJECTS

ISBN: 978-1-946435-52-1

Copyright © 2022 by Christine Pope

Published by Dark Valentine Press

Cover design by Lou Harper

Ebook formatting by Indie Author Services

Chapter 1
Double Vision

I paused in the living room, set my bags down on the tile floor, and released a relieved breath.

Home sweet home.

Or at least, this little rented house would be home for the next three months. That's how long the shoot on *Fool's Gold,* the limited-run western series MovieStream was producing, was supposed to last. Once filming wrapped, I'd have to decide whether to stay in Albuquerque or tell myself this particular life change wasn't really working out for me and I should pack it in and return to something a little more familiar.

Not that I had much to go back to in Southern California.

Drama much, Penny? I asked myself. In point of fact, I had a whole family back there—my mother and father and younger brother Cade, along with the usual complement of cousins and aunts and uncles.

What I didn't have was a marriage. No, Dave

Zelinsky, my ex-husband, had managed to smash the whole notion of a happily-ever-after for the two of us into a bunch of itty-bitty little pieces.

In hindsight, I probably should've seen the warning signs. My job as a prop shopper—i.e., the person who procures props and other items needed on set for film, TV, or theater—forced me to have some pretty crazy hours. When Dave and I first got married, I'd thought my non-standard work schedule wouldn't matter so much, since he was a cop with the Rancho Cucamonga police department and therefore didn't exactly work a nine-to-five, either.

But even though he sometimes had to work nights and weekends, he still wasn't putting in eighty-hour weeks the way I often did when I was on set... which left him plenty of time to get into all kinds of mischief.

It's the oldest cliché in the book—husband gets caught cheating with the wife's best friend. Then again, when it happens to you, it doesn't feel quite so formulaic.

I'd been sent home from the set early because the D.P. left abruptly after getting a call from his doctor to inform him he'd caught strep throat from one of his kids. Movie people will soldier through all kinds of illnesses, but when it's something that contagious, the production generally will get shut down until the person in question is well enough to come back to work, or at least isn't in danger of transmitting the crud to everyone else on the crew. Since my ex had that day off, I'd been visualizing all sorts of fun things we could do with my unexpectedly free afternoon—going to the movies, driving over to the San Antonio Winery in Ontario for some wine tasting.

What I hadn't visualized was walking into the master suite to find Dave in bed with my best friend, Casey.

I'd stared in frozen, horrified shock for about three seconds, and then I blurted out, "Excuse me," and ran right back to the garage so I could jump in my SUV and get the hell out of there.

About three minutes later, my phone started ringing. And ringing, and ringing...until I turned it off and threw it back in my purse while I was stopped at a traffic light.

I drove to the nearest bar—which happened to be an Applebee's—drank down a glass of chardonnay, and then checked into a Marriott Residence Inn. No luggage, but I figured I'd go back to the house later and collect my stuff.

Long story short, I was divorced three months after that little incident, and when the shoot here in Albuquerque popped up about a month later, it sounded like the perfect solution to all my problems. I'd be able to put a thousand miles between Dave and me, and get established in the booming New Mexico film industry.

What did I have to lose?

Dave got the house in the divorce, since it was his before we were married. He'd tried to offer a few token protests about my walking out, had tried to convince me to go to counseling and salvage our relationship, but with that image of him and Casey in our bed indelibly etched on my brain, I knew seeing a couples therapist would be a waste of time. Maybe someday I'd be able to forgive, but I knew I sure as hell would never be able to forget.

And now I was here in Albuquerque.

My rented house actually looked nicer in person than it had in the ad on Craigslist. Ida Martinez, the owner, was a nice lady in her early sixties who didn't seem to have mastered the fine art of composing photos for real estate listings, even though she apparently had at least five or six scattered around the greater Albuquerque metro area. Maybe she wasn't quite the real estate mogul my father was—Gerald Briggs had been flipping houses in Southern California since the early 1990s—but she seemed to be doing okay for herself.

The house, which was a little over a thousand square feet, felt old to me, with its thick walls and beamed ceiling in the living room. A far cry from the two-story tract home in Rancho Cucamonga I'd shared with Dave, and an even more distant shout from the large house in Pacific Palisades where I'd grown up, a mid-century masterpiece that always felt a bit like living in a museum.

But, as promised, the kitchen and single bathroom in my rented home were nicely updated, with quartz countertops and gleaming chrome fixtures, and everything was as neat and clean as the proverbial pin. There was even a second bedroom I could use as an office...not that I planned to be home enough to require that kind of space.

The key thing, however, was that this house, even though twice the size of the apartment I'd moved to after bailing out of the Marriott Residence Inn, was going to cost me half the rent I'd been paying back in California. To be honest, I was so jaded by real estate prices in SoCal that I was kind of shocked to see how affordable Albuquerque actually had turned out to be. I could have rented a much bigger house without putting much of a strain on my budget, but I didn't need it, not with the kind of hours I'd be working. This place would suit me just fine.

I took my suitcases into the master bedroom and set them down on the floor. There were a few odds and ends still sitting in my Hyundai Palisade SUV, now parked in the driveway, but I'd intentionally traveled light. No point in hauling along a whole bunch of extra baggage when the whole reason for this venture was to start over.

And even though I'd driven almost four hundred miles that day, I still made myself put my clothes away, get my toiletries arranged in the bathroom, and empty my vehicle of the few bits and pieces I couldn't quite allow myself to leave behind in Rancho Cuca-monga—a picture of me and my dad from a few Christmases ago, a gorgeous glazed vase I'd bought at an artists' fair the year before.

Once that was done, I called in for some Door-Dash. I'd made sure to arrive on a Friday so I'd have the weekend to explore the town a bit before production began on Monday, but I knew I'd reached my limit for the day.

Albuquerque would have to wait.

The first week of shooting was slated to take place at I-25 Studios, just a jump up the freeway from my new house, which was located in a neighborhood called Nob Hill, not too far from downtown. Even though I'd been working as a prop shopper—with a couple of credits as a property master and set dresser —for the greater part of seven years, I still always got those "first day of school" jitters when arriving on the set of a new production. Over time, those of us in the crew would form friendships and create a rough camaraderie achieved through working so many hours together on a show, but when things were new, they were always just a little nerve-wracking.

The morning air as I got out of my SUV felt awfully cool for mid-September, and I had to remind myself that we were at more than five thousand feet of elevation here in Albuquerque, and the nights got chilly in a way they really never did in the Inland Empire. I shivered a little in my leather jacket and hoped I'd get acclimated sooner rather than later. The shoot wasn't scheduled to wrap up until the middle of December, and I really didn't want to think about what those mornings would feel like.

But the coffee at the craft service table was excellent, as was the assortment of rolls and bagels and muffins that had been set out. Because I was used to eating on set, I hadn't bothered with any breakfast at the house, even though I'd gotten some frozen egg bites—yummy little nuggets of egg and cheese and bacon—and protein bars while grocery shopping over the weekend.

More people filed in to the big pavilion that housed the craft service and catering tables while I was sipping my coffee and munching my way through a plain bagel. Obviously, all of the newcomers were complete strangers to me, but I did my usual quick assessment to see who looked friendly, who seemed grouchy, who might turn out to be the sort of casual friend I could go out to have a drink with at the end of a long week of shooting.

Nothing about this group seemed that much different from the crews I'd worked with back in L.A., although I noticed there were a lot more people who appeared to be of Hispanic descent, which wasn't so strange. Los Angeles had a very large Latinx population, but New Mexico's was even bigger.

A pretty woman who appeared to be around my own age of thirty-two, or maybe a little bit older, smiled at me and headed over after getting herself a cup of coffee. "Hi," she said, although I noticed she didn't attempt to shake hands...probably because both of mine were full. "I'm Joy Zamora."

"Penny Briggs," I responded. I recognized her name from the crew list, since I did my best to familiarize myself with my new co-workers' names whenever I signed on to a production. Joy was the set hairdresser, someone who had a pretty impressive IMDB resume. It made sense the producers would hire someone with her kind of experience, since hairdressing a period piece like *Fool's Gold* was much more demanding than a contemporary shoot.

"How're you liking Albuquerque?" she asked next, a slight twinkle in her brown eyes. Even though film shoots tended to be casual in the extreme, her long, subtly highlighted hair fell in perfect waves over her shoulders, and her makeup game was definitely on point. Standing next to her, I looked like someone who should have been cleaning the toilets or something.

Trying my best to sound casual, I replied, "Is it that obvious that I'm a transplant?"

The small smile she was wearing didn't fade a bit. "Well, most of us have worked together before—we're kind of a tight-knit group. When I saw your name on the production team, I looked you up and saw you were from California. It's sometimes a bit of a culture shock coming here, so...."

"Oh, I don't know about that," I said easily. Just because I felt like the proverbial fish out of water didn't mean I wanted to admit it right off the bat. Also, I did my best to push aside the little niggling thought that wanted to question why she was being so friendly. Just because I'd had a lifetime of wondering whether I was worthy didn't mean someone like Joy, with her open, friendly expression, had any kind of ulterior motive for initiating the conversation. Keeping my tone light, I added, "I mean, you have Smith's instead of Ralph's and Safeway instead of Vons, but otherwise—"

"That's not exactly what I meant," she cut in, but in a friendly sort of way. A sip of coffee, and she added, "We do things a little differently in New Mexico."

About all I could do was shrug. True, I could tell it was going to take me a while to get the layout of the city figured out, since I'd managed to get myself lost once or twice even with the help of the nav in my SUV. Otherwise, though, Albuquerque didn't feel that foreign. There were a lot of the same national chains here, and although the outlines of the peaks were very different, I still found myself somehow comforted by the mountain range to the east of town, since it reminded me vaguely of the San Bernardino Mountains I'd left behind in Southern California, a range that had been a constant backdrop in the house I'd shared with my ex.

"That's probably a good thing," I remarked dryly, and she chuckled.

"I think you'll do fine."

Our conversation was cut short there, because the assistant director announced that everyone needed to be in their places in five minutes, and there was the usual hustle of people downing their coffee or running to the bathroom or whatever else they needed to do before the actual work got started. Even though the bulk of my work was already done, I was still expected to be on set to move props around if necessary, or—although it didn't happen very often

—make an emergency run to grab something the director had decided he needed.

Movies and TV shows were rarely filmed in chronological order, and so the first scene of the day was actually from the middle of the second episode, a scene that was intended to take place inside the office of the fictional town's doctor, who was supposed to be digging bullets out of our hero, who'd gotten shot in the previous scene. The actor playing the doctor—Jim Lincoln, a man whose IMDB credits list was longer than my arm, since he'd been playing character roles for more years than I'd been alive—reached for the wire-rimmed spectacles sitting on his desk.

Or actually, he reached for the spectacles that *should* have been sitting on his desk.

"Where are my goddamn glasses?" he growled.

"And cut!" the director called out, those two words packed with annoyance. His name was Troy Michaels, and he looked to be about ten years older than I, putting him in his early forties, with thinning brown hair and a permanent frown etched into his forehead...probably because of situations like this one. He shot an irritated look at the costume designer, a fragile, birdlike woman with light blonde hair pulled back into a no-nonsense ponytail. "Deanna, where are his glasses?"

"I put them right on the desk earlier this morning," she responded, her voice firmer than her appearance might have indicated.

"Well, they're not there now."

A hurried search of the set and the costume area

followed the director's comment, but the glasses didn't appear to be forthcoming.

"I can't believe I'm dealing with this kind of crap on the first day of shooting," Troy Michaels growled.

I couldn't blame him for his irritation. Yes, all kinds of annoying stuff could and did happen on set, but generally not on the very first day, when everyone was fresh and wanted to present their best faces. This sort of thing didn't make the costume designer look very good, since she—or, more likely, her assistant— was responsible for making sure every piece of a character's wardrobe, including accessories such as eyeglasses and watches and jewelry, was in the right place at the right time.

Usually, I was quiet on set and did my job without much comment. Right then, however, I remembered how I'd poked around an antique mall on Saturday afternoon and had spotted a large selection of vintage and antique eyeglasses at one of the vendors there. Shopping at antique malls and second-hand stores was a habit of mine from way back, since I figured it always helped to know where I could find obscure and interesting bibs and bobs that might be needed for a production, even if they weren't on the list of props I'd been given.

"Excuse me," I said, and the director shot me a vaguely surprised look, as if one of the chairs on set had suddenly started speaking.

"Who're you?"

"Penny Briggs," I replied, reminding myself I shouldn't be too offended that Troy Michaels didn't know who I was. After all, the production company had hired me, not the director. "I'm the prop shopper."

"And?" he returned.

"I stumbled across a vendor with a bunch of antique eyeglasses when I was out exploring this weekend," I replied, refusing to let myself be offended by his dismissive attitude. "If you want, I can run over to the antique mall and get a couple of pairs. It'll slow us down a little, but the whole errand shouldn't take me more than an hour at the most."

The director let out a breath, his expression still irritated. However, he obviously decided that it was better to lose an hour than a whole day, because he said, "All right. Go ahead and see what you can find."

I nodded, trying my best to ignore the way the entire cast and crew was staring at me. Some people might have liked being the center of attention, but I wasn't one of them...probably part of the reason why I enjoyed my job so much. It tended to be "fly under the radar" kind of work, only attracting notice when you screwed something up.

Given the go-ahead, I hurried out to my SUV and climbed in, then started to roll out of the parking lot while I was still putting on my seatbelt. The antique mall was located southwest of downtown—and luckily, I'd noticed when I was visiting over the weekend that it opened at nine rather than the usual retail ten o'clock. Otherwise, my promise of turning this errand around in an hour would have been a gross underestimate.

Traffic was a little cloggy but felt like barely anything at all compared to what I was used to back in Southern California. Within fifteen minutes, I'd pulled into the lot at the antique mall and had parked a few spaces down from a beat-up old minivan, the only other occupant of the lot. Clearly, antique shopping wasn't a first-thing priority on a Monday morning the way it had turned out to be for me.

But that was fine. I disliked tripping over people while trying to shop, so this worked out much better anyway.

I made my way to the stall at the back of the antique mall where I'd spotted the collection of eyeglasses over the weekend. Unlike most malls of its type, this one seemed to be run by a single proprietor rather than everyone managing their own little micro-shops, and I had to go in search of him once I'd determined that the glasses I wanted were still in the case.

The owner of the antique mall looked like he was probably in his late sixties, a slender Hispanic man not much taller than me, with thick gray hair combed straight back from his forehead and a tidy little Vincent Price mustache. I told him what I wanted, and he dug a set of keys out of his desk and followed me back to the stall where all the glasses were located.

"That pair," I said, pointing at the glasses on the top shelf of the case and slightly over to the right. I wasn't exactly sure what had drawn me to them, since there were several others in the case that also looked extremely similar to the ones I'd seen on the prop list for the production, but long ago I'd learned not to ignore that inner voice, or whatever you wanted to call it.

Instinct, I supposed. I'd always been very good at finding exactly the right thing for the occasion, whether the item in question was the perfect pair of Jimmy Choo sandals for my cousin's wedding at nearly seventy-five percent off, or scaring up a throw pillow with the exact combination of colors to match a friend's sofa. In fact, I was so good at that kind of stuff that for a while I'd considered becoming a personal shopper.

Of course, one mention of the career I'd been considering had made my mother practically recoil in horror.

"You want to *shop* for other people?" she'd demanded, looking like I'd just announced that I was going to shave my head and start handing out flowers to people in airports.

If that was even a thing anymore.

At the same time, I had a pretty good idea of exactly what had freaked her out so much. Her rich friends were precisely the types who would hire a personal shopper, and I had to bet that the notion of her daughter working for any of them was what made her worry I would embarrass her and, by extension, the whole family.

Not that she hadn't considered me an embarrassment pretty much my entire life.

At any rate, it wasn't too long after that little conversation that a producer friend of my father's had floated the whole prop-shopper idea to me, and

I'd gone along with it, mostly because it sounded like fun and yet was something that wouldn't make my mother cringe with mortification.

Funny how I was still so worried about pleasing her, even though her behavior over the years had pretty much proved that she didn't give a damn about me.

The antique mall owner pulled the glasses out of the case and handed them over. They had thin gold frames, and from the way the light caught in the lenses, I could tell they were just clear glass and not prescription.

Even better.

"I'll take them," I said, and the shop owner nodded.

"Anything else?"

It was on the tip of my lips to say no, but then I realized it would probably be smart to pick up a second pair, just in case of another mishap on set. There was another pair in the case that looked almost identical to the ones that had called to me, except they had a few grayish smudges of oxidation on the earpieces. Still, that was the sort of thing which could probably be buffed out if necessary.

"Those ones," I told him, pointing at the glasses in question.

He got them out as well, then told me he'd take them up to the front. I followed him to the cash register and watched as he carefully wrapped each pair in bubble wrap, and slipped them into a paper bag.

Fifty bucks later, I was back in my Palisade with the precious glasses riding on the passenger seat. Fifteen minutes after that, I walked onto the sound stage, where everyone appeared to be lounging around, awaiting my return. That might have seemed strange to someone not familiar with how film and TV worked—why not shoot another scene while they were waiting for me?—but it would have taken more time to get everything together on a different set than the amount I'd needed to run my little errand.

"Got them," I announced, and headed toward Deanna, the costume designer, bag outstretched in one hand.

"'Them'?" she echoed as she peered into the bag.

"I got a spare pair, just in case," I told her. "But they're not in quite as good shape."

Deanna pulled out both pairs of eyeglasses, unwrapped them, and looked at them with a critical eye. "These are great," she said after a moment, and I allowed myself to relax.

It looked like we'd be able to get back to work.

"All right," the assistant director called out as Troy Michaels stood next to him, still looking annoyed. Maybe that was his habitual expression. "Everyone, back in place."

The crew dutifully took up their assigned positions, and the "doctor" headed back to the set, where his replacement glasses now sat on his desk.

"And...action!"

I watched from the side, since there wasn't

anything else I needed to do at this point. At the same time, I found myself almost holding my breath. What if the new glasses didn't fit? What if they were more fragile than they looked, and one of the lenses fell out at a critical moment? What if...?

"What the fuck!" Jim Lincoln burst out. He'd just settled the glasses on the bridge of his nose, but almost as quickly, he pulled them back off and all but threw them onto the desk in front of him.

"Cut!" Troy Michaels barked, sounding more annoyed than ever.

Not that I could blame him. The eyeglasses I'd just bought were supposed to solve a problem, not create a new one.

"There is something *seriously* wrong with those glasses," Jim said. His whimsical eyebrows—probably part of the reason he got cast in these sorts of roles so often—were pulled together in a scowl, but I could have sworn he looked almost more frightened than angry.

"'Wrong' how?" Deanna asked. She'd also been standing off to one side, but a little closer to the director than my almost hiding place. "They're in very good condition."

"I don't give a shit about their 'condition,'" Jim retorted. "When I put them on, I felt like I was about to pass out."

Deanna and Troy exchanged a glance. I knew there were rumors that Jim Lincoln bent the elbow a little more than was preferable, and I could only guess that the director and the costume designer were wondering whether he'd tipped something into his morning coffee while I was out running my errand.

"Well, let's try the other pair," Troy said, his tone a little too soothing, as if he knew he needed to humor his actor if he was going to get any work out of him today at all.

The director had barely finished speaking before Deanna had hurried over and set down the replacement pair of spectacles and retrieved the ones that had given Jim so much trouble. As he set those ones down on his nose and announced they seemed to be just fine, she handed the original pair to me and said in a murmur, "Check these out when you have a chance. If there really is something wrong with them, then you should probably take them back."

I almost told her the antique mall didn't allow any returns, then decided it wasn't worth the effort. Instead, I nodded, wrapping my fingers around the glasses and then beginning to make my way toward the back of the soundstage. I figured I could surreptitiously try them on there and see if they really were defective in some way.

My own fault for not trying them on before I bought them, I supposed.

With Jim and his glasses apparently settled, filming began for real this time. Since I didn't think I would be needed for a while—and even if I were, I was still within earshot—I paused by the back door to the sound stage and set the glasses on my nose.

At once, the darkened stage around me seemed to disappear, and I saw a bright, sunlit canyon, its walls red rock, marked here and there by scrubby ever-greens that I thought might be junipers. A light wind stirred dry grasses, although the scene was utterly silent.

An ingrained habit of knowing to remain quiet at all times during filming stopped me from letting out a startled gasp. Instead, I lifted the glasses, and the ordinary darkness of a soundstage in use settled around me. I put them back on, and the canyon scene appeared in front of my eyes once more.

What the hell was the deal with these things?

I had absolutely no idea. Once more, I took off the glasses, except this time it was to scrutinize them as best I could in the dim lighting. Were they some kind of trick glasses that had some sort of weird virtual-reality mechanism embedded in them?

That theory didn't seem very plausible, though. For one thing, the VR headsets I'd seen were big, bulky things, not the flimsy, antique-appearing glasses I held now. And if someone had managed to invent VR spectacles this lightweight, I doubted something so rare would have ended up in a stall at a cut-rate antique mall in Albuquerque.

Gingerly, I put the glasses back on. In some part of my mind, I was probably hoping that the scene would disappear, that the whole thing had just been some sort of weird hallucination and nothing more.

Unfortunately, the canyon scene was back...with a slight difference this time. Yes, there were the red rocks, and there were the juniper trees, but a shadow passed over the dry grass, as if a hawk or a raven had flown overhead. The scene felt so real that I found myself flinching and glancing upward, as if I thought the bird was somehow here in the soundstage with me.

Heart beating a little faster now, I quickly pulled off the glasses and shoved them in my jacket pocket.

Just what in the *hell* was going on?

Chapter 2
The Enchanted Circle

Because we had a scene change after that first one, I didn't have much time to stew over the conundrum of the strange glasses. And even though it wasn't strictly kosher to sidle up to one of the leads and start asking questions, I couldn't quite stop myself from murmuring to Jim as he was walking off the set for a wardrobe change, "What did you see when you put on those glasses?"

He shot me a look that managed to be both irritated and a bit startled. Most likely, he was wondering why a lowly prop shopper would have the temerity to address him directly. "I didn't 'see' anything," he snapped. "I felt dizzy for a minute. Those things were garbage."

And then he pushed past me, headed to the wardrobe department. I didn't try to stop him, since I knew the director would not be happy if he found out someone as far down the rungs as me was preventing one of his leads from making a quick costume change.

When we finally took a break for lunch a little before two, I sat down with a salad and an iced tea at an unoccupied table a little ways away from the rest of the crew. In general, I'd try to sit with the crew even if I didn't know any of them, but the incident with the glasses had rattled me more than I wanted to admit, and I wanted to take some time to pull myself together. I still was a lot shakier than I would have liked, and thought I wasn't in any shape to be social.

However, I apparently wasn't going to be allowed my solitude, because Joy Zamora came over before I'd even taken the first bite of my salad, and settled herself across the table from me.

"Hey," she said after sipping from some bottled water. "Are you doing okay? You look a little shaken up."

"I do?" I responded, doing my best to repress a flicker of annoyance. Not at Joy so much, but more at myself. I thought I'd cultivated a better poker face than that.

"Don't worry," she said quickly. "I doubt anyone else noticed anything." A pause, and she added, "Was it something with those glasses? Jim was acting a little weird when he came back for his wardrobe change and a touch-up, but I knew better than to ask him about it."

Those damn glasses were still in my jacket pocket. Some part of me wanted to brush off the weird experience and pretend it had never happened, but I knew what I'd seen. And at least Joy seemed sympathetic. Why, I wasn't sure, since we were basically complete strangers, but maybe she was just one of those kind souls who was always looking out for lost puppies or newcomers who didn't quite seem to fit in.

"Maybe," I said. I pulled the glasses out of my pocket and set them on the tabletop. "Why don't you try them on?"

For just a second, she seemed almost reluctant, but then she gave a small lift of her shoulders, picked up the problematic spectacles, and set them on her nose.

Her eyes widened, and almost as quickly as she'd put them on, she pulled them back off again and put them down on the tabletop with a faint clang of metal against metal.

"That is messed up," she said as she blinked several times, apparently trying to clear her vision of whatever the glasses had just shown her. Although we were sitting outside, taking advantage of the mild early fall weather, she wasn't wearing sunglasses. Her lashes were so thick and long, I wondered for a second if they were false.

Envy-inducing eyelashes aside, I could completely agree with Joy's statement. "You saw it?" I asked, knowing I sounded way too eager. "The canyon, I mean."

My hopes got deflated instantly as she replied, "I didn't see a canyon. Just a weird blur of colors." Before I could say anything in response, however, she went on, "But that doesn't necessarily mean anything. Maybe you were able to get better resolution on whatever-it-was than I could."

"Or maybe I'm going crazy," I remarked sourly as I reached for my iced tea.

The corners of her eyes crinkled in amusement. "I kind of doubt that," she said. "After all, I did see something, even if it wasn't exactly what you saw. No, I think those glasses must be hexed or something."

For a second, I could only blink at her, at the completely casual way she'd uttered that crazy word. "'Hexed'?" I managed after a moment. "You mean, like cursed or something?"

"Or something," Joy said. She sounded absolutely calm as she made that statement, as if it wasn't a big deal that our conversation had suddenly taken a left turn at Albuquerque...so to speak.

"This is a joke, right?" I was doing my best not to get upset, even if I could have a temper to match my red hair if provoked enough. Although the people I'd met on set so far had seemed neutral, if not overly friendly, I couldn't help wondering whether they'd decided to play some kind of joke on the new girl.

If that was the case, I didn't think it was very funny.

"No joke," Joy said calmly, then took a bite of her sandwich. One eyebrow lifted as she continued. "Let me guess—you don't believe in hexes and that kind of stuff."

"Nope," I said, my tone flat. No one could ever have accused me of being the New Age, airy-fairy type. I knew I was a Pisces because I'd been born in late February, but that was about the extent of my esoteric knowledge.

"That's all right," Joyce said. She drank some of her bottled water before adding, "It exists whether you believe in it or not. There's definitely something funky going on with those glasses, though. I think you should talk to my cousin Isaac."

This *non sequitur* made me blink again. "Why should I talk to your cousin?"

"He owns a New Age kind of store in Santa Fe," she replied. "But, more important, he's also a *brujo*."

I was pretty sure I'd never heard that word before. "A what?"

"A male witch."

My suspicions about being the butt of a practical joke returned full force. "Like a warlock?"

At once, Joy shook her head, and her expression sobered. "No, it's not the same thing at all. Warlocks are users of magic who use their powers for ill. A *brujo* is a male witch, someone who walks the right-hand path."

All the words were English, but she might as well have been speaking Swahili for all that those words were making any sense. Tone dubious, I said, "So, you think I should talk to him because he might be able to figure out what's going on with these glasses?"

"If he can't, I don't know who else could." She paused there and started fishing around in her purse, and at last pulled out a handsome black business card with some gold lettering and a mystical-looking symbol on it. "That's his shop," she went on as she pushed the card across the painted aluminum tabletop toward me. "It's right in downtown Santa Fe. You should take the glasses to him and see what he has to say."

I was still skeptical, but since I didn't want to be downright rude, I went ahead and picked up the card, glancing at it before I tucked it into my pocket.

The Enchanted Circle. That must be the name of the shop, especially since it said right below that, *Isaac Zamora, Owner.*

When exactly I was supposed to go running up to Santa Fe, I had no idea, since we were scheduled to work until seven every night and the hours printed on the card were apparently ten in the morning until six in the evening, Monday through Saturday.

I didn't argue, though. No, I just sent Joy a wan smile and hoped I wouldn't have to deal with any more strange incidents...supernatural or otherwise... for the next few days.

As it turned out, the week that followed was surprisingly without incident. And since the union had enforced a five-day work week for the shoot, that meant I had Saturday off.

Which also meant I had the day free to go up to Santa Fe and see this Isaac Zamora person if I chose.

Except...I really didn't want to do that. I hadn't bothered to try returning the glasses to the antique mall, but had instead shoved them in an empty drawer in my bedroom dresser. Once or twice, I'd been tempted to pull them out to check whether they would still show me that odd scene in the canyon. However, my common sense had asserted itself and let me know they were probably better off being left alone.

So, I killed time by going to the grocery store and puttering around the house, tidying up and wiping down the counters in the kitchen and bathroom. The place really didn't need a lot of work, since I basically went home to sleep and shower before I headed back to the set the next day, but at least I felt as though I'd accomplished something during my free time.

However, those stopgaps only kept me busy until around three-thirty, which meant I still had plenty of time to get up to Santa Fe before Isaac's shop closed at six.

Damn it.

Common sense warred with curiosity, but eventually I let out an exasperated breath, fetched the glasses from their hiding place in the dresser, and did a quick primp in front of the bathroom mirror to make sure my hair wasn't a wreck and to apply some lipstick.

Not because you're trying to impress anyone, I reassured myself as I picked up my keys and headed out to the carport where my SUV was parked. *You just don't want to go to Santa Fe looking like a walking disaster area.*

Maybe that was even the truth. The wound from my divorce was still raw enough that I had absolutely no desire to pursue anything remotely resembling a relationship, even if Joy's cousin Isaac turned out to be someone interesting.

Not that I would even want to consider getting involved with a person who thought magic was real.

I pointed my Palisade north along I-25, telling myself that if nothing else, this would be a good opportunity to see something of Santa Fe. When I was first looking for a place to live here in New Mexico, I'd briefly considered moving to the state's capital city, just because it seemed somehow more exotic and interesting than Albuquerque. But an hour commute didn't sound like much fun, and I could tell right away that Santa Fe was a much more expensive place to live.

As I was sitting in the driveway, I'd entered the address for the Enchanted Circle into my Hyundai's nav system so I could have it guide me to the store. As Joy had said, the shop was located right in the heart of downtown Santa Fe, and on a beautiful Saturday in late September, the city was absolutely jam-packed with tourists. I circled the block where the shop was located a few times—no pun intended—before realizing that getting street parking just wasn't going to happen. Instead, I had to park in a large structure a few blocks away from the shop, and even then I had to go to the roof level before I found an open space.

As soon as I got out of my SUV, I noticed that the temperature here was a good bit cooler than down in Albuquerque, maybe even as much as ten degrees lower. I paused to get my leather jacket off the passenger seat and shrugged it on, then took the stairs down to street level. According to the map I pulled up on my phone, I just needed to head down San Francisco Street for a block, then jog down Galisteo so I ended up on Water Street. It looked like the store was in the middle of the block.

The sidewalks were almost as crowded as the streets had been, so my progress wasn't as fast as I would have liked it to be, thanks to having to dodge tourists who kept pausing to look in store windows, or stop to stare down at their phones to make sure they were going the right direction. My annoyance kept ratcheting up as I walked, and I wanted to scold myself for being so impulsive and coming up here on a wild goose chase. I could have just stayed home, put my feet up, and binged Netflix or Hulu, both of which had been thoughtfully included as part of my rent.

But I was here now, so the best thing to do was just to push on. Eventually, I found myself approaching the entrance to The Enchanted Circle, which had the store name printed in gold in an elegant, slightly Art Nouveau font on the glass. Deep blue velvet curtains framed a display in the front window, showcasing a variety of crystals and books and arcane-looking sculptures and instruments. The place had a certain late Victorian vibe to it, despite being housed in a typically Southwest building of pale blush-colored stucco, similar to many others I'd passed on my way here.

In other words, it looked just about like what I'd expected a metaphysical store to look like.

As soon as I walked in, a wash of incense hit my nose. However, it wasn't the sticky-sweet sort of incense I'd smelled before—mostly when friends in high school were trying to hide their pot use from their parents—but something sharp and spicy and aromatic.

"Can I help you?"

A man's voice, not quite deep enough to be a baritone, edged with the same faint accent I'd heard from Joy and some of the other people I'd met in Albuquerque. I couldn't even really describe that accent, not distinct enough to be Spanish, but somehow still evoking a population whose families had lived here longer than the United States had been an actual country.

Instinctively, I looked up...only to realize the man who'd spoken was sitting in a wheelchair in front of the display case that housed the cash register and a fairly impressive display of crystal specimens. I adjusted my gaze accordingly, noticing that he had jet-black hair and eyes to match, and wore a simple dark gray pullover top and jeans. A faint dark stubble dusted his jaw, and a certain tightness about his sculpted mouth spoke of pain dealt with and dismissed long before now.

Damn. I hadn't expected Joy's cousin to be quite so spectacular.

"Can I help you?" he said again, and I realized I'd been staring.

"Um, I'm not sure," I replied, and took a step forward, even as I wondered how he had ended up in a wheelchair. A congenital issue? Some kind of accident? Trying my best to sound casual, I went on, "Your cousin Joy told me I should come and talk to you about something weird that happened to me this week."

"I do specialize in weird," Isaac said with a flash of a smile.

Somehow, I managed to ignore the flush that hit my cheeks as our eyes met. This was ridiculous. Was I back in junior high or something?

"It's these glasses," I said, fumbling in my jacket pocket to get them out. "When I put them on, it's almost as if I'm watching a movie through them. What I'm seeing isn't anything that's actually in front of me."

"Let me take a look," Isaac said, and made a motion as if to roll his chair closer to me.

Since I didn't want him to make any extra effort on my account, I quickly closed up the space between us and handed over the glasses. This close, I could see a few lines around Isaac's dark eyes, and I guessed he was probably a few years older than I.

And I also couldn't help noticing how sooty and thick and black his hair was, the kind of hair that made you want to bury your fingers in it.

Since I wouldn't allow myself to do anything so remotely crazy, I stood there with my hands buried in my pockets, praying he hadn't noticed the way I'd apparently taken leave of my senses. To my relief, he wasn't looking at me at all, but instead kept turning the antique spectacles over in his hands, almost as though he was trying to detect some sort of vibrations in them.

Which seemed pretty damn woo-woo to me, but then, he was a *brujo*, right?

"Aren't you going to try them on?" I asked. Maybe it was just the silence in the room getting to me. I noticed we were the only two people in the store, which seemed kind of odd, considering how busy the other shops downtown had appeared to be. Maybe a New Age store wasn't most people's idea of a destination when visiting Santa Fe. For all I knew, Isaac Zamora and his store catered mostly to locals.

"In a minute," he said, his tone almost absent, as though he was focusing most of his attention on the glasses and didn't have much left over to spare for me. "I want to get a feel for them first." Then he glanced up, his expression slightly amused. "You can look around a bit while I'm working with these."

That sounded like a dismissal to me—maybe having me hovering around was messing up his juju or something—so I wandered over to one of the bookcases placed up against the back wall of the shop and began perusing the titles. It was definitely an eclectic collection, with volumes on everything from reiki healing to Area 51. In fact, the array of arcane subjects was just a little dizzying to a neophyte like me.

A few minutes passed, during which Isaac didn't seem to be doing anything except sitting there in his wheelchair and holding the spectacles lightly in his hands. I didn't want to seem too curious, but I still couldn't help glancing over my shoulder from time to time.

At length, though, he said, "Yes, they're definitely charged. What do you see when you put them on?"

I came back over to the spot where he waited in his wheelchair. "It's some kind of canyon with red rock and junipers. Would that be somewhere around here?"

"Possibly," he said. "We have some red rock here in New Mexico, although it's not as widespread as what you'd see in a place like Sedona in Arizona."

"Did you see the same thing?" I asked, since I'd caught a glimpse of him putting on the glasses briefly before taking them off again so he could once again balance them on the tips of his fingers.

"No," Isaac replied at once. "I got a blur of colors, but nothing more."

Which was just about what Joy had told me she'd seen. I mentioned that to Isaac, adding, "Is Joy like you? A witch, I mean."

The words sounded so awkward falling off my lips, I wished I could take them back. However, Isaac's mouth only lifted faintly at the corners as he said, "Not exactly. She has a few small gifts, but she chooses not to use them most of the time. All the same, I think that's why she was able to see something. Someone with no gift at all would most likely only experience an odd dizziness they couldn't explain."

Which was exactly what had happened with Jim Lincoln. I told Isaac about that incident, and he nodded.

"Yes, someone without any magic might feel a bit off when wearing the glasses, but it wouldn't affect them any more than that."

How weird was it that we were discussing magic and magical abilities as if they were no big deal? The practical side of my brain wanted to assert itself and remark that magic wasn't real. All the same, I couldn't deny that something very strange was going on here.

"Then why could I see a complete scene when you couldn't?" I asked, knowing how plaintive that question sounded.

"Because it responded to your magic differently," Isaac said, his tone calm.

All right, this was getting ridiculous. "I don't have any magic," I blurted out, but he only gave me another one of those Sphinx-like smiles in response.

"Oh, you do," he replied. "I sensed it the moment you walked in the door. Your family must be very powerful."

Since I didn't quite know how to respond to that statement, I just blinked at him. "My family doesn't have any magic," I said flatly. "They're just a bunch of regular people from Southern California."

"Oh, but they must," Isaac said. His tone wasn't remotely argumentative, but I could tell he wasn't going to back down from his position. "Or at least, your mother must. That's how magic is passed down

—through one's mother. My own mother was a powerful *bruja*, but she had no daughters, only sons, and I'm the only one of her children who has any magic. But the only way I could have children with magic would be for them to inherit it from their own mother."

Okay, a sex-linked trait that could only be passed through the female line. That made some biological sense...not that any of the rest of our discussion was making any sense at all.

Since Isaac had looked so serious as he tried to explain all this, I held back the laughter that had started bubbling on my lips as soon as he'd said my mother must have passed her magic on to me. If there was a less magical person on the face of the planet than Kara Briggs, I sure hadn't met her yet. My mother's entire existence revolved around socializing with the other "ladies who lunched" in our part of the world, as well as spending vast amounts of time organizing various charity functions of one sort or another. However, I didn't think any true charity was involved on her part... well, beyond the need to be seen as someone who donated her money and time to the trendy causes of the day.

Was I being harsh? Probably. But even though I'd certainly never wanted for anything in my life and on the surface we appeared to be the stereotypical happy, prosperous family, anyone who paid close enough attention would have seen soon enough that the lavish affection she showered on Cade, my younger brother and the "miracle" baby she'd had at forty-three, definitely didn't extend to her oldest child.

Which was fine. I didn't need my mother's approval. But even if I were willing to accept the existence of magic...and I didn't know whether I was... one thing I definitely knew was that Kara Briggs was no witch.

At least, not in the magical sense.

"My mother isn't a witch," I said flatly. "Not a chance in hell."

Isaac's arched brows drew together. I guessed he wasn't thrilled by my flat denial.

"Were you adopted?" he asked next.

I'd definitely wished for that to be the case quite a few times in my youth, but I knew I was my parents' child, even if they were still trying to figure out where my red hair had come from. Then again, it was a recessive trait that seemed to pop up out of nowhere sometimes, so my flaming mane wasn't exactly conclusive evidence that they hadn't contributed to my genetic makeup. Besides....

"No chance," I said, this time summoning an ironic smile. "I've seen the pictures taken at the hospital when I was born. I'm definitely not adopted."

Isaac fell silent for a moment. Then his shoulders lifted—broad shoulders, muscled enough that I guessed he was pretty dedicated to staying in good shape despite the wheelchair—and he said, "Well, we can worry about that later. Have you had any odd experiences in your life that made you wonder if you were somehow different from everyone around you? Any unusual traits you didn't seem to share with your friends or family?"

My life, prosperous as it had been, definitely wasn't anything close to strange or unusual. And yet....

"Well," I replied, hesitating for a second. Did I really want to go spilling all my deep, dark secrets to a guy I'd just met?

Then again, my "secret" really wasn't that much of a secret, considering it was partly what made me good at my job.

Isaac waited calmly for me to go on. I guessed that he'd had to cultivate a good deal of patience in his life, considering his disability.

"I'm good at finding things," I said at last.

"What sort of things?" he asked. It seemed he'd sat up a little straighter in his wheelchair as soon as he heard my reply, and his dark eyes were lively with interest.

"Anything," I responded with a helpless little shrug. "I mean, it's more like I need the perfect birthday present for a friend, or the exact right pair of shoes for a special event...or a prop for a movie shoot...and I just sort of stumble across it."

"Like these glasses?" he said, nodding toward the pair of spectacles he still held. Before I could answer, he went on, "Why don't you tell me how you found them?"

Was Isaac trying to imply there was some sort of mystical power behind my weird little ability to find the exact thing I needed? That seemed like a hell of a stretch to me, but whatever.

"Well," I said. "I knew I had to find something similar to the glasses that had somehow gotten lost on set. I'd already scoped out an antique mall in Albuquerque and had spotted some in one of the stalls there, so I ran over to see if I could find something that would work. And as soon as I saw this pair"—I inclined my head slightly toward the gold-framed glasses Isaac was holding—"I just knew they were the right ones. But I also grabbed a second pair, figuring it would be a good idea to have a spare, just in case. And good thing, too, because the actor who tried to wear the original glasses ripped them off his face almost immediately."

For a moment, Isaac was silent, as though pondering what I'd just told him. Then he said, "And this kind of thing happens to you often?"

"Yes," I replied, although part of me wanted to lie and say no, this was a complete fluke.

Problem was, I knew my current situation was anything but a fluke.

Isaac gave a very faint nod. From his demeanor, I guessed that what I'd told him had just corroborated a theory he'd already formulated.

"I think you're a lodestone," he said at last.

I blinked. "A what?"

"A lodestone is like a magnet," he told me, and I shot him an irritated glance.

"I know what a lodestone is," I snapped. "But how can a person be a magnet?"

The look he gave me next was almost...but not quite...pitying. "An ordinary person can't," he replied. "But a witch who's a lodestone has the very rare gift of attracting special items to her, especially magical ones. Have you ever stumbled across any objects with strange properties before this?"

"No," I responded at once. My head was spinning as it tried to absorb all the outlandish things Isaac had told me, but one thing I did know was that I'd never encountered anything strange and unusual before this. "I mean, unless you count getting a pair of Manolo Blahnik sandals sixty percent off at the Barney's warehouse sale as something strange and unusual."

Isaac smiled then, and I'd be lying to myself if I didn't acknowledge that his smile did something entirely unwelcome to my midsection. All right, the guy was good-looking. But I didn't have the time or energy to deal with physical attraction right now, no matter what my hormones might have to say on the subject.

"Interesting," he said. "And yet you had something almost fall into your lap when you'd only been here in Albuquerque a few days. It sounds to me like your *chi* got unblocked."

I was beginning to get a bit fed up with having all this esoteric stuff flung at me. "My what?"

Once again, Isaac wore that patient look on his face, like a teacher who was getting a little tired of having to explain basic principles to a backward student over and over again. However, he sounded unruffled enough as he said, "'*Chi*' just means your vital energy—your life force, so to speak. If it was blocked badly enough, then your full powers might not have been able to assert themselves."

Full powers. Right then, I thought I could use a drink. I'd passed several restaurants with bars on the walk over here. Maybe on the way back, I'd stop and have a margarita or something. Just one, nothing that would impair me too badly for the drive back to Albuquerque but what would, with any luck, help to ground me back in reality.

"And how does someone's *chi* get blocked?" I asked, trying my best not to sound too skeptical.

Isaac's head tilted very slightly as he considered my question. "There are many different ways, but probably the most likely is that you had a lot of negative energy emanating from the people around you, energy strong enough to keep you from staying in contact with your vital force."

It didn't take me too long to guess who might have been responsible for my *chi* blockage. Dave hadn't been the most supportive husband in the world, that was for sure. And that was even before I discovered what a cheater he was. For the last eighteen months or so, he'd been bugging me to quit the prop-shopper work and get something with regular hours closer to home so we could start a family. All his friends had kids, and I knew he felt left out, like they were all in a special club he needed to join.

But starting a family hadn't been on my radar.

Maybe someday, in some hazy future I couldn't quite envision, but not right now.

And when I really analyzed the situation, I had a feeling my reluctance hadn't stemmed from a desire to remain child-free indefinitely, but because I honestly couldn't imagine having kids with Dave.

Too bad I hadn't listened to my gut.

And before Dave, there had been my mother. Since she seemed to exist solely to nitpick pretty much anything I did, I could only imagine she'd done a damn good job of *chi*-blocking before my ex had even come on the scene.

"Yes, I can see that happening," I said, my tone neutral, but I had a feeling Isaac was perceptive enough to fill in the blanks without my having to go into any detail.

"Well, I think that's your explanation," he said. "Your powers were blocked, and now they're coming to the fore."

If magic powers were even a thing. But I knew what I'd seen when I put on the glasses, and there didn't seem to be much of an explanation for the phenomenon except that it must be some sort of magic.

"So, what am I supposed to do?" I asked next, hoping I didn't sound too desperate. "Am I going to have to worry all the time about some weird magical object falling into my lap?"

To my relief, Isaac didn't smile, or try to make light of my situation. No, he was silent for a moment, clearly thinking over my plaintive question. Then he said, "That's always a possibility. However, there aren't unlimited magical items in the world. I also think these glasses came to you because they thought there was something you could do to help them."

"'Help them'?" I echoed. "They're inanimate objects."

This time, he did smile. "Perhaps, but they still have a story to tell." He paused for a moment before adding, "I think you need to pay attention to it."

Chapter 3
Canyon Blues

After that, Isaac told me I should try to let my powers do what they wanted, and advised meditating to help clear my mind and ground me so I would be better mentally prepared just in case anything else odd happened to cross my path.

And then I drove back to Albuquerque, a drive that felt oddly anticlimactic. It wasn't as though I'd expected Isaac to invite me out for a drink or something, but it seemed as though he could have given me a little more direction.

Then again, he'd told me to call or text him in case I had any more questions or if anything else strange happened, and had handed me his card—a different one from the business card Joy had given me at lunch on Monday, this one pale blue stock with just his name and a different phone number from the one for The Enchanted Circle.

His personal contact information, I supposed, and told myself I should be glad he'd made the gesture. After all, he could have sent me on my way and washed his hands of the whole situation.

Since I didn't feel like cooking anything and definitely didn't want to go out again, I ordered in Door-Dash from a local Indian place that supposedly had high ratings, and tried to console myself with chicken korma washed down with some rosé I'd picked up at Trader Joe's the weekend before.

Let them tell their story.

I frowned at the eyeglasses, which I'd set down on the coffee table, several yards away from the high-top dining table where I was eating my solitary meal. Although I'd pulled them out of my pocket and put them there after I got home, I hadn't yet had the guts to try wearing them again.

Part of me really didn't want to see what they might show me. What if the scene they revealed was something new, something terrible? All right, I had to admit that an empty canyon that might or might not have had a hawk circling overhead wasn't the worst thing in the world, but my imagination was ready to manufacture scenes that might not have been out of place in some of the horror movies I'd worked on.

"Chicken," I scolded myself aloud. The sound of my voice was actually somewhat reassuring, since it sounded firm and no-nonsense, and not at all like the voice of a person who'd be freaked out just because they happened to see a scene that shouldn't be there playing out on the inside of some eyeglass lenses.

Well, that seemed to settle it. I'd eaten my fill of korma and rice anyway, and I knew better than to pour myself a third glass of wine. I'd already checked my email and my phone, and both had been conspicuously quiet. Then again, I'd already been in contact with my parents to let them know I was safely settled and everything was going well on set, so I didn't know why I would have heard from them. My mother would think her duty satisfied for the moment, and my father was so busy with work that he wouldn't have had the time for another chat.

As for the friends I'd left back in Southern California, well, although they'd all taken my side in the divorce since the evidence of Dave's cheating was pretty much indisputable, they didn't quite know what to do about me moving a thousand miles away to someplace like Albuquerque, a city in their minds that was overrun with meth dealers and had shootouts on the street every day. Too much *Breaking Bad* and not enough reality—the only actual crimes I'd witnessed so far had been some fairly heinous blowing through red lights, nearly causing an accident or two—but I hadn't bothered to try correcting my friends' misperceptions.

Anyway, I was out of sight, out of mind for most of them, so the lack of any contact shouldn't have surprised me too much.

The TV was on, playing an episode of some home improvement show or another. I'd mostly turned it on for background noise, since I didn't feel like listening to music but also hadn't wanted to contend with dead silence.

Coming to terms with living alone had been the

hardest part of the break-up, really. I'd lived with roommates before I moved in with Dave, and he and I had been together seven years. This was the first time in my life I'd been by myself.

Alone, and with my *chi* completely unblocked, according to Isaac Zamora. Once again, I found myself wondering how he'd ended up in a wheelchair. It didn't seem to have slowed him down very much, considering he appeared to run his store by himself. Maybe he had a part-time person to help with stocking the shelves and that sort of thing—I didn't see how he could possibly reach the top of the book-cases while sitting in a wheelchair—but they hadn't been around this afternoon. We'd had the shop completely to ourselves.

Honestly, I didn't quite know what to believe about the whole thing. On the surface, my talk with Isaac seemed completely ludicrous, what with lode-stones and hereditary witches and *chi* and God knows what else.

But since I hadn't yet been able to come up with a single logical explanation for what was happening to me, I decided to ride with it for the time being.

However, if Isaac was right and not just spouting some woo-woo lingo in an attempt to make sense of a completely whackadoodle situation, I didn't know whether I really liked the idea of my *chi* being unblocked. It made me feel vulnerable in a way I'd never experienced before.

"Stop being a baby," I told myself, and got up to take my dirty dishes into the kitchen. After I'd rinsed everything off and put it in the dishwasher—and put the cork back in the wine and returned it to the refrigerator so I wouldn't be tempted—I went back to the living room and retrieved the eyeglasses from the coffee table. The metal of their frames felt cool to the touch, but that was probably just because the room wasn't overly warm.

"What are you trying to show me?" I asked them, and of course they didn't react at all, only sat there, dangling from an earpiece I held between two fingers.

If I was actually expecting a pair of spectacles to talk to me, I really must be going crazy.

As the TV blathered on in the background about engineered-wood flooring and quartz countertops, I sat down on the couch and set the eyeglasses down on my knee. The backlight from the television revealed some new smudges on the lenses, probably from them being handled so much today.

Would those smudges interfere with the images they revealed?

Only one way to find out, I supposed.

Before I could lose my nerve, I lifted the glasses to my face and set them on my nose. At once, the prosaic living room around me disappeared, once again showing me the canyon scene with its red rock outcroppings, dark junipers, and dry grass waving in the wind.

And the dark shadow of a bird overhead.

This time, however, the bird descended in front of me, revealing itself.

It wasn't a hawk.

No, this was an ungainly dark bird, something I'd only seen in pictures and on TV before now.

A turkey vulture.

It made an ungraceful landing on a mound of reddish earth and began pecking at it with its beak. As it worked, a second and a third vulture landed next to it and began tearing at the ground as well.

Was that normal behavior for a vulture?

Since I had no point of reference, I really couldn't say. Soon enough, however, I realized why they were ripping up the earth with such gusto.

Beneath a shallow covering of dirt, a body began to be revealed. From my vantage point, I couldn't really tell whether the body was male or female, or what kind of clothes it was wearing.

But as soon as one of the vultures grabbed a gobbet of cheek and pulled it away, stretching the dead flesh like sickly pink taffy, I yanked off those horrible glasses and tossed them on the coffee table.

Part of me wished I'd thrown them hard enough to break the lenses—and therefore, whatever horrible enchantment had caused me to see these awful visions in the first place—but no such luck. They landed on the wooden surface with a metallic little *clink,* and barely avoided slipping over the edge.

My heart was pounding like crazy, and I found myself reconsidering my decision not to have another drink. After all, it was Saturday night. I could completely destroy myself and still be fine to go in to work on Monday morning.

But no, that was the coward's way out. I made

myself get up from the sofa and go into the kitchen to fetch some water from the fridge, and I took a few deep gulps of the cool liquid before returning to the living room.

The glasses still teetered on the edge of the coffee table. Although I had no desire to touch them again, I told myself that I'd never seen a vision until they were actually sitting on my nose, and so moving them to a safer place shouldn't be a problem.

Still....

I sucked in a breath and used the tip of one finger to slide them to a more solid position in the center of the table. Then I stepped back, heart beating, as though I'd expected them to bite me.

Honestly, a bite would have been preferable to what I'd just seen. Even though I'd worked on some fairly gory horror movies and had been unmoved, this was different.

This was real.

Or at least, it *felt* real. These visions could all be nothing more than my imagination, but I didn't think so.

For one thing, my imagination didn't generally conjure up images of anonymous corpses being devoured by vultures.

Were the glasses showing me these images so I could help the authorities find the body?

That made just about as much sense as any of the rest of this mess.

I sat down and made myself take in a breath, and then another. All right, if I was supposed to find justice for this unknown victim, it might have been nice if the glasses could have shown me something that was actually useful. The canyon didn't seem to have any landmarks in it that would help to identify the place—no structures, no trail signs, no abandoned vehicles or any evidence at all that human feet had ever set foot in the place.

Well, except that dead body.

In a way, I was glad of the angle from which I'd viewed this last scene. It hadn't been up close and personal, like from the point of view of one of the vultures or anything like that.

No, it had felt more like watching a movie.

A really disgusting movie.

My heart still pounded, and I drank some more water—not that it seemed to help much. And as I set the glass down on the table a few inches away from those damned spectacles, I realized my hand was trembling.

Had my hands ever shaken like that before?

Maybe after a nasty spin-out during one of Southern California's rare heavy rainfalls, but I couldn't think of any other time I'd felt this rattled. Usually, it took a lot to put me off balance.

The TV had continued to rattle away in the background during all this, but right then I didn't feel particularly comforted by those human voices. It wasn't as if they were here in the room with me; they couldn't protect me from what appeared to be weird supernatural forces.

It's just visions, I told myself as I swallowed some

more water. *They can't hurt you. You don't even know if they're real.*

Maybe it was the stress of the move and trying to start over in a new place. Maybe I really wasn't seeing anything at all.

But no, Isaac had claimed he'd glimpsed some sort of blur of colors when he put on the glasses.

What if he was lying, though? Trying to confuse me with all this crazy talk of witches and lodestones and visions?

No, that was ridiculous. I couldn't claim to have the world's best instincts about people—otherwise, I wouldn't have been stupid enough to get seriously involved with Dave—but something about Isaac seemed calm and almost soothing. He just didn't seem like the kind of guy to try to mess with a stranger's head.

Which led me back to the worrisome theory that all this might be real. And if that was the case, what would happen if I continued to attempt to unravel the story the glasses were trying to tell? Would it become real at some point, bleed over into my actual life?

I didn't like that thought very much. Although I'd had a few lows over the past few months as my life felt as though it was falling apart around me, I had absolutely no desire to end up in a shallow unmarked grave in a lonely canyon somewhere.

For some reason, I thought of the card Isaac had given me, the one with his personal phone number. Right then, I wanted to hear the sound of his voice, to hear him say everything was fine and I was getting myself worked up over nothing.

But it was Saturday night. I knew nothing about the guy, nothing about what his life was like, other than he ran a metaphysical shop in downtown Santa Fe, but it seemed awfully rude to be calling a near-stranger on the most social night of the week.

Then again, he had told me to reach out if anything else came up. This seemed exactly like that sort of situation.

And if it turned out he was busy, then he'd probably just ignore the call and let it go to voicemail.

No worries, right?

I sipped some water, then made myself get up and go into the bedroom, where I'd left my purse. After digging out my phone and Isaac's card, I stood there for a moment, gathering the nerve to make the necessary call. I'd always had phone anxiety anyway, this weird little niggling flaw in what I otherwise thought was some pretty tough armor. And to have to call some guy I barely knew on a Saturday night, just because I was having the screaming heebie-jeebies?

That was *no bueno*.

But since I knew I would give myself all kinds of unending crap if I didn't pull on my big-girl panties and make the damn call, I went ahead and entered the digits for Isaac's phone number.

It rang three times, and I wondered whether I'd be able to leave a message that didn't make me sound like either the world's biggest sissy or a raving lunatic.

But then he picked up.

"Penny Briggs?" he asked.

For just a second, I found myself wowed by his psychic powers. Then reason kicked in, and I realized he'd probably guessed from the area code who was calling him, even if I kept my name blocked on outgoing calls.

"Hi, Isaac," I said. "Yes, it's Penny. I really hate to be bugging you like this, but—"

"It's fine," he said at once. However, since I could hear a murmur of voices in the background, I had to believe he wasn't alone, and therefore I must be interrupting something. "What is it?"

"Did I call you at a bad time?" I returned. For some reason, now that the moment had come, I wasn't sure if I could just blurt out what had happened in that latest vision from the spectacles.

"Not at all," he said. "I know you wouldn't have called if it wasn't something important. Has something happened?"

Since he'd asked me outright, I knew I needed to go ahead and tell him. As briefly as I could, I explained what I'd seen in the glasses after I'd put them on after dinner.

"I know you told me to try to see what the glasses were trying to tell me," I finished. "But this was just awful. I didn't think I was going to see a dead body."

A pause. Then Isaac said, "I can see why that would be disturbing. But the things you see in those visions can't hurt you."

"So you say," I replied. "But I'm feeling pretty hinky right now."

"I can understand that." He stopped again, and I got the feeling he was trying to figure out the best way to proceed without making me feel that much more off balance. "I probably should have sent some black tourmaline home with you, just to be safe."

"'Black tourmaline'?" I echoed. I'd heard of pink and green tourmaline, but never black. "What's that?"

"A sort of protection stone. It absorbs negative energy."

I thought then that I could have used some black tourmaline during my marriage to Dave. Maybe if I'd been wearing some, I could have repelled him that first time he hit on me at a mutual friend's Halloween party.

Before I could say anything—not that I really knew how to reply to Isaac's comment—he went on, "But failing that, you should cast a protection spell."

Was he kidding?

"I don't know how to cast spells," I told him. "Hell, I'm not even sure I'm ready to believe I might be a witch."

A chuckle came through the phone's speaker. "Well, you are one, whether you want to believe it or not. So that means any spell you cast will have some decent power behind it. Can you give me your email address? I'll send you a simple charm, nothing too complicated."

Well, it sounded as though being a witch in the twenty-first century might be a little easier than it had in the past. Emailing spells had to be much less

complicated than passing around grimoires, or whatever it was that witches used to write down their
charms and hexes.

I gave Isaac my Gmail address, and he said,
"Okay, look for it in a few minutes. I'm at a social
kind of thing, or I'd try to come down there right
now."

"Oh, I wouldn't expect you to do that—" I
began, but he cut off my protests.

"I'd be remiss if I didn't. But this should keep you
safe for tonight. Tomorrow, though, I think you
should come up here so I can give you a crash course
in some of the basics. The shop's closed, but you can
come over to my place."

From anyone else, I might have viewed such an
invitation as a come-on. From Isaac, though, I got the
feeling he was only doing his best to make sure I
didn't get myself into the kind of trouble I couldn't
handle.

"Okay," I said, and oddly, I didn't feel as reluctant
as I probably should have.

Something in me wanted to spend more time
with Isaac, no matter how much the logical side of
my brain was telling me I was in New Mexico to
work, not to get involved with someone.

This isn't "getting involved," I told myself. *It's just
getting some help. That's all.*

Right.

"I'll send you my address along with the spell,"
Isaac said. "Does late morning work for you, say
around eleven?"

"Sure," I replied. After all, it wasn't as though my social calendar was overflowing with activities. I'd planned to do some laundry, and that was about it.

And maybe if I was really lucky, he'd suggest lunch after he was done teaching me his particular brand of hoodoo, or whatever it was that he practiced.

We said our goodbyes after that and ended the call. A minute or so later, my phone pinged, telling me I had a new email. Sure enough, there was the protection spell from Isaac, along with his address. I didn't recognize the street name, of course—I knew next to nothing about Santa Fe. The nav on my SUV would have to guide me in, just as it had the day before.

As for the protection spell, that didn't seem too complicated. It called for some kosher salt, but since I'd bought a canister of the stuff at the store earlier in the week, figuring I'd need some if I decided to do any real cooking, I thought I had enough on hand.

I just had to hope none of my neighbors would catch a glimpse of me out making a circuit of the property, laying a line of salt while I quietly chanted the incantation Isaac had sent me and visualizing a bubble of white light protecting the house and the small yard that surrounded it.

Thank God it was full dark already.

After fetching the salt from the kitchen's tiny pantry, I went outside and laid a thin strand of kosher salt across the threshold of the house, then did the best I could to continue that thread all around the structure. The house didn't have a back door, so I didn't have to worry about doing anything extra to protect an additional entrance. The whole time, I couldn't help feeling like a complete idiot, although, as I'd hoped, none of my neighbors seemed to be out and about, and so I didn't have any witnesses to my first foray into witchcraft.

The weird thing, though, was that when I returned to the front door, thus effectively closing the circle of salt, a strange little tingle traveled up and down my spine, and I felt oddly relieved, as if by doing so, I'd activated the circle of protection Isaac's spell had described.

Power of suggestion, I told myself, but something in me wasn't so sure.

What if there was more to this magic stuff than I'd thought?

Chapter 4
Master and Student

The next morning was so insanely bright—seriously, I'd never seen skies as blue as those in New Mexico—that its prosaic nature made all my heebie-jeebies of the night before...and the spell casting that had followed...seem like the crazed actions of someone who'd watched too many horror movies. There was no way that magic and the dark worries of the night could exist on a blazingly clear day like this.

But since I'd already told Isaac I would go see him, I knew I couldn't back out now. Instead, I had a relentlessly normal morning of coffee and toast and bacon, followed by some yoga. I missed the treadmill I'd left behind in Southern California, since my rented house didn't offer those sorts of amenities. And I wasn't quite comfortable enough with the neighborhood to go running, which was generally my fallback whenever my regular exercise equipment wasn't available.

The line of salt remained in place around the house when I peeked outside, and since it didn't seem as if it was going to rain any time soon, I had to assume my odd little protection device would remain where it was for the time being.

Under other circumstances, I might have fretted over what to wear for this visit to Isaac's house, since I couldn't remotely call it a date but also didn't want to look like I'd just rolled out of bed. But because I'd packed light for my sojourn in Albuquerque and had thought I'd be working on set the entire time, I didn't have a lot of choices available to me.

Just as well. I definitely didn't want Isaac to think I was trying too hard.

So I put on a black long-sleeved T-shirt, jeans, and boots, recalling how it had been chillier in Santa Fe than it was down here in Albuquerque. I'd bring along my leather jacket, just in case. To make the ensemble look a little dressier, I got out my sterling and leather choker with the heart in the center and fastened that around my neck. Put together, it all did look minimally chic, and would probably work even if we did end up going out to lunch.

Jumping the gun a bit, aren't you? I asked myself.

Probably. On the other hand, why would Isaac ask me to come over at eleven if he didn't plan for us to eat somewhere afterward?

Maybe he suggested eleven because he didn't know whether you were a morning person or not, I thought then, which also seemed plausible enough.

Well, I supposed I'd find out more about his intentions in the next couple of hours.

The traffic seemed a little lighter than it had been when I drove up the day before, which made sense. Not as many people out doing touristy stuff on Sundays, probably. Because I didn't have to contend with quite as many cars on the road, I got to Santa Fe a little earlier than I'd thought, and rather than show up on Isaac's doorstep before the appointed time, I drove around a little, trying to get more of a feel for the area. Albuquerque already felt old to me—at least, a lot of the neighborhoods around Nob Hill, although there was a sprawl of much more modern suburbs in all directions—but Santa Fe felt more ancient still. Some of the adobe houses looked as though they'd been there for hundreds of years...and probably had.

When I pulled up to Isaac's house, it had that same feeling of antiquity to it. Sure, a second glance told me the place probably wasn't quite as old as some of the buildings I'd passed on my way here, but still, I had a hard time figuring out exactly which home was his, since the entire neighborhood felt like kind of a hodgepodge of interlocking yards and properties, and very unlike the orderly grids of suburbia that I was used to.

But I had to admit the house was beautiful, two stories and bigger than I'd imagined, with large trees just starting to show a bit of autumn color providing shade in the front courtyard, and a covered patio that seemed to encircle the house. Although I couldn't see it, I thought I heard the faint gurgle of water, as if there was a water feature tucked away somewhere.

Almost as soon as I lifted my hand to knock on the door—I didn't see a doorbell—the door opened, and Isaac's cool brown gaze met mine.

I had a sensation of being knocked off-kilter, and in the next moment, I realized why. He wasn't sitting in his wheelchair, but stood there supported by a pair of metal crutches.

For some reason, I hadn't imagined he'd be so tall. I was just a hair over five foot seven, but he had to have a good five inches on me.

Maybe my mouth hadn't exactly dropped open, but it seemed he could tell I was just a little flabbergasted.

"I don't need the wheelchair all the time," he said quietly. "If I'm having a bad day, or if I know I'm going to need my strength for later on, like I did last night...then I'll use it."

"Um, that's great," I said, knowing I probably sounded like a complete idiot. "I mean, it must be nice to know you don't need it every day."

"It is nice," he agreed, although now there was an amused glint in his dark eyes, one that told me he'd acknowledged my awkwardness, even if he wasn't going to call it out directly. "But come on in."

He moved out of the way so I could enter the house. At once, I had a sensation of light and peace, despite the heavy beams crossing the ceiling overhead and the dark wood pillars that separated what appeared to be the living room from the entryway.

The main living area was nearly two stories high, open to a loft above, and bright September sunlight poured in through the tall windows that overlooked the courtyard.

"Would you like something to drink?" Isaac asked politely. "Water, or tea, or coffee?"

"Water would be great," I replied. Usually, I brought some bottled water along with me whenever I knew I was going to be in the car for a long time, but I'd forgotten this morning. I'd already had two cups of coffee with breakfast and didn't need to be any more amped up than I already was.

He nodded, and led me through the dining room and into the kitchen. It felt almost cluttered, thanks to all the plants growing on shelves mounted to the walls and on the counter itself, but once again, I had that feeling of light and peace and belonging. Never mind that most people would have said the room was horribly dated, with its green tile countertops and knotty pine cabinets with their wrought-iron handles, but at the same time, it suited the house perfectly...and Isaac himself. I couldn't think of a kitchen that would have looked more *brujo*-like.

The stainless appliances were completely up-to-date, however, and he got us both water through the entirely prosaic means of water in the refrigerator door. After he handed me a heavy blown-glass tumbler with a green rim, he said, "We can sit down here."

"Here" apparently meant the little drop-leaf pine table that had been placed up against a window overlooking the backyard. On it grew a cheerful little philodendron in a hand-painted pot whose colors echoed the greens and blues of the kitchen.

Isaac settled into one of the two chairs that flanked the table. I couldn't help noticing how he did so with some effort, maneuvering himself so he sort of dropped onto the chair rather than gradually lowering onto it. But he extricated himself from his crutches with the grace of long practice, and set them up against the wall behind him.

"So," he said, after taking a sip of water. "How did last night go?"

"It was fine," I replied, nothing more than the truth. Maybe it was some secret property of the salt circle that protected the house, or just my mind allowing itself to be lulled into a false sense of security, but I'd slept like a baby, even though I often woke up in the middle of the night and took an hour or more to get back to sleep. "I mean, everything seemed to be quiet."

"I'm glad the spell worked," Isaac said.

I lifted an eyebrow, and he grinned.

"I know you're thinking the spell had nothing to do with it," he told me. "And you can think that if it makes you more comfortable. But, as I told you, because you have considerable powers, any spell you cast will have power as well, even if you don't believe it does." A pause, and then he grinned at me and added, "Although those spells would definitely be stronger if you actually believed in what you were doing."

"Easy for you to say," I returned, doing my best not to be too affected by that grin. In repose, his face was quite serious, with the sorts of elegant angles that made me think of paintings I'd studied by Caravaggio back when I was in college, but when Isaac really smiled, he seemed to light up all over, those dark eyes of his showing glimmers of amber and gold in their depths. Since I didn't know how well I was doing at maintaining a poker face, I went on, "This is all super-new to me, remember."

His expression sobered slightly at my comment. "I know," he said. "And I also know I've been throwing a lot of stuff at you without too much context. So, why don't we do a kind of witchy 'ask me anything' to get started, and then we can see where we should go from there."

Ask him anything? There were so many things I wanted to ask...chief among them, *Are you single?*, but that seemed like extremely poor taste. Anyway, he definitely wasn't wearing a wedding ring, and I hadn't seen a single hint that he lived here with anyone other than himself.

And I also guessed that inquiring as to how he'd ended up in a wheelchair wasn't a very good idea, either. The house clearly had two stories, and I didn't see any evidence of an elevator or some other means of getting upstairs, which seemed to tell me he must have owned the place before he'd suffered the injury that had impaired his mobility.

Better to try sticking to safer topics.

I sipped some water before saying, "Well, I guess

we can start at the beginning. When did you know you were a *brujo?*"

For some reason, it seemed easier to refer to Isaac in those terms rather than trying to make myself think of him as a male witch.

"Early," he said. "But that's partly because my mother was looking for signs in all of her sons. She never came right out and said it, but I know she was disappointed that she didn't have any daughters. I know she was very relieved when she realized she'd passed her powers on to me."

I leaned back in my chair. At that angle, I could barely see the crutches propped up on the wall behind Isaac's seat. This just felt like a friendly convo between two new acquaintances and nothing more.

Of course, I knew better than that.

"But *how* did you know?" I persisted. "Did you start throwing lightning bolts or turn one of your brothers into a toad?"

Another of those brilliant smiles illumined Isaac's face, and he shook his head. "Nothing quite so spectacular, I'm afraid."

Even more curious now, I asked, "But is that possible, though? Throwing lightning bolts and turning people into toads, I mean."

Although he still smiled, something in his expression seemed to darken slightly. "It's possible," he replied. "But it requires a great deal of the witch's energy and isn't something to be taken lightly—even if you set aside the very bad karma of turning someone into another life form. By doing so, you consciously remove them from the path they were on and put them on another, and the repercussions of doing such a thing can be very serious." He stopped himself there, his dark eyes brightening a bit. "But we don't need to worry about that right now. To answer your question, my first bit of magic was making my bed."

"'Making your bed'?" I repeated. That seemed like an awfully prosaic use for magical powers.

He nodded, and sipped some more water. "I hated making my bed, but I had to do it every day, or I wouldn't get dessert with supper. My mother was very strict," he added, as if that hadn't been pretty obvious from his explanation as to why he'd used his magic to do such a thing.

I refrained from mentioning that the first time I'd had to make my own bed was when I went away to college at eighteen. Before then, our housekeeper Eliza had always done it for me.

"Anyway," Isaac went on, "I remember thinking I wanted that darn bed made so I wouldn't miss out on that night's *dulce de leche* cake, and the sheets and blankets and quilt all started to move. In the next moment, the bed was made."

"But how did your mother know it was magic and not you?" I inquired, thinking it seemed like kind of a leap to accuse your kid of using magic instead of doing an ordinary household chore on his own.

"It was much neater than I could have ever managed," he responded, mouth quirking a bit. "I would pull up the covers and call it done, even though the bed was still a lumpy mess. But this time it had hospital corners, something no six-year-old could have managed on his own."

No, probably not. "So, you were six?"

"Yes. And as soon as my mother realized I had powers, she started teaching me her ways—how to use spells to focus my magic, how to create potions for all sorts of ailments and conditions."

If he could really brew magic healing potions—and I thought the jury was still out on that one—why hadn't he used a potion to heal himself?

The question must have been obvious in my face, even if I hadn't uttered those words out loud, because his expression turned wry.

"I suppose you're wondering why I still have to use these crutches—or a wheelchair—if I can heal people."

A denial sprang to my lips, but then I realized it was probably stupid to protest. All I could do was shrug.

For a moment, Isaac was silent. Then he said quietly, "After the accident, the doctors said I could never walk again, and would probably have only limited use of my arms and hands. I knew I would have to prove them wrong—and I have. My physical therapist says it's a miracle that I'm where I am now, but it's no miracle."

"Only magic," I said, my tone equally soft.

"Exactly. I'm not all the way there yet, but I will be someday."

He spoke with such confidence, fine chin lifted

proudly, that I knew better than to say anything. And honestly, if what he was telling me was true, and his prognosis really had been that dire, then something had to be at work here, whether it was magic or sheer dogged will. If he could make it this far after being told he would be the next thing to a quadriplegic, then who was I to say that he couldn't keep going, couldn't one day put aside the wheelchair and the crutches and resume the life he'd once known?

Although I hadn't intended to, my glance slipped upward, to a second floor that must be inaccessible to him a good deal of the time.

"Yes," he said. "I owned this house before the accident. Luckily, the master suite is on the ground floor—I used the bedrooms upstairs for an office and storage. I still do, actually. I just moved my base of operations down here, but if I need something, I can usually manage to get it if I'm having a good day. Otherwise, someone in the family will come over and help out."

It sounded as though the Zamoras were all pretty close. For some reason, I couldn't quite hold back a flash of envy. My own brother and I barely spoke—not out of enmity or sibling rivalry, but more because almost twelve years separated us, and we had hardly anything in common.

"That's pretty amazing," I said, and stopped there.

"But...?" Isaac responded.

"But how do you know it's really magic that got

you where you are now, and not just grit...determina-
tion...whatever you want to call it?"

To my relief, he didn't appear offended by the
question. "I understand your skepticism," he said.
"You weren't raised around magic and don't have any
real reason to believe it truly exists. But that's easy
enough to prove."

Just as soon as he stopped speaking, our two
water glasses rose about a foot above the table,
hovered in the air for a moment, and then just as
easily descended to the tabletop.

What the hell?

I blinked, and Isaac raised an eyebrow.

"You see?" he said. "Magic is real."

My breath didn't seem to want to come, as
though someone had just punched me in the gut.

In a very real sense, that was pretty much what
had just happened.

Even so, reason hadn't deserted me to the point
where I kept myself from passing a hand over both
glasses, half expecting to encounter an invisible wire
or some other means of making the tumblers levitate
above the table.

"It wasn't a trick," Isaac said, now looking more
amused than anything else. "Just my abilities working
on physical objects, in the same way I got my bed to
make itself when I was a little kid."

Was it possible?

It had to be, because I couldn't see any other way
he could have gotten those glasses to rise into the air.
I'd been to the Magic Castle in Hollywood and had

seen some of the magicians there performing up-close tricks, but I'd never seen them do anything like that.

"Well, then," I said, knowing I sounded shaky but apparently helpless to do anything about it. "I guess it's time to start teaching me a few things."

A slow smile spread over his sculpted lips.

"Yes, it is."

Not that he ended up showing me how to levitate objects. No, he worked with me on a different, stronger spell of protection, and gave me a little bracelet of faceted black tourmaline beads on stretchy elastic.

"This will also help to keep you safe," he said as I slid it onto my wrist. We stood out in the court-yard, the bright September sun shining down on both of us. Isaac supported himself on his crutches, but in an almost negligent way, as though he regarded them as an afterthought. "If some kind of magical danger is close by, the bracelet should turn warm to the touch, warning you to keep your guard up."

"And what am I supposed to do if 'danger' is somewhere near?" I inquired. "Maybe you should teach me to throw lightning bolts."

"That sort of thing attracts a lot of attention," Isaac returned without missing a beat, although I noticed that amused quirk at the corner of his mouth again. "I'm not saying there haven't been magical battles between witches over the years, but most of the time, we try to be discreet."

I could see that. Brewing healing potions and casting protection spells was one thing; a layperson could always attribute any positive results to good luck and nothing more. But lightning bolts would be a lot more difficult to explain away.

"Anyway," he went on, "because you've wrapped yourself in so much magical protection, the chances of any hostile witch or other entity trying to get through it would be pretty low."

"'Entity'?" I echoed, not liking very much the way my voice squeaked a bit on that last syllable. "What do you mean by that?"

His expression became guarded. "We share this world with beings who aren't precisely from it. But, chances are, there's no reason in the world your path should have to cross with any of them."

Great. I guessed that was his oblique way of referring to ghosts and spirits...or maybe demons and angels. After all, if you were willing to accept that magic was real, then that meant all other sorts of things could be real as well, right?

I didn't like that idea very much.

"Well, let's hope for the best," I said brightly.

Isaac nodded. "A good philosophy. And now that you're adequately protected, I think you should try looking in those spectacles again."

I made a face. "Seriously? The last time I took a peek, I saw a vulture eating a dead guy's face."

At least, I assumed it was a guy. The body had

been decomposed enough that it was hard to tell what it had started out as.

It appeared my new mentor—or whatever Isaac was to me—didn't have too much patience for that kind of squeamishness. His expression turned almost stern, and he said, "Sometimes magic shows us unpleasant things. That doesn't mean we should turn away. Especially in this case, where it seems clear enough to me that those glasses are doing their best to tell a story you need to see."

Fine. If I could stand off to one side and watch as the makeup guys painted a mixture of food coloring and Karo syrup on some extras to make them look like victims of a zombie attack, then I could watch this. After all, it was just images, not something that was actually happening in front of me.

I'd stowed the spectacles in my jacket pocket, and so I pulled them out now and dangled them hesitantly from my fingertips. "You're sure about this?"

"Absolutely," Isaac said, his tone unwavering. "And remember, I'm right here with you. No matter what you see, it can't affect you. You're perfectly safe."

Easy for him to say. Then again, I had to admit that it did feel a bit better to have him standing only a few feet away from me, to have the bright sun beating down on my head and seeming to reassure me that nothing too awful could happen on such a lovely day. And because the property was ringed with high adobe walls and the trees provided their own shelter, I knew I didn't have to worry about any of Isaac's neighbors seeing what we were up to.

All the same, I drew in a breath before I settled the spectacles on the bridge of my nose.

There was the canyon again, unchanged from the last time I'd seen it. Or rather, the landscape was the same, but the vultures appeared to be gone. In the next moment, I understood why.

The shallow gravesite the carrion eaters had been raiding seemed to have disappeared.

"It's not there," I breathed.

"What's not there?" Isaac asked. Obviously, I couldn't see his expression because the vision in the glasses was obscuring my sight, but he didn't sound overly concerned.

"The grave I saw the last time I put these on," I replied.

"Was it dug up?"

"No," I said, and squinted at the spectacles, even though I didn't know whether that would really help or not. "It's just not there. The ground appears completely undisturbed." Frowning, I took them off, and saw him standing there, one arm propping him up on his crutches while he rubbed his chin with the other hand.

"Interesting," he said.

Which could mean pretty much anything. "Interesting how?" I asked.

"It's possible that the spectacles aren't showing you whatever happened in that canyon in a linear way," Isaac replied.

I absorbed that comment for a moment, then said, "You mean I'm getting bounced around in time?"

"Something like that." His brows drew together, and then he shook his head. "I'm just making an educated guess, though. This is the first time I've ever encountered anything like this. But if the grave is gone, then it seems as though either you've jumped back to a time before the person you saw in your previous vision was murdered...or you've skipped far enough ahead in time that any evidence of the crime has vanished from the scene."

Great. If Isaac was right, then it seemed as though I had a pretty narrow window in which to figure out who the victim was, and who had killed him.

And let's not forget the whole reason why the glasses had somehow recorded the incident—or however you wanted to refer to it—just so they could pass that information along to the first hapless witch who came by.

Namely, me.

"Well, how does that help anything?" I demanded, starting to feel just a little cranky. Probably low blood sugar—it was now inching toward one o'clock, and all I'd had to eat that day was some toast and bacon six hours earlier.

"I don't know," Isaac replied. He actually looked almost apologetic, even though none of this was his fault. "It could be whatever enchantment was placed on those glasses is not working properly, or it may be starting to fade."

Even better news. If the spell or whatever it was went away altogether, how could I have any hope of solving the mystery?

It's not your job, I told myself. *You're not a cop.*

No, but I'd drawn the glasses to me, apparently, and so I felt as though I now had a responsibility to see this thing through to the end.

Wherever and whenever that might be.

"So, what are we supposed to do now?"

Isaac paused for a moment, then glanced upward, as though gauging the position of the sun in the sky. "Now," he said, "we go to lunch."

Chapter 5
Cousin Confessions

I saac took me to a cute restaurant a few blocks away from his house that served a mishmash of Central and South American and New Mexican food. I didn't recognize a lot of the dishes, but everything was pretty fabulous. And even if the food hadn't been great, I was so hungry it probably wouldn't have mattered too much.

On a Sunday afternoon, the place was fairly crowded, with people filling all the booths and most of the tables, and so we didn't talk about what we'd been up to. No, Isaac spoke about growing up in Santa Fe, about his family and the store. It had been his mother's, and she'd left it to him after her untimely death in her mid-sixties from a massive heart attack. I didn't ask why Isaac had gotten the place and not either of his older brothers; since he'd already told me they didn't have any magic, running a woo-woo kind of shop like The Enchanted Circle really wouldn't have made much sense.

It seemed the name of the store was sort of a play on words, since Isaac explained that the Enchanted Circle was also the name of a drive you could take in the northern part of the state, a route that took you from Taos out to a place called Angel Fire, then down through Red River and back into Taos.

"And casting a circle is an important part of magical practice," he added, but left it there, probably realizing that going into any great detail wasn't a good idea right then.

I nodded, but since my mouth was full of something amazing called *chile nogado,* I couldn't respond beyond that.

The conversation wended its way here and there, with me talking a bit about what it was like to work in film and television. Isaac seemed duly impressed by the whole thing.

"So, what do you plan to do when filming on the current series wraps up?" he asked.

I shrugged, and reached for my glass of water. He'd almost studiously avoided the alcoholic offerings on the menu and had asked for only water, so I'd followed suit...even though a margarita had sounded like it might be a good idea after yet another round of having to look into those damn enchanted...or whatever they were...glasses.

"There are always new productions starting up," I told him. "And once I have this show wrapped and under my belt, then it'll be that much easier to get another one, since now I'll have a reputation here in New Mexico and people who know me."

"Is it hard, though, to not know what's coming next?"

My parents had asked me almost that same question on multiple occasions. Or rather, my mother had been more worried about me not being able to support myself and ending up back home, unemployed and underfoot—at least before I got married, after which time she probably figured I was Dave's problem—but I got the impression that Isaac's inquiry was based more out of genuine concern for my well-being.

"Maybe it was at first," I said, and then took a bite of a yucca fry. "But then it became pretty clear that I wouldn't have a problem getting that next job, and so I just rolled with it. And it's fun doing something different every few months or so, instead of going to the same office job year after year."

Even as I spoke, I hoped he didn't think I was disparaging steadier kinds of work—like running his store, for example. But then, you couldn't really compare owning a New Age shop to working in the accounting department at a Fortune 500 company.

Also, there was an odd sort of camaraderie that tended to spring up on the set of a production, this feeling that you were leading a sort of gypsy existence but had come together to make magic—screen magic, that is—happen. I'd never gotten that feeling when working the couple of part-time office jobs I'd had during the summers while I was still in college, and I couldn't deny it was some of the lure of my chosen profession.

"But that's why I found a place in Albuquerque that's month-to month," I continued. "If I really can't find anything else, then I'll head back to L.A."

Was it my imagination, or had that remark made a flicker of disappointment cross Isaac's face?

Wishful thinking, probably.

"It's always good to have contingencies," he said, his tone neutral. Clearly, he didn't have any intention of getting too intimate during this lunch date...if that's even what it was. More like, we were both hungry, so it just made sense to go out and get something to eat.

That impression was borne out after our meal, when we made our laborious way—Isaac had wanted to walk to the restaurant, even though it seemed a long distance for him to be on crutches—back to his house. He told me to keep up the protection spells, and to call him if I saw something new in the glasses, but that seemed to be that.

And as I drove home, even though part of me buzzed with uneasy excitement that all this stuff seemed to be turning out to be real, I couldn't help feeling a little disappointed.

I'd wanted something to happen between us... even as I realized that was a very bad idea.

Isaac was helping me, and nothing more. Expecting anything else was stupid and misguided. After all, I didn't have the time or energy for a personal life right now. I needed to focus on work and starting over...and apparently dealing with this new magical intrusion in my life...and I didn't have the headspace for anything else.

If only I could actually believe that.

Work was busy enough on Monday—we were shooting four scenes, and would probably be on set until at least eight o'clock—that I was able to shove Isaac Zamora to the back of my mind. Or at least, I was able to remain reasonably distracted until his cousin Joy came over and sat down at my table. So far, she was the only person working on the production who'd made any truly friendly gestures toward me, and I couldn't help thinking the crew here seemed a little clannish.

In Joy's case, though, I could tell she wanted me to tell her what had happened with Isaac, and that she was all too glad we didn't have to share the table with anyone else so we could speak frankly.

"So, did you talk to Isaac?" she asked, almost as soon as she settled her paper plate on the table. It seemed barely able to stand up to the flat, New Mexico–style enchilada it held, laden with cheese, green chile, and shredded beef, and I found myself wondering how Joy managed to stay so thin when both times I'd seen her eating, it was food guaranteed to fill up a linebacker.

Maybe having the metabolism of a hummingbird was her magical superpower.

"I did," I said, and took a quick look around. Everyone at the other tables was chattering away, and so I thought it was probably safe enough to spill the beans. "I went up to his store on Saturday so I could talk to him in person."

"And?"

"Oh, he thinks I'm a witch," I responded, doing my best to sound airily unconcerned about the whole thing.

"I knew it!" Joy exclaimed triumphantly. "I could tell right away."

I tilted my head at her, mouth curling slightly. "How? We didn't even exchange the secret handshake."

That comment got me a grin, one which showed off the Zamora family resemblance, even though otherwise, she didn't look all that much like her cousin. "Oh, I can usually tell. It's nothing concrete, really...more like a feeling. But didn't I tell you that you couldn't possibly be seeing things in those glasses if you weren't a witch of some kind?"

Since Joy had said pretty much that exact thing when we'd sat in this same spot and had lunch on Friday, I couldn't really argue with her. I shrugged, and took a bite of my neglected BLT. "And then I went to his place on Sunday so he could show me a few basics of protection magic."

This revelation made her eyes widen a bit. "He invited you over to his house?"

"Yes," I said, trying to sound casual.

"Wow." A pause, and then she said by way of illumination, "I mean, he *never* has anyone over. His brothers sometimes, because they help him with the stuff he can't manage, but he definitely doesn't entertain, not even family. I just figured it was hard for him, because...." The words trailed off, and she made a vague wave with the hand that held a fork.

I guessed she was referring obliquely to his disability, and figured I probably wouldn't get a better opening than this. "So...what happened?"

Joy took a bite of her enchilada, expression subdued. "He was heading back home on I-25 after coming down to Albuquerque for some kind of trade show. A wrong-way driver plowed right into his car. For a few days, we weren't even sure he would live."

Damn. I'd already surmised that the accident must have been a pretty bad one for the doctors to give him a prognosis of possible quadriplegia, but I hadn't realized how close he'd come to death. I stared at Joy, wide-eyed, and she nodded.

"Yeah, it was really bad. And then when the doctors said his spinal cord was severed, and that he'd never be able to walk and might not ever get control of any of his limbs...well, it was pretty devastating for all of us, especially since my Aunt Angelica—his mom—had passed away only six months before." Joy reached for her bottle of water and took a sip, and then brightened a little. "But the doctors were wrong, or at least, they didn't know they were dealing with a *brujo*. Isaac swore he would walk again, and he did. It took more than two years, but these days, almost three years after the accident, he doesn't use his wheelchair very much."

"He was in it when I went to the store," I said, and Joy gave a philosophical shrug.

"Then he was probably having a bad day. It happens. But he's still pretty self-sufficient—he has one of those custom vans, you know, with the special foot pedals and the ramp for his wheelchair, and so he can drive himself to and from work, and he was able to stay in his own house, thanks to the family helping out."

"It does seem like he has everything pretty well dialed in," I agreed. It definitely looked to me as though Isaac had managed a minor miracle, being able to keep the store going and live an independent life even after everything he'd been through.

"Mostly," Joy said. She ate a few bites of her enchilada before stealing a sidelong glance at me. "So...you went over to his house. And?"

"Like I said, we went over some protection magic and took another whack at the glasses, but they didn't show me anything new. And after that, we had lunch at a place downtown."

Once again, her eyes widened. "He took you to lunch?"

"Well, we went Dutch," I said, wanting to disabuse her of the notion that Isaac's and my meal had been anything close to resembling a date. And actually, he'd tried to pick up the entire tab, but I'd insisted on paying for my share and he'd relented without too much argument, as if realizing that protesting too much would make the situation more than awkward.

"Still," Joy said, and paused. "He really doesn't do much of anything with anyone. I mean, he went over to his brother Richard's house Saturday night because it was one of the kids' birthdays, but...."

So, that was why I'd heard a murmur of voices in the background when I made my panicky call to him. Now I felt even worse for interrupting Isaac, since he'd been at a family get-together.

I didn't have time to say anything, though, because Joy continued, voice dropping a bit even though I could tell no one was paying any attention to us. "He was engaged when it happened."

"Really?" I asked, not bothering to hide the shock in my voice. Isaac seemed like such a solitary person, it was hard to imagine him planning to share his home with someone. "Was she hurt in the accident?"

Joy's full mouth compressed. "No, she was in Santa Fe when it happened."

"Then...." The word trailed off, since I honestly didn't know what I'd intended to say.

"Her name is Lena Alvarez," Joy said. "She's sort of like me—she comes from a witchy line but doesn't have much in the way of powers. Works in real estate. Anyway, when it became obvious that Isaac wasn't going to bounce back right away and might be in a wheelchair forever, she bailed out."

"That's cold," I remarked, and meant it. Maybe

the couple hadn't been married yet, but you'd think even an engagement would have an implied "in sickness and in health" clause in there somewhere.

Joy's pretty face turned grim. "I know, right? Of course, Lena had to make it all about her, and cried and apologized and said that Isaac deserved better than her and that she didn't want to stand in the way of his recovery. Isaac being Isaac, he didn't bother to argue or try to get her to stay. I guess he just told her he understood, and that was the end of it. Now she's dating some big-shot developer from Houston who's almost twice her age."

The curl of the lip that accompanied those words told me exactly what Joy thought of the situation. I couldn't even blame her. This Lena Alvarez had pulled a pretty dirty trick on Isaac, that was for sure.

Then again, I couldn't help thinking it was probably a good thing that Isaac's former fiancée was safely out of the way.

Which I knew was a stupid thing to let even cross my mind. Isaac hadn't shown the slightest interest in me—well, beyond doing his best to help me navigate my way through this new, witchy world I'd stumbled into—and I needed to take my cue from him. The guy had enough on his plate...and so did I.

"That sucks," I said with feeling.

"It does, even though the whole family is glad she's out of the picture. She probably thought Isaac was a good prospect because he owns his own business and his own home, but there should be a little more to a relationship than that." Joy returned to her enchilada, probably no more than lukewarm by that point, and took two bites before adding, "I'm still not sure how Isaac fell for her act in the first place. He's usually a better judge of people than that."

Maybe that was true, but I'd seen first-hand in my own life that we often didn't make the best decisions when the heart was involved. "Well, at least it's good to know that the trash took itself out in this case."

My comment got me another grin. "You're right about that." Joy sent me a sideways glance. "So... when are you going to see him again?"

Well, no one could ever accuse her of being subtle. At the same time, though, I couldn't help but feel a little encouraged she apparently thought highly enough of me that she thought I might be good relationship material for her cousin.

Not that it would ever happen. Isaac was wrapped up in his own stuff, as he should be, and I needed to focus on work, or I could kiss any hope of a professional future here in New Mexico goodbye.

"We left things kind of open-ended," I replied. "I mean, if I see something new and earth-shattering in the glasses, then I'll call him, but otherwise, I think that's probably it for the moment. Work is the most important thing right now."

"Mm-hmm," Joyce responded, but didn't say anything else. I could tell she didn't think that would be the end of it.

I found myself hoping she was right.

The day went even longer than I'd thought it would, so I didn't get to slog my way home until past nine o'clock. At that hour, traffic was pretty light, but I still felt as though I was dragging the whole way.

I just hoped that one or two of the local restaurants would be still open for delivery. No way did I have the energy to fix anything, even if the food prep involved nuking a few dishes and nothing more.

As soon as I pulled into the driveway, though, I knew I wouldn't have any sort of restful evening ahead of me.

The front door was standing wide open.

Every single nerve ending in my body went on high alert, and adrenaline started shrilling in my veins.

I knew I'd locked both the regular lock and the deadbolt before I left for work that morning. The house suited me just fine, but its major drawback was that it didn't have a garage, just a carport, and so I always came and went through the front door.

My hand shook slightly as I reached into my purse and pulled out my phone, then dialed 9-1-1. It seemed as though it took forever for the call to go through, but eventually I heard a bored-sounding woman's voice.

"Nine-one-one, what's your emergency?"

"Someone broke into my house. I came home to the front door standing wide open."

"Are you inside the house now?"

"No," I replied. "I'm sitting in my car in the driveway. I didn't think it would be a good idea to go in just in case the robbers are still somewhere around."

"All right, ma'am. I'll send someone over. Stay where you are."

Like I planned on going anywhere. Thank God my SUV locked itself as a matter of course as soon as I got in and fastened the seatbelt. Of course, if the intruders were still lurking somewhere on the property, they could have tried to rush the vehicle anyway, but I didn't think such a maneuver would work too well for them. My Palisade might not have been quite as big as a Suburban or a half-ton truck, but I guessed it would still do plenty of damage once it got rolling.

"Okay, I'll wait," I told the dispatcher, and she ended the call.

Furtively, I glanced around the yard, now nicely illuminated by my SUV's headlights, but I didn't see anything obviously out of place...well, besides the gaping dark hole of my front door. When I'd left that morning, I'd told myself to leave a light on inside, since I'd known I would be coming home late, but that resolution had obviously slipped my mind.

I glanced down at the phone. A nagging voice in the back of my head told me I should call Isaac, but on the surface, that seemed like a silly impulse. What could he do, after all? Drive himself down here in his specially equipped van and fight off the bad guys with his crutches?

Right.

After all, I had no reason to believe this was anything but an ordinary break-in. Half the houses in the neighborhood had bars on the windows, telling me it might not be the safest place in the world, even though the rental had been quiet enough during my short tenure there. Anyway, what good were bars if an intruder could just kick in your door or pick the lock?

It took the cops almost an hour to show up, an hour during which I sat in my SUV and fumed, and also realized how frigging hungry I was. I'd heard horror stories about how notoriously understaffed and overworked the Albuquerque P.D. was, and it looked like I was suffering the effects of those issues firsthand now.

Eventually, though, a black-and-white squad car pulled up into the driveway behind my Palisade. Two officers got out, with one coming up to my window while the other shone a flashlight toward the house's tiny front porch.

The first officer made a gesture toward my window, obviously directing me to roll it down. I pushed the button, and it descended.

"Penny Briggs?" he asked.

"Yes," I said. "I'm renting this house. I came home from work to see the door standing open."

"Anything missing?"

I thought of those damned spectacles, safely tucked into the pocket of my leather jacket. "I don't know," I said. "I didn't go inside—I thought it better to wait here until the police showed up."

An hour late, I added mentally, but knew better than to say anything out loud. I might not have been in the demographic to get a lot of pushback from the cops, but I wasn't stupid. If nothing else, being married to an officer for almost seven years had taught me how to behave myself around the police.

"Okay," the officer said. "We'll go take a look."

He headed over to meet his partner, and the two of them went up onto the porch and then peered inside, shining their flashlights all around. It looked as though they both shook their heads, but since the porch light was off and the only real illumination was from my headlights and a streetlamp half a block away, it was hard to tell for sure.

However, since the cavalry had shown up, I figured it was safe to get out of the car. I unlocked the door and wearily climbed out, trying to ignore how heavy my limbs felt and how I would've liked nothing better than to put my feet up and sip some merlot while I waited for DoorDash to bring me Chinese takeout.

That sort of relaxation didn't seem to be in the cards for me this evening, however.

As I made my way onto the porch, the lights inside suddenly blared on, showing me the chaos the darkness had hidden.

Every single stick of furniture looked as though it had been overturned, and the couch cushions had been slashed open, with stuffing and foam fill spread everywhere. I could only see the living room from where I stood, but I had to guess that the rest of the house was in just as bad shape. The utter destruction took my breath away, although I tried to hold it together. Police officers were used to people having emotional breakdowns in front of them, but I told myself I was made of sterner stuff.

I hoped.

"You can come in," said the cop who'd spoken to me through my car window. With the lights turned on, I could see he was probably in his early forties, dark enough of complexion that I guessed he was Hispanic or maybe a member of one of New Mexico's Pueblo tribes. His deep brown eyes were sympathetic. "The place is a mess, but it's hard for us to tell if anything was taken."

"There's not much to take," I said, more worried about what the wreckage might mean for my landlady. She had to have homeowner's insurance, of course, but I doubted it would pay to repair or replace the furniture. And I had renter's insurance as well, which should help to mitigate some losses.

Right then I was just glad that I'd traveled as light as I had, and that I'd left the few pieces of jewelry I really cared about in a safety deposit box at my bank in Rancho Cucamonga. That morning, I'd put on my silver heart choker, even though I didn't wear it to work all that often, and so it was safe as well.

"You should take a look around, though," the officer said. "We'll dust for fingerprints, but I can tell you now that we usually don't recover much from break-ins like this."

"It's okay," I said, an automatic response, since

nothing about the situation was remotely all right. "I didn't have much to take."

His expression turned almost skeptical—after all, my Palisade was less than a year old, and quite obviously expensive—but he didn't say anything, only went to join his partner in the master bedroom. A peek inside told me the intruders had torn up the bed and that all my clothes appeared to have been summarily tossed on the floor, although it didn't seem as though anything was missing.

At least the front door didn't appear to have been kicked in; the locks were intact, and the frame looked undamaged. They must have picked the lock, even though the deadbolt was a heavy-duty Schlage and something that should have deterred most casual burglars.

Even with the door uncompromised, I knew there was no way in hell I could spend the night here, not with the furniture destroyed and the mattress shredded. I supposed I should count myself lucky that I was living in a big city, and therefore shouldn't have too much trouble finding a hotel room for the night.

Still, what a pain in the ass.

I waited for the cops to complete their inspection of the crime scene, then gave a brief statement. The officer who'd spoken to me before asked, his tone almost gentle, "Do you have someplace you can stay tonight? The place is pretty trashed."

Voice too calm, I replied, "I'll get a hotel room, and then I'll be in touch with my landlady tomorrow morning to see what she wants to do. Thanks for coming out."

They nodded and excused themselves, and I closed the door behind them, engaging the deadbolt even though I knew doing so was an empty gesture at best.

For a moment, I stood in the wreckage of the living room, and then I pulled in a breath.

First things first.

As I'd thought, they'd tossed my clothes on the floor, but everything still seemed to be there. I hung up the things I wouldn't need right away, and then made a pile of stuff to get me through the week. Out came my suitcases from the closet in the second bedroom, and I mechanically packed the clothes I'd pulled for work, and went into the bathroom to get any necessary toiletries.

After that, I sat down on the floor and pulled up the Booking.com app on my phone, then made a random selection from the downtown hotels that still had any available rooms. Right then, I didn't really care where I ended up, just as long as it had room service or a restaurant nearby.

Once that all-important task was handled, I took my suitcase out to the SUV, tossed it in the back, and pulled out of the driveway, heading toward down-town. The hotel I'd booked was called the Andaluz, and was apparently some kind of historical landmark, but I didn't care about its cultural significance right now.

No, the important thing was that they'd had

availability, and I could order in from the restaurant until eleven o'clock at night.

In the morning, I'd try to figure all this out. In the meantime, I just had to hope I'd be safe where I was going.

Chapter 6
Crawling Through the Wreckage

As soon as I'd gotten installed in my hotel room —and was happy to see it had been updated in a sleek, fun sort of way that still worked with the building's vintage style—I called Ida Martinez, my landlady, to let her know what had happened at the house. To my dismay, she insisted on meeting me at the property the next morning so she could survey the damage. I tried to tell her that she could let herself in and check it out, but she stood firm.

"I don't want to be there without you," she told me. "It's in the rental agreement."

True, the contract had said that the landlord wasn't allowed to enter the property without the renter being present. Still, I would have thought my verbal permission would be enough for me to skip the entire process.

Apparently not, however. I ended up agreeing to a nine o'clock meeting and ended the call. Great. Now I'd have to contact Jake Mills, the guy from the production company whose job it was to keep tabs on all the crew, and let him know I was going to be late.

That sort of thing generally didn't go over very well when a production was already midstream.

But since there wasn't much I could do about it, I sent the email anyway, promising I'd be in as soon as I could and assuring him that this sort of thing would never happen again.

Famous last words, I thought as I sent the email, although I remained somewhat hopeful. After all, my house had already been ransacked, and the intruders hadn't found what they were looking for. Surely there was no reason for them to come back.

With those necessary tasks handled, I finally ordered some room service, then stared down at my phone, brooding. I kept wondering whether I should call Isaac, or at least send him a text to give him an update. After all, he'd told me to get in touch if anything unusual happened.

Except I knew that was fudging it a bit. He'd told me to get in touch with him if something strange happened with the eyeglasses. I still had absolutely no idea whether the break-in at my rental had anything to do with those freaky spectacles or not.

Besides, it was now almost ten o'clock on a Monday night. While I knew that was a little better than trying to reach out at 3 a.m. or something, it seemed like a pretty huge imposition.

Okay, I'd message him on Tuesday morning after I met with Ida. That way, he'd still be in the loop, but

I wouldn't have sent the signal that I was so needy, I couldn't go even a few hours without his input or advice.

That particular issue resolved, I unloaded my suitcase while I waited for the room service to arrive.

I could only pray I'd actually be able to get a decent night's sleep.

Somewhat to my surprise, I slept much better than I'd thought I would. Maybe I'd been lulled into a false sense of security by staying in a place where I was surrounded by people, or maybe it was just the simple luxury of realizing I didn't have to get up at the crack of dawn, since I didn't have to meet Ida until nine and the house was less than ten minutes away from the hotel that had given me some temporary shelter.

More room service for breakfast—I thought I could get used to this—and then I went ahead and got ready, dressing simply since I knew I'd have to head straight over to I-25 Studios once I'd wrapped up the meeting with my landlady.

It was another brilliantly sunny day, without a cloud in the sky. I reflected that it was hard to believe something so awful had happened the night before when everything around me looked to be promising a cheerful week ahead.

Appearances were deceptive, though. I'd grown up in sunshine and warmth, and yet there'd been plenty of skullduggery going on beneath the surface back in Los Angeles.

However, I did my best to push those grim thoughts away as I pulled up to the house and parked at the curb out front, since Ida's meticulously maintained older-model Cadillac sat in the driveway. She was already waiting on the front porch, looking anxious, although I'd arrived only a minute after the hour.

"I am so sorry about all this," she said as soon as I approached. "This is normally such a safe neighborhood."

"It's okay," I assured her, since her pleasant, round face was creased with worry. Normally, she had the sort of comforting presence that made me think of grandmothers from greeting cards and Hallmark holiday specials, quite unlike my own grandmothers. My mom's mom seemed to be doing her best to keep up with my mother in the Botox department, and my paternal grandmother, who lived in the Pacific Northwest in a town called Bellingham, spent most of her time outdoors hiking or working in her garden, and was lean and taut and weathered, not a series of adjectives that could possibly be applied to Ida Martinez.

"Still...." Ida said, and then let the word trail off, as if she'd hoped something else inspiring might have come to mind and then wasn't sure what to say when it didn't.

"We can go inside," I offered. "I have to warn you that it's pretty bad, though. Maybe I should have tidied up before I left for the hotel, but honestly, I just wanted to get the heck out of here."

"I can understand that," she replied. Her gaze moved to the front door. "There wasn't any sign of forced entry?"

I shook my head. "Nope. The cops thought the burglar probably picked the lock."

Ida bent down and peered at the deadbolt, dark eyes narrowing behind her bifocals. "I don't see any scratches or anything."

Figuring I might as well add my own eyeballs to the inspection, I leaned down, too, and gave the deadbolt a once-over. As I'd noted the night before, it was obviously something she'd installed right before I moved in, and as far as I could tell, the surface seemed unmarked.

Then again....

"Would someone picking the lock even leave marks behind?" I asked, knowing how dubious I sounded. "I mean, you just insert the pick right inside the lock, right? It's not as if the thieves would have to really mess with the surface much."

Ida's unnaturally dark penciled brows pulled together. She'd probably had deep brown hair before it turned iron gray, but clearly she planned to keep the eyebrows of her youth even if they looked obviously drawn on.

"I don't know," she said, and her mouth pursed slightly. "This is the first time I've ever had to deal with a break-in."

Which seemed to support her assertion that this was actually a pretty safe neighborhood.

"I guess we'd better go in," I said. "I don't see much of anything out here, and neither did the cops."

Judging by the way Ida's round shoulders seemed to square themselves at my suggestion, I could tell she wasn't any more eager to confront the wreckage inside the house than I was. But time kept ticking by, and I really needed to get this over with so I could go to work before I was fired. That might have sounded extreme, but I'd seen people canned over the years for a lot less. Producers and directors tended to have a short fuse when it came to people not being on set when they were expected to be there.

Ida didn't protest, however, so I went ahead and put my key in the lock. It turned easily, indicating that whoever had picked the thing, they'd been enough of a pro that they hadn't damaged the inner mechanisms.

Which begged the question why they'd go to all that trouble, only to trash the house and take nothing. None of this made any sense.

As soon as the door swung inward, Ida made a sound of dismay. I couldn't blame her, since I'd let out a similar gasp when I arrived home the evening before.

"Well, thank God you weren't home," she said. "Who knows what might have happened?"

That scenario was something I really didn't want to contemplate. True, the intruders seemed more intent on mayhem than anything else, but if they'd stumbled across a woman on her own....

My gut clenched, and the excellent *huevos rancheros* I'd had for breakfast seemed to do a somersault in there. "Yes, thank God for that," I agreed.

Ida's mouth tightened again, and she pulled a surprisingly new-looking iPhone out of her purse and started taking pictures—for her insurance, I assumed. Since I'd done my duty by letting her in and being there while she inspected the place, I decided to stay out of the way and hang back in the living room as she made a circuit of the rest of the house, snapping photos the whole way. When she came back, she looked tired.

"I'll submit a claim to my insurance," she told me, expression troubled. "But I don't know how long it's going to take me to get the house put back together."

"It's okay," I replied. There was no need for her to look so worried. None of this was her fault...even if it was a huge inconvenience for me. "The people at the hotel told me I could have the room through Friday. If this isn't settled by then, I'll just find another hotel to move to."

This assurance didn't seem to calm her very much. "But for you to be paying for a hotel when you've already paid rent here—"

I couldn't help noticing how Ida hadn't offered to help cover my expenses, or maybe prorate my rent so I wasn't paying for the days I'd be spending at the Hotel Andaluz. Most likely, she operated on fairly thin margins and didn't have the cash on hand to be very expansive.

Whereas I really didn't need to worry about the money involved, even if my hotel stay ended up extending indefinitely.

"It's okay," I repeated. "You just do what you need to do, and keep me updated. While I'm here, I'll get the rest of my stuff out, but then I need to head to work."

I got the impression she wanted to protest, but my comment about work had probably let her know I'd given her just about as much time as I was able. She nodded, and I got the second suitcase from the office and proceeded to pack up what remained of my belongings, although I didn't worry about the food in the fridge. It wasn't as though I was permanently vacating, only giving Ida some space so she could get the repairs handled without me being underfoot.

She was on the phone when I trundled my rolling suitcase through the living room, so I just gave her a thumbs-up as I headed out the door. That gesture got me another nod, followed by an extended pinkie and thumb held near her ear, signaling she'd call me when she had some more information to impart.

Our business handled, I loaded the suitcase into the back of my SUV and closed the hatch. I didn't really like having something so conspicuous in the cargo area, but I didn't want to waste the time it would take to drive over to the Andaluz and haul it up to my room. My parents had drilled into me from an early age that I shouldn't leave anything valuable visible when parking my car in a public place—a habit that had saved my laptop from the burglary, since it had been safely stowed under the passenger seat of the Palisade when the break-in occurred—but I had to hope the parking lot at the studio would be safe. People were always coming and going from their cars, and also, the studio had its own private security, a couple of guys in golf carts who didn't seem to do too much except drive around all day and try to look busy.

It would have to do.

By the time I got to the studio, the hour was a little after ten o'clock. As luck would have it, there seemed to be a break between shooting scenes, since a lot of the crew was milling around outside, drinking coffee and chatting. I spotted Joy Zamora, who seemed to be deep in conversation with Lily Smith, the show's makeup artist. Joy gave me a head nod, as if inviting me to come over, but I only made it a few steps before Jake Mills intercepted me.

"Nice of you to drop in," he said sarcastically.

I did what I could to maintain a neutral expression. Jake was sort of a bulldog, the kind of personality trait that suited him well in wrangling finances and making sure he built the crew the director wanted. When it came to social situations, though, his pugnacious attitude left just a bit to be desired.

About twenty different retorts popped into my brain, but I told it I needed to behave myself. "I got here as fast as I could," I said, then couldn't resist adding sweetly, "but I'll make sure to schedule my next break-in with the burglars so I don't inconve-nience anyone."

Jake's almost nonexistent brows pulled together. He was one of those fair-haired, ruddy types whose lashes and eyebrows seemed to blend in with his perpetually sunburned skin. "Yeah, well, try not to get broken in to at all," he groused. "Doesn't your house have a security system?"

That it did not. I didn't know why Ida hadn't installed one; maybe she'd been relying on her supposedly "safe" neighborhood to keep her from having to invest in a burglar alarm.

"No," I said shortly. "So, we're on break, right? I can just slide right in when we start shooting again. It'll be fine."

Jake didn't look too convinced by those words, but at least he didn't waste my time by arguing further. Instead, he called out, "Five minutes!" and then headed back into the building.

Technically, it was the assistant director's job to tell everyone when they were due back on set, but I noticed no one protested. No, people just finished their coffees or snacks, threw the trash in a nearby bin, and headed inside.

I was one of the first people back in the building, mostly because I'd been closer to the door when Jake made his announcement. Because of that, I didn't have a chance to talk to Joy, who sent me a ques-tioning look but made a beeline to her station, where one of the actresses was waiting to have a few stray strands of hair pinned back in place.

After that, the day progressed normally enough, although we didn't get a chance to break for lunch until nearly two. I decided to head away from the studio and grab a bite to eat from a local burger joint, partly because I wasn't sure I wanted Joy picking my brain, but also because I knew I needed to call Isaac and let him know what was going on.

Once I'd gotten my burger and parked the SUV under a convenient shady tree to shield it from the bright sun, I waffled for a moment over whether to call his personal number or the number at the shop, and then decided I might as well call his personal cell. If he was busy at work and couldn't answer, I'd just leave a message.

However, he picked up after the second ring. "Penny? Is everything okay?"

"Mostly," I said. "I mean, I'm fine, but someone broke into my house yesterday."

"Oh, my God," he said at once. "You weren't home?"

"No, it happened while I was at work," I replied. "As far as I can tell, they didn't take anything."

Isaac didn't answer right away. I could almost see him frowning, almost see the way the fine lines of his jaw tensed with worry.

"They must have been looking for the spectacles," he said.

Although that had been my suspicion, too, I certainly didn't have any evidence to back it up...and that meant I shouldn't allow Isaac to let his theories move in that direction.

"There's absolutely no evidence that's what happened," I told him. "It's not like Albuquerque is some kind of low-crime small town. Break-ins happen all the time here."

"Maybe so, but if they didn't take anything—"

"There wasn't anything to take," I cut in. "I mean, I don't keep cash lying around, I don't have any expensive jewelry, and my laptop was at work with me...and so were those stupid glasses. Whoever broke in didn't find anything worthwhile, so they trashed the house and left."

"They 'trashed' it?" Isaac repeated, now sounding even more alarmed. "How bad?"

"Bad enough that I'm staying at the Hotel Andaluz until my landlady can get it sorted out," I replied.

"I want to come down and check it out," he said, his tone firm, as if he knew I was going to argue but wanted to head me off at the pass.

"You don't need to do that—" I began, but I didn't get any farther than that.

Isaac wasn't the sort of guy who needed to raise his voice, but somehow he managed to push past my protests. "Yes, I do," he said. "I might be able to figure out who broke in."

"You can do that?" I asked, startled. All right, he'd gotten me halfway convinced about the whole magic thing, thanks to that little demonstration he'd performed with our water glasses on Sunday morning, but still. It was probably going to take a while for me to accept he might have ways of conducting an investigation that had absolutely nothing to do with gathering physical evidence.

"Maybe," he said, surprising me again. Most guys I knew would have asserted that of course they could come breezing in and figure out who the perp was, no problem, but apparently Isaac Zamora didn't operate that way. It was refreshing to have met someone who didn't see the need to convince the world he was infallible. "Magic isn't an exact science, but it still provides me with resources that the police couldn't possibly have. What time do you get off work?"

Well, there was a good question. There was no such thing as a fixed eight-to-five when it came to working on a movie set. "I'm not sure," I replied. "We're supposed to wrap around six-thirty or seven today, but I probably won't have a really good idea until later this afternoon. I'll have to text you."

"That's fine," he said. "Send me a text when you can—along with the address—and I'll meet you there."

The request for my address was oddly reassuring, if for no other reason than to tell me Isaac wasn't all-seeing and all-knowing, couldn't use his magic for every little thing.

Unless he was being disingenuous, and already knew exactly where I'd been living.

Oh, you're a trusting soul, Penny, I scolded myself, even though I knew it wasn't completely my fault. Being married to a cop—especially a cop who'd turned out to be a huge cheater—did tend to create some trust issues.

"Sounds like a plan," I responded. "But now I have to go—my burger's getting cold."

"Enjoy your lunch," Isaac said, now sounding almost amused. "I'll see you later."

We ended the call there, and I picked up my Whataburger. Oddly, I felt almost cheerful.

The day had started out pretty shitty, but at least I'd get to see Isaac that night.

Chapter 7
Ghost Prints

To my relief, the rest of the day at work went smoothly—or at least as smoothly as any day on set could be—and I was able to escape a little after six-thirty. During the afternoon break, I'd filled Joy in about what had happened at the house, and she'd been properly horrified.

"You need a security system," she told me, and I'd given a resigned shrug and said I'd think about it. Unfortunately, that sort of thing was out of my control. Maybe Ida Martinez would decide to install one, but I somehow doubted it. I had no idea how much something like that cost—Dave had one at the house we'd shared in Rancho Cucamonga, but it was already there when I moved in, and so the only cost I knew about was the monthly charge for monitoring the system, which ran about a hundred bucks. Even if Ida decided to bite the bullet and get some kind of alarm, I had to believe she'd pass that cost on to her tenants.

But at least Joy hadn't asked too many probing questions—mostly because, with everything up in the air, I didn't have a lot of answers—and I'd been able to make my escape. Because Isaac had to drive down from Santa Fe, that meant I had time to get back to the hotel and get myself freshened up a bit before heading over to the house. Ida hadn't told me to stay away, but it still felt a little strange going there with the place still in such disarray.

In fact, I sat down on the front porch to wait for Isaac, figuring I could enjoy watching the sunset, which turned out to be spectacular, thanks to some high clouds that had moved in during the afternoon. The sky blazed with scarlet and gold, and then began to shift to coral and aqua just as Isaac's van pulled up into the driveway behind my SUV.

It took him a while to get out, but I made myself wait patiently for the motorized lift to lower his wheelchair to the pavement. He had his crutches with him, though, and raised himself from the chair so he could insert them under his arms and make his way up the front walk toward me.

"Evening," he said casually, and I smiled at him.

"Thanks for coming down." I figured I wouldn't mention his maneuvering with the wheelchair; it looked as though he probably drove while sitting in it, using special hand controls, even if he didn't want to sit in the chair once he'd gotten to where he was going. "So...what are we looking for?"

"I'll let you know when I find it," he said with a quick flash of a grin.

Oh, there went my knees again. Did the guy have any idea the sort of effect he had on me?

Since he went straight to the front door after that, I had to believe he didn't. Just as well. Even if I couldn't seem to control my atavistic reactions to him, I could at least try to act like an adult. Maybe with enough practice, I could tell my hormones to take a hike.

I stood off to one side of the porch and watched as Isaac passed his hands over the doorframe and the deadbolt, palms less than an inch above the surface, obviously being careful not to touch anything directly. His lips moved, but I couldn't hear the words he was murmuring under his breath.

Reciting some sort of spell?

Probably.

After a minute or so, he turned back toward me, expression grim. "Someone definitely used magic to open this door. That's why there wasn't any sign of forced entry, or any indication that the locks had been picked."

I digested that piece of unwelcome information as best I could. "People can use magic to unlock doors?"

"Yes," he replied, dark eyes troubled. "Magic just *is*—it's up to the practitioner to decide whether to use it for good or ill."

Great. Good to know that witches—male or female—were running around using their powers to break and enter. I crossed my arms and said, "If that's the case, then why trash the house? They could have come in, not found what they were looking for, and gone right back out without me realizing anything was going on. You'd think that would be the smarter thing to do."

Isaac glanced over his shoulder, but the neighborhood was quiet. Probably, everyone had gotten home from work and was making dinner, or maybe already eating it. Anyway, I didn't see any of my neighbors. The two of us might have been the only living beings on the street, ruddy-hued with the last dregs of sunset.

"I honestly don't know," he replied, apparently satisfied that nothing we were saying would be overheard. "It could have been out of a simple need for intimidation and nothing more. Do you mind if I look around inside?"

"No, that's fine," I said. "But be careful—I don't know if Ida has had anyone come in yet to get things straightened up, so there could still be crap all over the floor."

"I'll watch my step."

That was probably something he had to do on a daily basis. I could tell he tried to use the crutches as much as he could, and traversing downtown Santa Fe wasn't necessarily all that easy, considering how crowded the sidewalks often were and how those sidewalks weren't terribly even, thanks to the age of the place.

I went ahead and unlocked the door, then entered first, flicking on the lights as I headed deeper into the house. Behind me, I thought I heard Isaac make a faint sound of protest, as if he thought he should go first, but that didn't make much sense. If someone attacked us the second we stepped inside, it was way more logical for the person who wasn't on crutches to bear the brunt of the assault.

No attack came, however. In fact, even though the furniture was still a total disaster, it was clear to me that someone had come in and done their best to tidy up, whether that was Ida herself or the gal who cleaned her rental properties and got them ready for new tenants.

"It's fine," I said, somewhat unnecessarily, since Isaac was right behind me and could see for himself that the house wasn't the utter wreck I'd prepared him for.

He nodded as he made his way past me, sharp dark eyes taking in every detail of the damage that had been done, from the shredded sofa cushions to the deep scratches on the coffee table and TV stand. After he was done surveying the living room, he poked his head in the kitchen, but there wasn't much to see. For whatever reason, the intruder—or intruders—had left that space alone.

"And the rest of the house?" Isaac inquired as he turned back toward me.

"There's a bathroom and two bedrooms down the hall," I said, pointing in that direction. "You can take a look if you want."

This time, I let Isaac go ahead of me, since it seemed pretty obvious that whoever had done this was long gone and didn't appear to have any intention of coming back any time soon...if ever. Isaac turned on the lights as he went, pausing every once in a while as if to try to drink in the energies around him.

I couldn't feel a damn thing. Some witch I was.

Well, despite Isaac's arguments to the contrary, I still thought the jury was out on that one.

He poked his head into the bedroom I'd been using as an office, but the only thing to see in there was an office chair with the seat ripped up and a desk with its legs broken off. After another pause, he headed into the master.

Even though I'd only slept there for a week or so, it still felt odd to have Isaac in what seemed like an especially intimate space. Here as well, things had been tidied up, the slashed mattress back on the bed frame and the lamps returned to the nightstand, even if their bulbs had been shattered and their shades looked as though someone had put their foot right through them. However, the ceiling fan overhead had a light kit and was relatively undamaged, so he switched it on.

"What about your personal stuff?" he asked.

"Like, my clothes and things?"

He nodded.

"They were fine," I said. "Everything was still hanging in the closet where I left it, and it didn't look as though any of the toiletries in the bathroom had been touched."

"Interesting."

I cocked my head at him. "What's so interesting about that?"

Isaac's cool gaze met mine, eyes unreadable behind their fringe of heavy lashes. He didn't look particularly worried, but more speculative, as if a number of thoughts were passing through his mind and he needed to decide which of them was worth articulating.

"The furniture and bedding were destroyed, but not your clothing. If someone was truly trying to intimidate you, I'd think they'd want to wreck your personal belongings and not just the furniture. It almost seems as though their main goal was to make this place uninhabitable so you'd be forced out."

There was an idea I didn't like very much. A little shiver passed over me, even though the room was almost stuffy, thanks to being closed up on a day that had gone into the upper seventies.

Isaac went on, "Does anyone know you're staying at the Andaluz?"

"You do," I said. "And your cousin Joy. I told my producer I had to get out of the place I was renting, although I didn't go into any more detail than that. Same with my landlady—she knows I'm staying at a hotel right now, but I didn't tell her which one."

To my relief, he looked almost approving. "That should be all right. You can trust Joy—she knows how to keep things to herself."

Honestly, I didn't know if that was exactly an accurate assessment. After all, she'd told me more about Isaac's personal life than he probably would have preferred. In that case, though, she was probably just trying to help things along between the two of us...not that there was much to help along.

Probably a good thing, even if the crazy half of my brain wanted more.

"So, you think I'm safe at the hotel?" I asked.

"For now...probably," he said, which wasn't the world's most reassuring reply. "Public places with lots of people are always safer. As to where you'll go next...well, we'll just have to figure that out."

I didn't like the sound of his remark very much. Hands on my hips, I said, "The only place I'm going is back to this house once it's cleaned up. I don't have time to be bopping around from house to house— I'm on thin ice at work already and don't need any more disruptions."

Isaac's expression was almost studiously neutral, which told me he didn't think much of my protests. Rather than argue, however, he gave a very small lift of his shoulders and said, "From the looks of it, it's going to be a few days before you can come back here, and in the meantime, you're in a safe place. You're still wearing the black tourmaline bracelet, right?"

In answer to his question, I pulled up the sleeve of my jacket an inch or two so he could see the little line of faceted black beads glittering on my wrist. "I don't take it off," I told him. I could feel a frown pulling at my brow as I asked next, "And what about those protection spells you had me cast? They don't seem to have done a very good job of keeping the bad guys out."

"Maybe not," he returned, looking remarkably unperturbed. "But you were safe, right? The break-in occurred when you weren't home."

That sounded just a little bit like equivocating to me; one would have thought the lines of salt I'd drawn across the threshold and around the entire house should have been enough of a barrier to keep out any magical bad guys.

"Also," he went on, "no spell is infallible, and this was one of the first real spells you'd ever cast. I still can't get a read on who broke in here, but if they're someone who's been practicing magic for years and years, then it's not so implausible to think they could have easily gotten past your protection spell."

This was getting better and better. What was the point in doing magic if someone bigger and stronger could come along and just blast one of my spells into nothing?

"So, I might as well not have cast that spell in the first place," I said, not bothering to keep the annoyance from my tone.

"Not at all," Isaac said. He still sounded calm and not particularly worried about the whole thing, which only served to increase my irritation. It was easy for him to sit there on his lofty perch after practicing magic almost his whole life, and act as if it was no big deal that my puny little spell hadn't been of any real use. In the back of my mind, I'd been thinking it should have been enough to keep me safe, but clearly, that particular view wasn't anything close to reality.

"Really?" I asked with a lift of my eyebrow.

"Really," he repeated. "It could have slowed them down a bit. Or maybe it was just enough to keep them from destroying your personal belongings. I wasn't here and am trying to look at things after the fact, so about all I can do is offer an educated guess. If nothing else, it gave you a chance to practice your magic, and that's always a good thing."

"If you say so," I returned. Right then, I was more tired than anything else. Although I'd slept okay last night, I'd still had a long day at work afterward, tense the whole time because I kept worrying during my entire shift that Jake Mills was going to jump down my throat for one transgression or another.

Also, my stomach was telling me that the burger I'd scarfed down at lunch had been a *very* long time ago.

"How about we table this for now?" I suggested. "Have you eaten anything? There's a brewpub not too far from here that has great tacos."

Isaac gazed at me for a moment, and I wondered what I would do if he turned me down. This wasn't anything like a date, only a chance to get some desperately needed food in my stomach, but what if he didn't look at the situation the same way?

Then he said, "Sure. That sounds great."

Sagging with relief would have been way too obvious.

"Let me lock up here, then."

The brewpub was too far to walk, and Isaac was blocking my Palisade with his van, so I ended up letting him drive. I did my best not to stare as he expertly piloted the specially equipped van via its hand controls, but I had to admit the setup was pretty slick.

At the same time, I wondered how much a van like this must have cost. Probably a lot more than the SUV I was driving. It didn't seem as if The Enchanted Circle was all that busy, and yet Isaac had the van and a fairly large house in the heart of Santa Fe, both pretty high-ticket items. How could he afford all this stuff?

I told myself it wasn't any of my business. Maybe he'd inherited some money from his mother after she passed away, or maybe he'd gotten a big settlement after his accident. He could have gotten grants to help pay for the van. There were a million different explanations, and if he wanted to volunteer that information to me, then he would.

In the meantime, though, I made myself push the speculations away as I gave him directions to the brewpub. Soon enough, we were pulling into one of the handicapped parking spaces near the entrance.

Since it was a little past seven, the place was pretty packed. Luckily, though, a group of four was leaving as we came up to the hostess stand, and she told us we could have the table as soon as it was wiped down. Isaac and I waited off to the side, and then a few minutes later, we were seated, with him carefully lowering himself into the booth after propping his crutches up against the wall next to it.

"So, the tacos are good?" he asked as he picked up a menu.

"Yes," I replied. "So are the burgers, but I had one for lunch, so...."

He nodded, and our server came by then and asked what we wanted to drink. I requested the lager, since I didn't want anything too heavy, and Isaac ordered an IPA. We also went ahead and ordered our food, since it seemed we were both ready for some tacos that evening.

And once the waitress had left—after promising to be back with our beers in a couple of minutes—an awkward little silence fell. Even though we'd sat across from one another at that restaurant in Santa Fe a few days earlier, this somehow felt different.

I said, "Thanks for coming down here. I really didn't know who else to call."

Isaac smiled, although his expression still seemed somehow serious. "It's not a problem. I just wish I could've found something more conclusive."

Because the booths to either side of us were occupied, I thought it better not to go into any specifics. "Well, but you did find something. At least that tells me we're not dealing with some kids looking for electronics to steal so they can buy this week's meth supply."

That comment earned me a grimly amused nod. "No, that's definitely not what we're dealing with here. Something felt off about the place, about the traces of magic I found on the front door, but I can't really put my finger on it."

"Maybe you'll have a stroke of inspiration after a beer."

He didn't even bother to argue, only gave a small shake of his head. Our server came by with the drinks and promised that our food would be out shortly, thus effectively cutting off that particular topic of discussion.

Just as well. It wouldn't take too much for the conversation to veer someplace I really didn't want overheard.

We clinked glasses, and I said, "*Salut*." The beer was light and cool, and just what I needed right then.

And we would keep it at one beer. Santa Fe wasn't all that far, but Isaac still had about an hour drive ahead of him after our meal.

A drive on a freeway where he'd had his life changed irrevocably a few years earlier.

I told myself that lightning wouldn't strike twice, that thousands of people drove that route every day without incident. Just because I had the heebie-jeebies, thanks to some unknown witch breaking into my house, didn't mean anything bad would happen to Isaac.

To my relief, we kept the conversation pretty light after that, talking about the restaurants I'd found in Albuquerque so far and which ones I liked best, and Isaac describing a few of his favorites up in Santa Fe. Just the sort of normal talk a couple of friends might share over a glass of beer and some tacos.

Afterward, he drove me back to the house so I could get my SUV, although he didn't offer to climb out when I did—not that I would have allowed him to, considering what a procedure it was to get him in and out of that van. He'd parked on the street so I'd be able to back out right away, and he remained there until I'd turned down Central, heading toward downtown and my temporary home base at the Andaluz.

Nothing about that dinner had been particularly earth-shattering, and yet as I rode up in the elevator, I found myself a lot more cheerful than I had any right to be. I'd gotten to see Isaac again, and once again he'd told me to reach out if anything strange happened.

As I slipped the electronic card key into the lock for my hotel room, though, a nervous little tingle moved down my spine. What if I opened the door and found the same wreckage I'd discovered at my rented house the day before yesterday?

When I stepped inside, though, I saw at once that the room looked just fine, the bed made, the ten-dollar bill I'd left out for the housekeeping staff now gone from the nightstand.

Maybe one of these days I'd stop trying to scare myself.

The bottled water had been replenished, too, so I opened one and took a long swallow, then went about getting ready for bed. Yes, it was barely nine o'clock, but we had a five-thirty call on set the next morning, and I needed as much sleep as I could get.

I set the alarm on the clock radio next to the bed for four-thirty, then climbed between the crisp, cool sheets. The place was so quiet, I could hear the faint hiss of the hotel's HVAC system as it pushed air through the vents.

Perfect. I closed my eyes, and was instantly out.

In my dreams, I saw the canyon again. A different day, though, one with a sky not so brightly blue, but thick with storm clouds. In fact, I thought I heard thunder somewhere off in the distance, even though I hadn't glimpsed a single flash of lightning.

And this time, the canyon wasn't empty. Ahead of me ran a figure covered from head to foot in a long black cloak, a piece of clothing so bulky, I couldn't tell whether the person beneath it was a man or a woman. They were moving quickly, though, threading their way among the tumbled rocks and boulders as though desperately trying to evade some pursuer I couldn't see.

Maybe I was that pursuer.

"Wait!" I called out, but they didn't turn around or slow down the slightest bit. If anything, their pace increased.

Even though I knew it was a dream and therefore not something I could necessarily control, I knew I had to try again.

"Stop!" I yelled. "I'm trying to help you!"

Once again, no response. I ground my teeth in irritation and did my best to speed up...only then it seemed as if someone or something grasped my shoulder in a grip of iron, bringing me to an abrupt stop. I tried to look up to see who had caught me, but there was only darkness, the darkness of a well where I was suddenly falling, falling...

...only to sit up in bed, eyes blinking against the bright day slipping past my hotel room's heavy blackout curtains. On the nightstand next to me, the alarm was shrilling, sounding somehow tired, as if it had been doing that for a very long time.

Eyes adjusted now, I stared at the clock, a sinking feeling clenching my gut.

Oh, shit.

Shit.

The time displayed on the clock was nine-thirty. I was supposed to be on set four hours ago.

How the hell had I managed to sleep for twelve whole hours...and also sleep through an alarm that must have been going off since five-thirty? It was a wonder no one had called the front desk to complain about the noise, although I had to admit that these rooms seemed pretty well soundproofed.

Shoving aside the shreds of the dream that still clung to my brain, I jumped out of bed and ran to the bathroom, took the world's fastest shower, and then pulled my hair back in a messy twist and applied a single coat of mascara and one of lip gloss, just so I wouldn't look like I'd rolled right out of bed.

Even if that happened to be exactly the case.

Ten minutes after I'd woken up, I was on I-25 heading north to the studio. My phone showed six missed calls, although everything had gone ominously silent after about 7 a.m. Probably by that point, Jake had given up on me.

At least by that hour, the morning rush hour had mostly subsided. I made it to the studio in record time, and pulled into the parking lot just a hair before ten. As if on cue, people started walking out even as I clicked the fob to lock my SUV.

Just my rotten luck that I'd gotten here right in time for the morning break. Considering when shooting had started today, this should have been more like lunch, but I guessed the midday meal wasn't going to happen for a few more hours.

I spotted Jake going over something on a clipboard with Seth Whitman, the A.D., and pulled in a breath. Never in my life had I been this heinously late to work, and I honestly didn't know the best way to handle the situation.

Seth walked off, heading toward the craft service pavilion, and I knew this would be my best opportunity to talk to Jake without having an audience overhear our conversation.

As I got close, I saw the way his eyes narrowed behind his sunglasses.

"Penny," he said, his tone an irritated drawl. "So nice of you to grace us with your presence. Another break-in? Or maybe you decided to spend the morning getting spa treatments instead of showing up for work."

There was no real way to defend myself—I knew I'd screwed up royally. I only said, "I'm really sorry, Jake. I don't know what happened—I had the alarm set for four-thirty, but I never heard it. I got here almost as soon as I woke up."

"Right." He paused, and I could feel my whole body tense up. "We don't have room for that kind of mistake. Not with this shooting schedule."

Once again, he stopped, pale eyes now glinting behind his Ray-Bans. I got the feeling he was enjoying this.

"Penny, you're fired."

Chapter 8
Change of Scenery

F or one horribly long, agonizing moment, I just
stood there, staring at Jake. My stomach felt
exactly like the time Dave had coaxed me onto the
Tower of Terror at Disneyland—as though I'd left it
roughly five floors above where I now stood.

"What?" I finally managed.

"You're fired," Jake replied, looking even more
pleased with himself than he had when he'd told me
those fateful words the first time. "Two strikes, you're
out. Have a better one."

And then he sauntered off toward the studio
doors, giving the slightest nod at the security guard
who stood there. Ostensibly, the guy's job was to
make sure nothing valuable walked off the set, but I
had no doubt he'd stop me if I tried to follow Jake
and plead my case.

Not that I would even bother. I didn't like the
guy, but he was right about one thing.

In this industry, you didn't get three strikes.

At least no one had been close enough to over-hear the exchange, and so I'd be able to slink off toward my car without any of the cast and crew noticing. I didn't see Joy anywhere around, but I figured she'd find out what had happened soon enough.

When I got to my SUV, I climbed in, shut the door, fastened my seatbelt...and sat there, staring blankly through my windshield at the Dodge truck parked in front of my Palisade.

What the hell was I supposed to do now?

It wasn't even about the money, because unlike most people, I was sitting on the kind of cushion that would keep me off the street for a long, long time. Not too long after Dave and I had broken up, my father asked me to meet him for lunch. I'd thought he wanted to see me to lend some moral support—I knew better than to expect anything like that from my mom—and in fact, he said some nice things about knowing I'd be just fine and how I shouldn't be too hard on myself for the marriage falling apart—but at the end of the meal, he'd pushed an envelope across the table toward me.

"Just wanted to help," he said, his tone quiet but firm, telling me there was no point in trying to tell him I didn't want it.

No, I'd just murmured a thank-you...and waited until I was back in my car before opening it.

Inside that envelope had been a cashier's check for half a million dollars.

I'd stared at it blankly, then blinked away some

tears and shoved the envelope in my purse. Part of me had wanted to send it right back via registered mail, but the rational side of my brain and intervened and told me I shouldn't let my pride get in the way of practicalities. It wasn't that my father couldn't afford to give me that much money...and a whole lot more if necessary; I'd never asked point-blank how much my parents were worth, but I knew they were millionaires many times over. Maybe not Elon Musk or Jeff Bezos territory, just enough so that they—or anyone else in the family—would never have to worry about money as long as they didn't do anything too monumentally stupid.

So, I'd paid off my Palisade, figuring that saving four hundred bucks a month from the car payment could only make me that much more flexible, and then I'd put a hundred grand in an interest-bearing savings account and the rest of it in the highest-yield, lowest-risk investments I could find. Most of the time, I did my best not to think about my extremely unexpected nest egg, but in situations like this, I couldn't help but be grateful for my father's generosity.

All right, so I didn't have to worry about ending up living out of my car any time soon. However, I was also in a weird sort of limbo right then. I couldn't go to my rented house, since it would be unlivable until Ida could get everything sorted out with her insurance company, but I also really didn't feel like going back to the hotel—especially since I'd slid the "please make up room" sign on the handle as I ran out of there, and I had absolutely no idea when housekeeping would actually get around to straightening up the place.

With my luck, they'd be in my room right as I arrived at the Andaluz.

And it was way too early to start day drinking, although I was sorely tempted.

Without thinking, I pointed the SUV north on I-25, heading toward Santa Fe. Maybe it was a spectacularly bad idea to drop in on Isaac like this, but I didn't know where else to go. Also, he and Joy were my only real friends here in New Mexico, and since she was otherwise occupied, he seemed like the logical choice.

I could really use a sympathetic ear.

If it turned out the shop was busy when I dropped in, I'd just excuse myself and go wander around the Georgia O'Keeffe Museum for a couple of hours. I'd been meaning to go there anyway when I had the chance.

Well, it looked like that chance might have just presented itself.

Since I didn't have any real idea how long I was going to be in Santa Fe, I went ahead and parked in the big public structure on San Francisco Street, then walked the couple of blocks to Isaac's store. Although it had been bright and sunny in Albuquerque, up here, a scrim of high clouds covered the sky, and the day felt almost gloomy.

Good. I liked it when the weather matched my mood.

A tall, thin older woman with her white hair pulled back into a sleek ponytail and an impressive turquoise squash blossom necklace adorning her simple black dress was leaving the store just as I walked up. Her gaze passed over me for just a second or two, and I became acutely aware of my messily knotted hair and simple work clothes.

Well, I hadn't come up here to impress random strangers.

True, I would have preferred not to look like ten miles of bad road in front of Isaac, but I had to hope he'd forgive me, considering the situation.

Today, he wasn't in his wheelchair, but standing on his crutches behind the counter. His dark eyes widened in surprise as he realized who his latest "customer" was.

"Penny!" he exclaimed. "What brings you up here?"

"I got fired," I said shortly.

His eyes couldn't really go any wider, but I could tell my flat statement had shocked him by the way his shoulders appeared to tense. "'Fired'?" he repeated. "For what?"

"For oversleeping and missing my call time by about four hours," I replied. Once again, the shop was empty except for the two of us, so I didn't have to worry about unburdening myself in front of any strangers. I had a feeling the impossibly elegant woman who'd just left the store wouldn't be the most sympathetic audience in the world.

"That seems harsh," Isaac said.

Maybe it was. But there just wasn't much wiggle room in a production schedule, especially one for a TV show that needed to have ten episodes wrapped in the next ten weeks.

"Well, I already had one strike against me after coming in late because of the break-in," I told him. "This was just the last straw."

He was quiet for a moment, studying my face as if to get his own read on my reaction to this latest calamity. "How are you?"

In a way, I was relieved that he hadn't tried to probe any further as to the fairness of my getting canned. It was what it was, and no amount of complaining or analyzing was going to change that.

"I'm okay," I replied, moving closer to the counter. Once again, the air smelled of that aromatic incense I'd already begun to associate with Isaac. One of these days, I'd have to ask him what it was. "Kind of numb, I guess. I'm not sure what to do now."

He grasped his crutches and came around the counter so it wasn't separating us. Not for the first time, I thought of how tall he was, how imposing his presence despite having to lean on those crutches. His tone thoughtful, he said, "Maybe you should take this as a sign from the universe."

"A sign of what?" I retorted. "That my producer is an asshole?"

A slow smile spread across Isaac's lips. "It sounds like you didn't need a sign from the universe to figure that out. No, I meant working on this show. I'm getting the impression it just isn't your destiny."

Oh, boy. If he was going to start talking about destiny and that kind of crap, then I was definitely going to need a margarita or at least a glass of wine. Eleven had come and gone on my drive up here, so I figured the hour was close enough to a socially acceptable time to begin drinking.

"Seriously, Isaac, if you start talking about destiny or some sort of 'chosen one' kind of b.s., then we need to head to a bar."

He grinned at that remark. "I don't think we've gotten to 'chosen one' territory yet."

I planted my hands on my hips and slanted him a sideways glance. "What about this whole lodestone thing?"

Maybe his smile faded a little, but he still looked amused. "Being a lodestone is just a special kind of witchy ability," he said. "It's not like it's never happened before and will never happen again. However, I do think you're wasting your talents by fetching and carrying for people who have absolutely no idea what your true gifts actually are."

This little speech was delivered in the sort of calm, thoughtful tone that was exceedingly difficult to counter. While I wanted to tell him that I couldn't think of doing anything else except working in the film and TV business, the truth of it was, my current career wasn't something I'd dreamed of since I was a little girl or anything like that. No, I'd sort of fallen into it when I couldn't figure out what to do with my life...or at least, had partly fallen, been partly pushed, since I'd gotten my first job in the industry thanks to my father putting in a word for me with one of his producer friends.

"So, what do you think I should do with these so-called talents?" I countered, and Isaac shifted on his crutches.

"I'm not entirely sure yet," he admitted. "But we don't have to figure out your entire future just now. Let's start with the basics."

"Which are?"

"Your living arrangements," he replied. "If you're not tied to that place in Albuquerque—"

"I'm not," I broke in. "I mean, I'm there month to month, and it'll be October on Saturday, so...."

"Perfect," Isaac said. "Then there isn't anything stopping you from moving up here to Santa Fe."

For a second or two, I could only stare at him. Then I found my voice and repeated, "'Santa Fe'? Why in the world would I move here?"

"It would be safer," he said without a second's hesitation. "When you're living down there in Albuquerque, there's only so much I can do to protect you. But here you'd be in a position to work on your magic more, get your defenses up."

It was on the tip of my tongue to tell him that I didn't need any man to protect me. However, this wasn't about some kind of strong man/weak woman stereotype, but the very bald fact that someone had broken into my house looking for those damn eyeglasses, and I hadn't been in much of a position to protect myself or my property.

On the other hand, the very notion of moving to Santa Fe sounded beyond crazy.

Well, if nothing else, I could always fall back on practicalities when it came to offering more arguments.

"Have you looked at the rental market in Santa Fe lately?" I demanded. "Even if I wanted to move here, there's hardly anything available."

Isaac didn't look too troubled by that pesky little detail. "Nothing that appears available to an outsider," he said. "But if you're part of the local network, you can find places that never hit Craigslist or Zillow."

"And I assume you're part of this 'local network'?" I inquired.

His smile looked almost smug.

Almost.

"My family's been here for generations," he said. "So yes, I have a few connections. I can make some calls." He paused there, smile fading slightly. "If things are going to be tight for you—"

Oh, no way was he going to try to loan me money. I cut in, "I've got some money. That's not the issue."

He didn't exactly relax, not propped up on those crutches like he was, but the set of his jaw looked a little less tight. "Okay. Then why don't you keep an eye on things out here, and I'll go back in the office and make a few calls."

I didn't see why he couldn't handle that business in front of me, since it was my possible future housing we were talking about, but I didn't argue. No, I just said, "Okay," and he disappeared through a small door set into the wall behind the counter.

It seemed quiet enough that the chances of any customers coming in were probably pretty low. At the same time, I wondered what I would do if someone did show up. I'd never worked retail in my life, and I certainly didn't know enough about the wares Isaac had for sale here that I'd be able to give anyone any concrete help.

To my relief, though, he was back out front within five minutes. "Found something," he said. "It's only an eight-month rental, because the owners will be coming back in June, but still, it's a fully furnished house on the other side of the Plaza. Great location."

Eight months? Did he really think I was going to be in New Mexico eight months from now?

Judging by the way his level gaze met mine, I got the feeling he did.

"Fully furnished?" I said dubiously. "Aren't you forgetting what happened to the last furnished place I rented?"

Isaac didn't look too troubled by that pesky little fact. "That's not going to happen again," he said, his tone full of a confidence I certainly didn't feel.

"Oh, really?"

"Really," he replied. "Because I'll help you set up a cloaking spell, and then whoever's looking for you won't be able to tell where you are."

Despite myself, I let my lip curl in amusement.

"'Cloaking spell'?" I echoed. "You mean like a Klingon spaceship?"

"Not exactly the same thing," Isaac said without missing a beat. "But I suppose the end result is about the same. Why don't we go over and look at the house, and then you can decide what to do?"

This was all moving way too fast. All right, I'd be the first to admit that I'd partly driven up here because I was hoping for some advice as to what I should do next, but I certainly hadn't expected to jump right into a real estate deal.

On the other hand, I needed somewhere to live. I couldn't stay at the Hotel Andaluz indefinitely, and my little rented house in Nob Hill was looking less and less appealing, even once Ida got it put back together.

Whether it would be terribly smart to live quite so close to Isaac Zamora was an entirely different can of worms, but I figured I'd worry about that later.

"What about the store?" I asked. "I don't want you to close and miss out on business just because of me."

"It's fine," he assured me, and I had to admit he didn't look terribly worried. "Did you see the woman who was leaving the store as you came in?"

I nodded.

"She bought that huge amethyst specimen I had in the front window. Wanted it shipped to her home in Bel-Air. Twenty-five hundred dollars. So, I think I can close for the day."

Twenty-five hundred bucks for a hunk of rock? A pretty rock, but still.

But I could see Isaac's point. After making that huge a sale so early in the day, he probably wasn't too worried about missing out on selling a book here or a pendulum there.

"If you're sure—" I began, and he nodded.

"I'm sure. I got the tip from my sister-in-law Rosa—she works at a property management company here in town—and it's not even on their website yet. She said she'd hold it until the end of the day, but after that they're going to start advertising the place."

And even with an eight-month lease, it would probably go fast if the location was as good as Isaac said it was.

"I'm in the Sandoval parking garage," I told him. "Do you want to wait here while I get my car, and then I can drive us over?"

To my relief, he didn't try to convince me he could walk, or try to insist on driving. He said that sounded like a good idea, and I headed off to get the Palisade out of hock. Since I'd only been parked there for twenty minutes or so, it cost me a whole buck.

Isaac was waiting for me outside, one of those little signs with a clock on it and the words "be back at" printed above the clock now hanging from the door. It looked like he'd set it for one-thirty, making me wonder if he planned to go have lunch after we were done looking at the property.

Fine by me. I definitely wasn't going to pass up a chance to go out to eat with him again.

Once he was situated in the passenger seat, he directed me to make a circuit of the downtown area, coming out on what I thought was the northwest side, only a few blocks from the Santa Fe Art Museum, on a quiet, tree-lined little street with well-maintained adobe-style houses and meticulous front yards. I had to admit it looked much more prosperous than where I'd been living in Albuquerque, where not all of the homes had been kept at the same level of repair.

"How much?" I asked, thinking that a house in this neighborhood had to be pricey. Just because I had a chunk of change in the bank didn't mean I could go completely crazy.

"Twenty-two hundred a month," Isaac said. "Normally, it would be more, but the owners are trying to keep it low because the place won't have a full year lease."

That was four hundred more than I'd been paying for the Nob Hill house, but if this place was at all nice on the inside, I'd consider it money well spent to be living in an area like this one.

"That's doable," I said, and he smiled.

"Good to hear."

He directed me to pull up to the square adobe house, which had a gorgeous, old-fashioned front yard full of hollyhocks and roses, and with a lovely weeping willow off to one side. The walkway and the front porch were reddish tile, as were the interior floors I saw after Isaac entered the combo in the lockbox and got out the key.

And the house really was lovely, in that wonderful, mellow Santa Fe style, with dark beams overhead, hand-painted tile set into the molded-plaster fireplace, and Navajo rugs underfoot. The furniture was understated, a soft brown leather sofa and tables in the same dark wood as the beams. I had no doubt that my friends back in Southern California, all with their fashionably gray-toned homes, would have thought the place hopelessly old-fashioned, but I liked it.

I felt safe here.

"What do you think?" Isaac asked.

"It's nice," I said neutrally. No point in gushing when I hadn't seen the kitchen or the bedrooms yet.

But those were equally wonderful, the kitchen larger than I'd thought it would be. Tile counters, yes, but they matched the house, whereas I didn't know whether granite would have worked as well in here. The appliances were stainless, though, and looked almost brand-new, as did the fixtures in the two bathrooms.

The backyard was just as nice, with a built-in barbecue and bar area, and a spa hidden away behind some evergreens. I didn't know how much longer it would be warm enough to sit out here and enjoy that spa, but I wanted to find out.

"Okay, it's amazing," I told Isaac after we'd completed our little tour. "I'm ready to sign on the dotted line."

He appeared relieved, as if he hadn't been quite sure that even this home's numerous charms would be enough to convince me to move to Santa Fe. "I'll send Rosa a text," he said.

"Perfect."

We went back inside, and I watched as he typed out a quick message to his sister-in-law. It was actually quite a feat of dexterity, the way he was able to maneuver his phone while holding himself up on those crutches. Almost as soon as he'd sent the text, his iPhone pinged, and he looked back down at the screen and nodded.

"Okay, we're set," he said. "Her office is just about to close for lunch, but she said you can come by after one o'clock."

For some reason, the way he'd said "you" rather than "we" relieved me a bit. I had to be grateful for the way he'd found this home for me, but it would have felt weird to have him watching as I sat there and signed the lease papers.

"Great," I said.

"But that leaves time for lunch," he went on. "Sound like a plan?"

"Definitely," I replied. "We can celebrate with margaritas."

"I know just the place."

It turned out he did, because after that he directed me to the La Fonda Hotel, a gorgeous historic building right off the Plaza. We didn't go to the main restaurant, however, but instead headed to the bar, where they served a variety of margaritas—

and also a menu that included some of the tastiest dishes offered at the hotel's restaurant.

"I could get used to this," I said after I took a sip of my prickly pear margarita. The place was dark and clubby, with a small stage off to one side that told me they probably had live entertainment here in the evenings.

"They do make good margaritas," Isaac agreed. Apparently, he'd thought my finding a place in Santa Fe was cause for celebration, since he'd ordered a classic margarita on the rocks. I already knew he wasn't a complete teetotaler, because he'd gotten a beer at the brewpub a few nights earlier, but still, this was the first time I'd seen him have anything alcoholic during the day. But then his expression turned serious, and he went on, "So, what's the plan?"

"'The plan'?" I echoed as I took another sip of prickly pear. Mmm. Yet another thing about Santa Fe I could definitely get used to. "Well, I suppose I'll go back to Albuquerque after I sign the lease papers, then check out of the hotel and head up here." A thought occurred to me, and I added, "Oh, and swing by the house and clear out the kitchen. All my personal stuff is already at the Andaluz, but I didn't bother to get the food out of the kitchen. Still, I should probably be back in Santa Fe by late afternoon."

"Let me know when you get here," Isaac said. "We'll want to cloak the house as soon as possible."

That whole concept sounded so silly to me.

However, since his expression was serious, almost grim, I didn't even bother to argue. "Sure," I said.

He relaxed against the back of his chair. "Good."

And that seemed to be that.

After lunch, I went to the property management office, signed the lease papers, and put all the deposits on my debit card. Thank God that was an option, or otherwise I would've had to run over to the bank to get a cashier's check.

Still, I was on the road by two o'clock, headed south to Albuquerque so I could close out my life down there.

For better or worse, it seemed as though my future lay in Santa Fe.

Chapter 9
The Woman in Black

"I'm sure the house will be safe now," Ida Martinez protested, and I tried not to scowl down at my phone, which I had on speaker. This was the last bit of business I needed to handle before getting on the road, and I'd been purposely putting it off.

Confrontations and I really didn't get along.

"It's not the house," I said. "I'm going to be working in Santa Fe now, so it just makes sense for me to move someplace closer."

That was a bald-faced lie. Isaac could talk about destiny all he wanted, but that didn't hide the fact that I was now unemployed for the foreseeable future. I had no doubt that stories about what a flake I was had already begun to circulate in the New Mexico filmmaking community, which didn't bode well for my continuing career as a prop shopper.

But since I really didn't want to tell Ida I'd developed witchy powers out of the blue and apparently was some sort of magnet for magical objects, the story about getting a new job was a useful fiction.

"Well...." She dragged out the syllable, clearly unhappy with the situation, but also realizing she didn't have any way of getting me to keep renting her house, since there was no lease, only a month-to-month agreement. "Best of luck in Santa Fe, then. You can just leave the keys in the house after you're done there. I'll come by and get them later."

"Thanks, Ida," I said immediately, glad she wasn't going to try to prolong the argument. "I'll be done in a little bit. You have a good day."

"You, too."

We ended the call there, and I shoved my phone in my purse with some relief. Honestly, I was just about done—I'd swung by Trader Joe's to get a bunch of their reusable shopping bags, and now the contents of the freezer and fridge resided in a couple of insulated carriers, while the stuff from the pantry had already been stowed in several brightly colored totes covered with New Mexico motifs, like green chiles and the Zia sun symbol.

I took the shopping bags out to the Palisade and placed everything in the cargo compartment next to my suitcases. It still felt a little weird to think that my whole life was in the back of that SUV, but on the other hand, there was something to be said for being mobile.

Speaking of which, time to get on the road.

By then, it was a little after four o'clock, and the start of the afternoon rush hour had already begun to clog I-25. However, the traffic was still so light compared to what I'd had to deal with in Southern California that I couldn't complain too much. I got off the highway right around five, and by a quarter after, I was pulling into the driveway of the house that would be my home base for the next eight months.

Well, unless I got chased out again.

I pushed that gloomy thought to the back of my mind. This was a fresh start, and I had to hope things would work out better here. Maybe Albuquerque had also been blocking my *chi*.

The property had a real two-car garage, although it was detached from the house. Still, I felt a lot better knowing my SUV would be safely locked up, and since I had to cut through the pretty yard to get to the back door, I got to enjoy looking at the garden all over again. In January, the walk might not be so nice, but I told myself I could still enjoy it for now.

It didn't take very long to get the food put away, and only a few minutes more to hang up my clothes and set my bag of toiletries down on the vanity in the master bathroom. By that point, it was almost five-thirty. I thought Isaac's store didn't close until six, but even if he came over now, he wouldn't be missing out on too big a portion of his workday.

I sat down on the sofa in the living room with my phone and sent him a quick text.

Okay, I'm here. Ready for cloaking whenever you are.

The reply didn't come back for a few minutes,

making me wonder if I'd been a little too flip in my message.

To my relief, though, his reply just said, *Okay, finishing up with a couple of customers. Be over when I can.*

I supposed I had to be satisfied with that.

To while away the time, I poked around in the kitchen and discovered a nice set of Riedel wine-glasses, some sturdy-looking cutlery, and a very attractive service for eight of some red-glazed dinnerware. Not that I was planning on entertaining that many people—the dining room set only had four chairs, and I didn't even know four people in Santa Fe—but it was still nice to know I wouldn't be eating off paper plates. Likewise, the laundry room was well-stocked with all-natural detergent and a bunch of other organic-looking cleaning supplies. Clearly, whoever owned this house had left behind all the important stuff.

And when I turned on the TV, it looked like it had pretty much every streaming service known to man. Isaac's sister-in-law at the property management company had told me all those channels were included in the rent, but I still hadn't quite believed I wouldn't have to pay extra to keep up with my favorite shows.

Obviously, pretty much any kind of television viewing I wanted wasn't going to be a problem.

I'd just set down the remote for the TV when someone knocked at the door. Almost at once, my nerves started shrilling with alarm...until my brain kicked in and told me that was just Isaac coming over, and not a bunch of criminal witches trying to pat me down for those stupid eyeglasses, which were still tucked into my jacket pocket, now hanging in the coat closet.

As I'd thought, there was Isaac standing on the front porch. At once I stepped out of the way so he could come in; he was using his crutches, yet something about the painful way he pushed himself into the living room told me he probably should have switched over to the wheelchair but was too stubborn to do so.

"Go ahead and sit down," I told him. "Do you want some water? That's about all I have."

Well, that and a few bottles of wine from TJ's, but I didn't know whether I should bring up drinks this early in the evening.

"Water would be great," he said. He looked a little less tired now that he was sitting down, but I still got the impression he'd been pushing too hard today.

I headed into the kitchen and got a pair of glasses from the cupboard, then filled them both with water from the refrigerator door. After I returned to the living room and handed one of the glasses to Isaac, I sat down on the love seat opposite him.

"Getting settled in?" he asked.

"Yes," I replied. "Not that I had much to settle. But this is a great house—thanks again for finding it."

"It wasn't a problem," Isaac replied. "It helps to have family in the real estate business."

Since my own father was something of a real

estate mogul, I couldn't really argue with that comment. To be honest, I'd always gotten the impression he was disappointed Dave had already owned a house, because I had a feeling my dad would have loved to find one for us. "True," I said. I sipped some water, then ventured, "So...how does this whole cloaking thing work?"

"It's not so hard," Isaac replied, then put his own glass of water down on a coaster so he could reach into the breast pocket of his shirt and pull out a folded piece of paper. "This is the spell," he added, pushing it across the coffee table toward me.

Oddly, I found myself reluctant to pick it up. Maybe that was just because I knew if I took this spell from him and did my best to make it work, then I really was admitting that magic was real and that I might—just *might*—be able to work with it. True, I'd cast that protection spell back at the house in Nob Hill, but if I'd left it at that and never tried anything else along those lines, I could have dismissed the whole thing as sticking my toe in the water and nothing more.

This, though...this felt much more significant.

I picked up the piece of paper and looked down at the lines of text it contained, written in a neat, precise hand. Isaac's handwriting was much better than mine, that much was obvious.

"*With these words I utter here, conceal this place from those I fear.*" I paused there and glanced over at him. "That's all?"

"Well, it's a translation," Isaac told me, looking

almost embarrassed. "My mother passed all her spells down to me, and they're written in Spanish, so I had to do my best to come up with a workable English version. It's the intent behind the words that's most important."

That statement made me lift an eyebrow. "And you're sure it'll work as well in English?"

"There's no reason why it shouldn't."

He sounded pretty confident. Then again, he had much more experience with this sort of thing than I did, so I supposed I should believe him.

"Is that how it works?" I asked next. "I mean, is magic a family kind of thing?"

"Yes," Isaac said. "Well, in most cases. There are definitely instances where the line has been lost, so to speak, and so while people might realize having psychic gifts runs in their family, they don't know that they're actually witches. Also, every family's magic has a little different flavor, for lack of a better term. My mother inherited her grimoire—her spell book—from her mother, and then added her own spells to it. Then it came to me, and I've been doing the same thing. Magic is always a work in progress."

Although what I knew about magic could basically fit in a thimble, I had to admit I sort of liked that idea, liked the thought of magic being a living, growing thing, and not a bunch of ossified rules that had to be followed to the letter.

"And I'll be able to use your spells?" I asked, knowing how dubious I sounded. "I mean, I'm not a Zamora. I don't even know what I am."

"You're you," Isaac said, now smiling slightly. However, I didn't get the impression he was laughing at me, but more that he didn't see any reason for me to be worried. "And that's enough. There's nothing that specifically bars a witch from using spells from another family. It's more that we tend to stick with what we know."

"And since I don't know anything, I have to start somewhere," I remarked.

"Well, I wouldn't go that far," he returned. "I just want you to know that you'll be fine working with these spells. Go ahead and read it over, and then when you're ready, hold this."

From his pocket, he produced a shiny black stone.

Obsidian? Maybe. I had to admit I wasn't an expert. The black stone could also have been onyx or even jet.

"What's it for?" I asked.

"To help you strengthen your energies and amplify the spell. We want to make sure it's as powerful as possible."

I couldn't argue with that. After what had happened to the house in Albuquerque, I wanted to turn this place into the Fortress of Solitude.

Once again, I looked down at the paper Isaac had given me. It was going to feel beyond embarrassing to say those few lines out loud, but it needed to be done.

Or rather, he thought it needed to be done. Right now, I still didn't know whether I could admit to myself that magic just might be real.

Well, time to bite the bullet.

I took the piece of obsidian and held it in my right hand while I grasped the paper with the spell and pulled in a breath. Time to focus, to see if this magic that supposedly resided within me could be put to some use.

"With these words I utter here, conceal this place from those I fear."

Once I was done, I set the paper and the obsidian stone down on the coffee table and looked around. As far as I could tell, absolutely nothing had changed.

"Did it work?" I asked.

Isaac nodded. "Oh, yes. I can feel it. The air is... charged, for lack of a better word. There are protective energies swirling all around us. Now anyone who's looking for you won't be able to tell that you're here at all. In fact, I think you probably won't have to worry about anyone knocking on the door that you didn't expressly invite over here."

As far as I was concerned, that was a good thing. Not that I had to deal with solicitors or over-aggressive Jehovah's Witnesses too much, since I was hardly ever home during the day, but it was still nice to know I wouldn't have to deal with too many interruptions here.

Well, except for Girl Scouts selling cookies. I sent a silent message to the universe that I was just fine with them dropping by any time they wanted.

"Okay," I said, then sat there, feeling oddly deflated. So, I'd supposedly protected my house, but what was I supposed to do now?

Either Isaac had picked up on my mood, or the question had been plaguing him ever since I showed up in his shop that morning, fresh from my firing. "So...do you want to talk about what happened this morning? What made you sleep in so late?"

Good question. I was not the sort of person to sleep through an alarm. In fact, I was one of those annoying people who could wake up and be pretty functional even without coffee, although I hardly ever skipped it, just because I liked having a latte or whatever to start the day.

"It was weird," I said. "I was dreaming about the canyon."

Isaac didn't bother to ask which canyon. "You were?" he asked, dark eyes lighting with interest, although he couldn't exactly lean forward on the couch the way most people might. I'd already noticed that once he got himself into a position, he tended to stay there until it was time to stand up. Probably, there was too much effort...and pain...to do otherwise.

I nodded, then reached for my glass of water and took a sip.

Too bad it wasn't merlot.

"The dream itself felt really short," I told him. "That's why I couldn't quite believe it when I woke up and saw how late it was. In my dream, I was running after someone in the canyon. They were wearing a long black cloak with the hood pulled up, so I couldn't really tell anything much about them."

"Man or woman?" Isaac inquired.

About all I could do was give a helpless lift of my shoulders. "I couldn't tell. They were running fast, though, and I was doing my best to keep up. I kept calling out that they didn't need to run, that I was trying to help them, but they never turned around or even slowed down. And then it almost felt as if something grabbed me by the shoulder and yanked me out of the dream. That's when I woke up."

Isaac rubbed a hand across his chin, brow furrowing slightly. "What did the canyon look like?"

"The same, as far as I could tell," I responded. "Oh, but it seemed stormy this time, and I thought I heard thunder."

"Monsoon season," Isaac said in musing tones.

Right. My research on New Mexico had told me they got some pretty wild thunderstorms in the state during the summer. Supposedly, the official season ended on September thirtieth, although I hadn't seen a single storm since moving here. Too bad, because thunderstorms were rare in Southern California, and I would have liked to experience at least one of the fabled monsoons before they disappeared until next year.

I made a noncommittal sound, and he went on, "It sounds to me like the glasses are still trying to tell you something, and are reaching out in a different way."

Great. So, now I was going to have to worry about having nightmares every time I went to sleep?

I crossed my arms and remarked, "Well, if that's the case, they could have been a little clearer."

Yes, I knew I sounded grumpy, but right then, I didn't care too much. I was having a hell of a week, and it was only Wednesday.

The corners of Isaac's mouth lifted slightly. "That's not how these things work. Visions and dreams come of their own accord and on their own schedule. But I do have a suggestion."

"What?" I asked, trying not to sound too wary. I'd had enough shake-ups and shocks that week to last me a good long while.

"Put the glasses under your pillow tonight. That way, whatever they're trying to transmit might come through a little more strongly."

I didn't like the sound of that proposition very much, but I also had to admit I didn't have any brilliant ideas of my own. "You're sure about that?"

"It's worth a try." He paused there, then said, "Well, now that you're situated here, I should get going. I have a meeting I need to get ready for."

The disappointment that rushed through me at those words was as strong as it was unexpected. I didn't even know what I'd been thinking—maybe that the two of us could crack open a bottle of wine and order something in, and he would stay here a bit to help ease my transition to a new city.

Apparently, Isaac didn't think I needed that much hand-holding.

"Oh, sure," I said at once, hoping he hadn't been able to read anything of the conflicting emotions that had just erupted within me at his announcement. "Thanks for coming over."

"It's no problem." He took hold of his crutches and awkwardly got to his feet. "Give me a call tomorrow to let me know how it went with the glasses, or stop by the shop."

"Will do," I replied.

I went with him to the door, and he slowly made his way down the front walk to his van. Part of me wanted to remain standing there and watching, just in case he needed some help getting inside, but then I realized that was the last thing he'd want. He'd been doing this for years on his own, and probably wouldn't be thrilled to have me act as though he didn't have it all handled.

Instead, I closed the door.

Time to open that bottle of wine, even if I'd have to drink it alone.

It felt completely silly to slide the glasses under my pillow that night. In fact, I pulled them out and set them on the nightstand, only to heave a breath a moment later and put them back beneath the pillow.

Nothing ventured and all that. Besides, it wasn't as though I would have any witnesses to this latest evidence of my insanity.

The house had one of those little white-noise generator gizmos sitting on the bedside table, and I'd already turned it on to rain sounds, figuring I could manufacture a monsoon storm even if I couldn't experience it in real life. This was a quiet street anyway, but now I knew I wouldn't be able to hear anything that was happening outside...which could be a good or a bad thing, depending on how you looked at it.

Still, since it had been a very long day...and since I'd had two glasses of wine with my takeout dinner...I fell asleep almost as soon as my head hit the pillow. I didn't know how much time passed before the dream stirred in my subconscious, but there I was in the canyon again.

As before, thunder cracked overhead, and dark clouds covered the sky. I was running, running like I hadn't run in real life for more years than I could count, my feet driving me forward as though they knew I had a date with destiny, even if my conscious mind still couldn't quite comprehend what was happening here.

I couldn't see the figure in the black cloak. No birds circled overhead, and despite the tumult of the storm, the canyon felt oddly still, as if it held its breath, waiting for me to reach my destination.

No, there, up ahead. I squinted past the bright copper strands of hair that whipped around my face, caught in the nearly gale-force winds.

A dark figure, lying prone on the ground, the black cloak still concealing anything of the person who lay beneath it.

This time, though, I was able to approach, was able to kneel down in the reddish, powdery dirt. My hand shook as I reached out to grasp the fallen person by the shoulder and turn them over.

The hood fell away from their face, and my dream-self gasped.

It was me.

No...wait.

I blinked, realizing that this woman was a stranger, for all she resembled me so closely. The same fiery red hair—although hers was much longer, lying in waves over her shoulders and almost down to her waist—the same swoop of eyebrows and full, almost amused lips, although her face was a touch wider, more heart-shaped than oval. Her eyes were shut, but I had no doubt that if she opened them, they'd be the same cool gray as mine, touched with just the barest hint of green.

What the hell?

Did I have a long-lost sister or something?

As that thought passed through my mind, though, I realized I was dodging around the truth because even in this dream...vision...whatever it was... I didn't want to acknowledge the reality of what I was seeing.

This woman couldn't be my sister.

This woman was my mother.

Chapter 10
Unburying the Past

I sat bolt upright in bed, my breath coming in gasps, cold sweat dripping down my back even though the room was warm enough. A blink, and I took in the time on the clock next to my bed.

Three o'clock.

Not an hour that was exactly conducive to texting Isaac. Besides, I couldn't go running to him every time something strange happened to me.

I pushed back the covers and went into the kitchen so I could get myself a glass of water, flicking on lights as I went. While nothing about the dream had been gruesome in the way that vision with the vultures had been, I was still far more shaken now than I was when I caught a glimpse of that shallow grave.

Now I had a pretty good idea of who had been in that grave.

A couple gulps of cold water helped to steady me a bit, although my knees still felt like rubber and my hand shook as I lowered the glass to the tile counter. My brain kept tracing the features of the woman I'd seen in my dream, taking in all the similarities to my own face while noting the differences. In fact....

I always kept a little pad of paper in my purse for jotting down notes or making quick sketches, and I hurried back to the bedroom to fetch it. For some reason, though, I felt safer in the kitchen, and so that was where I went, and set the pad down on the tile counter so I could draw the woman's face before it disappeared from my memory.

Not that such an outcome seemed particularly likely at the moment. The stranger's features were probably engraved on my brain for all eternity.

Thank God for all those art classes I'd taken in college. I'd never had any ambition to be a true artist, since I knew I was a good draftsperson but not particularly inspired. In the back of my head, I'd thought that maybe one day I could get a career doing storyboards for the movies. But then I'd sort of fallen into the prop-shopping thing, and that was the end of that particular notion.

Still, I was able to create a fairly decent rendering of the woman from my dreams, again near enough to me in appearance that she had to be a close relative, even though my conscious mind was already rejecting what had seemed like such a resonant truth while I was dreaming.

She *couldn't* be my mother. All right, there had been the usual family jokes about where my red hair had come from when my mother was blonde and my father sandy brown, but even so, it was generally accepted that redheads sometimes popped up in family trees almost out of the blue. And while I didn't resemble either of my parents that much, so what? I had lots of friends who didn't look much like their parents, either.

And yet....

Some more water down my throat, something to help ground me in reality. Unfortunately, I got the feeling that an ocean of water wouldn't be enough to erase the doubts that began to creep around the corners of my mind, doubts I was finding it harder and harder to ignore.

What if my parents really *weren't* my parents?

Isaac had told me magic was hereditary, was passed down through the mother, and yet I knew beyond a shadow of a doubt that my mother wasn't a witch any more than I was President of the United States.

Some kind of adoption charade, then? I honestly wouldn't put it past my mother to fake going to the hospital and having a baby just to cover up the fact that she hadn't actually given birth at all.

It had to have been a pretty elaborate fake-out, though, since we had pictures of her in the delivery room, sweaty and with no makeup on, holding a brand-new me, all red-faced and not too happy about being introduced so rudely to the world.

Well, these were all mysteries I wouldn't be able to solve right away. I could only imagine my parents' reaction if I called them in the middle of the night demanding to know whether I was adopted.

No, anticlimactic as it seemed, I needed to go to bed and try to figure this out in the morning.

First, though, I was taking those damn eyeglasses out from underneath my pillow.

Surprisingly, I slept just fine the rest of the night, and didn't wake up until almost eight the next morning. Not having to get up at the crack of dawn to be on set was something of a luxury, and I allowed myself a nice stretch before I got up, put on my robe, and wandered down the hall to make some coffee.

The sketch of the woman from my dream still lay on the counter. I allowed myself to pause and stare down at it, once again marveling at how much she looked like me, although I thought she was probably a little younger, in her middle twenties rather than her early thirties. The sketch was just pencil, of course, but I remembered how her hair in my dream was almost the same shade of red as mine, a bright copper that people always thought had come out of a bottle, even though it had been the same shade ever since it darkened a bit during puberty. That color red wasn't exactly common.

Maybe it would help me to figure out who she was.

If she was real at all. The dream had felt real enough, true, and yet it seemed somehow wrong to let myself go down this particular path. Hadn't I always prided myself on being tough and matter-of-fact, even if my imagination did have a tendency to get away from itself from time to time?

Still, if I was simply manufacturing all of this drama for some obscure reason, why would I have thought up all those minor differences between the strange woman's face and mine? Wouldn't it have been more conclusive to have her look exactly like me?

I didn't know, and before I tried any more pondering on the issue, I figured I'd better get some caffeine in me. The kitchen was equipped with a Keurig and a pretty impressive collection of K-cups, and so I chose hazelnut cream just to be decadent. Rosa at the management company had told me I could use whatever I wanted, and just needed to replace it when I moved out, so I wrote a quick note to myself as to what I was drinking that morning, although I knew the smartest thing to do would be to take a couple of photos of the contents of the pantry so I'd know exactly what to get when that day came, some eight months from now.

Having some coffee in me definitely helped, and when I discovered a package of bagels in the freezer, I felt that much happier. Consuming some carbs might help to improve my mood that much more.

The makeshift little breakfast did help, as did the shower and morning prep that followed. All the same, I knew I was tense, on edge. I wanted to talk to

Isaac, but I also knew there was someone else I really needed to speak to first.

My father.

No way in hell would I approach my mother with this—I could only imagine her reaction if I tried to insinuate she might not be my genetic parent—but I guessed my father might be a little more understanding. Or at least, if he thought I was leaping to crazy conclusions, he would still try to find a way to let me know it was okay and he'd be there for me no matter what.

By that point, it was just a smidgen before ten o'clock. My father usually got into his office some time between eight-thirty and nine, which meant—since California was an hour behind New Mexico—I had a fairly decent chance of catching him at work. There was always the off chance that he might not be at the office yet, might have had to go do a site inspection or check out a new piece of land he was thinking of acquiring, but I decided the odds were probably in my favor.

If not, I'd try again later.

I checked my appearance in the bathroom mirror, making sure I at least didn't look like a crazed madwoman. Maybe I appeared a little tired, but that wasn't so strange. My parents were used to me being exhausted half the time, thanks to the hours I usually worked.

Right then, I felt almost relieved at the thought of not having to get up and drag myself on set for the foreseeable future. I had no idea what the future might hold for me, but at the very least, in the meantime I'd be able to catch up on some sleep.

Back to the living room, where I sat down on the couch. I'd opened the blinds once I was dressed, and so a mellow morning light flooded the room, making it appear serene and welcoming. I still didn't know for sure whether that cloaking spell really was working or not, but I definitely felt safe here.

I unlocked my iPhone and pulled up FaceTime. Usually, I just called or texted when I got in touch with my parents, but in this particular case, I wanted to see my father's face while we were talking. In his business dealings, he was much harder to read, but I could usually glean a lot from watching the shifts in his expression.

The phone buzzed a couple of times, and then my father appeared on the screen. He looked obviously startled to have me reaching out to him like this.

"Penny?" he asked, blue eyes piercing as he regarded me through the screen. "Is everything okay? Why aren't you at work?"

"They let me go," I replied. Somehow, that sounded better than saying I'd been fired. "But it's all right."

"They 'let you go'?" he repeated, looking flabbergasted...and more than a little indignant that someone would have the balls to shit-can Gerald Briggs' daughter. "What happened? What are you going to do now?"

"It's a long story," I said. Maybe at some point I'd

give him all the details, but I didn't think that was necessary right now. I could tell he was genuinely concerned about me losing my job...even though he really didn't need to be, thanks to the huge cash cushion he'd given me following my divorce. "And I'm not totally sure what I'm going to do next, but I'll figure something out. I did relocate to Santa Fe, though—a friend found me a great place to land."

My father's brows lifted slightly, although I thought I detected a certain relief in his clear blue eyes. I knew he hadn't been super-thrilled about the whole Albuquerque thing, which just seemed silly to me. Being there certainly wasn't any more dangerous than living in L.A.

But because I didn't want to get into that, I went on, "Anyway, I have kind of a weird question to ask you."

"What?" he responded.

Now that the time had come, I found myself wishing I'd never initiated this damn call. I should have talked to Isaac first and seen what he had to say on the subject. But no, I really needed to get this out of the way. It was entirely possible that my father would say there was no way what I'd been thinking could be true, and that would be the end of the matter.

Never mind that this wasn't a genie I'd be able to put back into the bottle. Once I asked the fateful question, it would be hanging out there for all eternity.

I shifted my phone to my other hand and said, "Is

there...is there any way that Mom couldn't be my biological mother?"

Since I was staring intently at my phone's screen, I didn't miss the way something in my father's expression seemed to fall, as if all the muscles in his face had suddenly lost their elasticity.

His next words weren't what I was expecting.

"How did you find out?"

I blinked at his image on the phone screen. "'Find out'? You mean she *isn't* my biological mother?"

The muscles in his throat moved as he swallowed. Eyes not quite meeting mine, he said, "She never wanted you to know."

Clearly, or they would have been up front with me from the beginning. My voice shook a bit as I demanded, "Dad, tell me what the hell is going on!"

He glanced over his shoulder, although I could tell from the backdrop of bookshelves and serene watercolors of the Pacific Ocean that he was in his office, and probably had the door shut. No chance of eavesdroppers there. However, I could understand his caution, considering what he said next. "The doctors told your mother she couldn't have children...that her eggs weren't viable, even though she could carry a child to term. So...we got an egg donor. I'm your biological father, but your mother doesn't have any actual genetic connection to you, even though she carried you for nine months."

The room was spinning around me. Or rather, it seemed as if my surroundings had gone blurred and strange, and refused to resolve themselves into anything resembling normal furniture and walls and windows.

Thank God I was sitting down.

I blurted out the first thing that crossed my mind. "What about Cade?" I asked.

My father looked wearier than ever. He ran a hand through his short-cropped, gray-dusted hair and said, "He's your mother's. That's why she always called him her 'miracle baby.' It wasn't just that we didn't think she could get pregnant at forty-three—it was more that she shouldn't have been able to get pregnant at all."

No wonder she lavished so much love on my younger brother, and barely had any to spare for me. I'd never lacked for anything material growing up, but the only true affection I'd gotten had been from my father. One would have thought my mother might feel connected to me simply because she'd carried me in her womb all those months, and yet it seemed that biological relationship wasn't enough for her.

Maybe she'd sensed she was carrying something alien, a cuckoo placed in their comfortable suburban nest.

A witch's daughter.

A lodestone.

Just because my father had given me one answer... a staggering one, true...didn't mean I didn't have plenty more questions to ask. "Do you know who the donor was?"

He shook his head. "No. We worked with a very

discreet fertility specialist who got the donor egg for us. All we knew was that she was in her early twenties, with red hair and gray eyes, no known health issues or anything that would send up a genetic red flag. It sounded like a perfect match for us, and I suppose your mother and I were both hoping you'd get my brown hair. But when you showed up and were a redhead from the moment you were born...."

The words slipped away into the ether. Although my father hadn't completed the sentence, I thought I could guess what he was about to say. If my coloring had favored my father...if I hadn't looked so much like the woman who'd contributed half of my genetic material...then it would have been a whole lot easier for my mother to pretend I was hers, and to tell herself—and her friends—that I resembled my father's side of the family, that's all.

But since I didn't look much like either of them, they'd had to fall back on flimsy fictions about recessive genes and a great-great-grandmother who'd had red hair.

"And you really thought I'd never find out?" I demanded.

My father passed a distracted hand across his chin. He was impeccably clean-shaven as always, so the gesture had been a nervous one and nothing more.

"We hoped you wouldn't," he said. "Or at least, your mother kept hoping. She told me there was no point in telling you that you weren't her biological child, since the egg donor was anonymous and there was no way you could ever track her down."

I found that hard to believe. Why should finding that mysterious red-haired stranger be any more difficult than it had been for those people who'd managed to find the woman who had given them up for adoption years and years before?

"What was the name of the fertility clinic?" I asked. My voice probably sounded harder than I'd intended it to, but now that the shock had begun to wear off, a cold, sharp anger had started to take its place.

They'd kept this from me. They'd lied to me my entire life.

"Dr. Lightman retired years ago," my father said. "His practice is closed. That's a dead end, Penny." He stopped there, ocean-blue eyes somehow sad and piercing at the same time. "How did you even think to ask these questions?"

Because I saw my mother in a dream, I thought. *And because she's dead, and I'm sure she was murdered.*

If I said any of that out loud, my father would think I was certifiable. Just letting those words pass through my mind was enough to make me wonder the same thing.

"A lot of reasons," I said. I would have to lie, but in this case, I thought doing so was justified. The truth was just too unbelievable, was based on dreams and feelings, absolutely nothing that could be quantified. "A lot of stuff that just didn't add up. Maybe being here in New Mexico gave me the distance I needed to get some perspective." I stopped there. My father's worry was so palpable, I could practically feel it coming off my phone's screen.

Was that worry for me...or for my mother, a fear that I would now confront her with the truth?

"I'm not going to say anything to Mom," I went on. "I mean, I can't promise that I'll never bring it up, but I'm definitely not going to initiate some kind of long-distance confrontation, if that's what you're worried about."

"I'm worried about *you*," he countered at once, an edge entering his tone. "I knew it was wrong to keep this from you, and I should never have let your mother's wishes override what I knew was the right thing to do."

Easier said than done, probably. My father was pretty much ruthless when it came to his business—although I'd never heard a whisper of him doing anything outright illegal—but my mother still walked all over him in private. It was almost as if he still couldn't believe such a beautiful creature had consented to marry him, and so, almost forty years after they'd taken that vow to love and honor one another, he still did whatever it took to keep her happy so she wouldn't walk out and leave him alone.

"I'm fine," I said, and oddly, thought that assertion might have been nothing more than the truth. It was going to take a while to come to terms with all this, but at least I wasn't living a lie anymore...or not much of one, at any rate. I had a feeling it would take a lot longer before I dared confess to anyone that I was also a witch.

As my mother had been. Who had she been running from? What had chased her into that desolate canyon, where she'd obviously died alone?

"You're sure?" my father asked, and I nodded.

"Thank you for telling me the truth," I said. "I mean it. My whole life, I've felt as if I was missing something, as if there was some dynamic going on beneath the surface that I just couldn't figure out. Now I know what that something was."

"I'm sorry we kept it from you this long," my father said. He still looked pale and strained under his tan, but I could tell the shock was starting to wear off as he regained his equilibrium. "And I'm glad to hear you're in Santa Fe, but if you want to come back to California—"

At once, I shook my head. "No, I think I've landed in the right place. I just need to figure out what my next steps should be."

"But you'll be home for Christmas?"

When I'd left, I'd promised my parents I'd come home for the holidays, since by then the shoot would have been over, and even if I intended to stay in New Mexico, I would have had a few weeks off, if not more, depending on when the next gig landed.

Now I had even more free time, and yet I found myself hesitating. Was it just that I didn't know whether I'd be able to face my mother any time soon? And okay, Christmas was still almost three months off, but still....

"I don't know yet," I said, the only honest answer I could give him right now. "I'll just have to keep you posted."

My father's expression was more resigned than anything, as if he'd known that was the only possible response he could expect. "All right. You take care, Penny, and if you need anything—"

"You've already done enough for me, Dad," I broke in, but gently. "I'm going to be fine. And you take care, too. Love you."

"Love you," he responded.

I ended the call there, realizing that my eyes had begun to tear up, and I didn't want him to see me cry. Not that he hadn't plenty of times before, but....

This wasn't any time to fall apart, though.

I needed to talk to Isaac.

And then...and then, I needed to find out who'd killed my mother.

And why.

Chapter 11
Bloodlines

After some dithering, I decided to walk over to Isaac's shop that morning. I knew I'd rather discuss such sensitive topics in person, and besides, it seemed silly to waste a gorgeous early fall day when his store was only a ten-minute stroll from my new digs.

This time, he actually had a few customers, and so I had to hang back and pretend to browse one of the bookcases until he'd bagged up his patrons' purchases and they'd headed out the door. He'd acknowledged me as I walked in with a small head tilt, but now he came out from behind the counter, concern etched in the faint line between his dark brows.

"Something's happened," he said, and I raised an eyebrow.

"So, you're psychic, too?"

"Not exactly," he replied without missing a beat.

"But I can sense things about people, and you feel different."

Different. Yes, I could definitely state that I felt different. Maybe learning you weren't actually who you thought you were could do that to a person.

"I saw the woman in the cloak in my dream last night," I told him. "I saw her face. She looked like me."

A flicker of surprise passed over Isaac's elegant features. "'Like you'?" he repeated, tone almost uncertain.

I nodded. "Not exactly like me, but close enough. Seeing her face made me wonder about a whole lot of things, and so I called my father."

Isaac looked slightly nonplussed by this particular *non sequitur,* and so I continued.

"It turns out my parents used an egg donor to conceive me," I explained. "That's how I could be a witch when my mother obviously isn't one."

Comprehension dawned, lighting up his warm brown eyes. "Of course," he said. "That makes perfect sense. I have to admit I've been trying to puzzle out how you could be so powerful after you told me there was no way your mother is a witch." A pause, and then he asked, his tone gentle, "How are you doing?"

"I'm all right," I said briefly, my standard response when I knew the truth would be too uncomfortable.

Isaac sent me a penetrating look, but it seemed he

was going to allow me my little lie, as he didn't say anything, only waited for me to go on.

"So, it looks like my biological mother passed her witchy talents on to me," I continued, then cocked my head up at Isaac, since he was on crutches again today, rather than using the wheelchair. "What are the odds of that happening, anyway? Inheriting witch talents, I mean."

"For women? Almost fifty percent," he replied. "For boys, the chances are much lower, maybe only ten or fifteen percent. That's why my mother was so relieved when my own magic started to appear. She was worried the magic of her line would end with her."

I could imagine. And with odds like that of having your child inherit your magical talents, I supposed that was why the world wasn't overrun with witches.

After acknowledging his comment with a nod, I went on, "My biological mother died in that canyon. I don't know how, or why. But she was running from something. She was frightened."

For a moment, Isaac remained silent. Then his mouth tightened, and he deliberately went to the shop door and turned around the sign in the glass inset so the "closed" was facing outward.

I wanted to tell him that particular measure wasn't necessary, but I maintained my silence. He knew how much business he needed to keep the shop viable, and I didn't.

"This is making more and more sense," he said, and I frowned.

"Want to clue me in, then?" I returned. "Because none of it makes any sense to me."

Although he didn't smile, something in his expression warmed a bit. I didn't get the feeling he was laughing at me, though, but rather that he wanted me to know he'd be here to help me through this whole mess.

And I couldn't help but be grateful for that. True, my father and I had cleared the air somewhat, and at least he was no longer hiding such a huge lie from me even if my mother apparently was fine with continuing to do so until the day she died. But there wasn't much my father could do to guide me through this search to figure out exactly what had happened to the woman who'd contributed to half my genetic makeup.

No, that was a job for a witch.

"Let's go in the back room," Isaac suggested. "We can sit down and have some coffee."

That sounded like a great idea. With the door to the shop locked and the "closed" sign clearly displayed in the window, we could talk without being interrupted.

So, I followed him behind the counter and through the door I'd spotted the first day I came into the shop, and down a short hall with storerooms on either side. At the end of the hall was clearly the break room; it had a mini microwave, a coffeemaker, and an electric kettle on a small table off to one side, and in the center of the space was a beat-up wooden bistro set.

Isaac pointed at one of the two chairs. "Go ahead and take a seat. I hope Italian roast is okay—that's the bag I'm working through right now."

"Sounds great," I said as I sat down. Although I'd wanted to offer to make the coffee myself, I knew I needed to let him do it. I still couldn't pretend I knew him all that well, but it was pretty obvious to me he was fiercely independent and wanted to do whatever he could to prove he could get along just fine despite his disability.

And, to be fair, he got the coffee going with a minimum of fuss, showing he'd done the same thing hundreds of times before and so had the procedure pretty much down pat by this point. A few minutes later, he was placing a cheerful red and brown glazed mug full of coffee in front of me.

"Do you need any cream?" he asked, nodding toward the mini refrigerator off in one corner. "Or sugar?"

"Black is fine," I responded. I didn't always drink my coffee that way, but I'd already indulged myself with hazelnut cream that morning and didn't think I needed any more sugar.

"Okay."

Apparently, he drank his coffee black as well, because he brought his own mug over to the table without doctoring it at all. A moment to settle himself in the chair opposite mine, crutches deposited on the floor, and then we were settled.

"Tell me about what you saw," he said.

The coffee was too hot to drink, but I picked up my mug anyway and blew on the liquid inside. If nothing else, it felt good to hold that warm mug between my chilled hands. No real reason for that, since the day was shaping up to be mild enough, but I guessed my cold fingers didn't have much to do with the weather outside.

And then I launched into a description of my dream, and of the woman I'd seen in it. Through all this, Isaac sat quietly, his fingers wrapped around the handle of his own mug, although, like me, he was clearly waiting to drink it.

When I was done, he said, "You just knew she was your mother? How?"

My certainty on that subject was much more difficult to explain. It was as if the realization had come from somewhere deep within my gut, a bone-deep knowing I couldn't really quantify.

"I just knew," I said. "And it made sense."

"Made sense how?"

I gazed across the table at him, at the lean, elegant bones of his face, the faintly hooded dark eyes under the level brows. They were features that echoed bloodlines carried down through the centuries from the original conquistadors who'd come to these lands, although I somehow doubted any of those early Spanish warriors would have looked quite so gentle, so patient.

Now we came to the part of the story I wasn't sure I wanted to relate. Isaac and I had only known each other for less than a week. Did I really want to spill my guts about the troubled relationship I had with my mother, especially when I wasn't sure whether my story was going to come off as some poor little rich girl complaining that not everything was perfect in her insanely entitled world?

But I realized I needed to tell Isaac the whole truth, because otherwise, a lot of this wouldn't make any sense.

"My mother and I never got along," I said quietly. "Or rather, I always got the feeling she resented me in some way, even though on the surface, I was a model child. I got good grades. I never got into trouble...I mean, nothing more than sneaking a beer at a party or something. I always tried to do whatever I could to make her happy. And yet...it wasn't enough."

I stopped there, wondering if I was being just a little disingenuous. All of that was true, but I also couldn't help thinking about the way I'd zeroed in on Dave when I met him at a mutual friend's party. In the back of my mind, I'd known at once my mother wouldn't approve of him, would think he was too loud and coarse, not the doctor or lawyer or producer or whatever else she would have found much more appropriate.

Then again, I'd met my ex when I was twenty-four. By that point, I'd pretty much given up on ever trying to please my mother. Instead, I'd decided to do whatever I could to tick her off...and had succeeded pretty spectacularly.

Of course, I'd also managed to shoot myself in the foot at the same time. My bad.

Isaac's fingers tapped against the side of his mug. "And so you think this friction with your mother was because you weren't her actual child, genetically speaking."

About all I could do was lift my shoulders, then take a cautious sip of coffee. It was still a little too hot, but not enough to scorch my tongue.

"It makes the most sense to me," I replied. "My whole life—at least, once I was old enough to really process what was going on between the two of us—I kept wondering what I'd ever done to make her be such a bitch. Now I think she just never bonded with me, for whatever reason."

"I'd say she still has some serious problems to work out," Isaac commented, and allowed himself a sip of coffee as well. "After all, hundreds of thousands of women adopt children or even carry children that aren't biologically theirs, and yet I have a feeling they'd be offended if anyone suggested they weren't attached to those kids simply because they didn't share the same genetic material."

Since I couldn't really argue with that statement, I just shrugged again. "You're probably right. But I guess that's for her and her shrink to work out. Frankly, I'm tired of dealing with her crap. Right now, I'm much more interested in finding out who my biological mother really was...and who killed her."

Isaac reached up to run a hand through his hair. A single lock fell over his forehead as a result of the mussing, making him look even more distractingly gorgeous, and I did my best not to stare. I had to hope at some point I'd stop reacting to his every gesture, because I had much more important things to focus on.

"Are you sure about that?" he asked, but he sounded genuinely curious, not as though he was trying to be challenging just because. "That she was murdered, I mean. After all, you haven't yet seen the actual moment she died."

And thank God for that. While I supposed I should be grateful that I'd begun to uncover my past, there were some things I wasn't sure I wanted to witness.

"No, I haven't," I admitted, and sipped some more coffee. It had finally cooled to the point where I thought it would be safe to drink without worrying about burning my mouth if I took a real swallow. "But I saw the way she was running. That was a woman running for her life. And besides, if she'd dropped dead of natural causes—which seems kind of weird for someone who looks to me like she was in her mid-twenties at the most—why would she have ended up in a shallow grave? Someone had to be trying to cover up her murder."

"Good points," Isaac said. His hands were still wrapped around his coffee mug, but it didn't look as though he intended to drink any more any time soon. "And since part of being a witch is having good intuition, I'm willing to go with your gut on this one."

Too bad my "good intuition" hadn't steered me

away from Dave all those years ago. Then again, according to Isaac, my *chi* had been pretty well blocked back then, thanks to my mother's animosity. I guess my gut had been biding its time, waiting for an opportunity to steer me in the right direction.

Which apparently had been New Mexico. Had those instincts guided me here because my mother had died somewhere in this large and mysterious state? After all, when I'd been perusing all the listings for various productions starting up over the next few months, there had been a bunch in California, along with the usual stuff up in British Columbia, mostly a lot of Hallmark Channel movies. I could have gone with something like one of those productions and still been at least a thousand miles away from my ex.

But I'd come here, following an impulse I hadn't really understood at the time. Even though that was a pretty woo-woo assessment of the situation, I had to admit there must be some logic to it.

"I have no idea where to start, though," I said. "I know what she looked like, but that's it. I don't have a name or date of birth or anything at all to go on, in something that's got to be a cold case from more than thirty years ago."

"Well, let's start with what you do know," Isaac replied. If he was at all daunted by the task that lay ahead of us, he showed no sign of it. "You know what she looked like."

"Yes." I'd actually folded up the sketch and stashed it in my purse, so I reached around to where I'd slung the bag off the back of my chair, dug inside for a moment, and then pulled out the piece of paper and set it on the table. "I drew this earlier this morning, while the dream was still fresh in my mind."

Isaac reached for the sketch and smoothed it with one hand, expression intent as he stared down at the paper. "This is very good. You didn't mention you were an artist."

Unwelcome pink flushed my cheeks as I replied, "It's because I'm not. I mean, I majored in art, and I took a lot of studio classes, but I don't call myself an artist. Once upon a time, I thought I might try doing storyboards, but...."

"Maybe you still can," he said. "After all, just because you got fired from this one job doesn't mean you have to walk away from the entertainment industry completely."

Well, I had to give Isaac that much—he was awfully good at finding something positive in almost any situation. An image flashed into my mind of myself sitting in my light-filled living room, an easel in front of me as I sketched away at a board based on a director's notes.

It would definitely beat getting up at 4 a.m. to come in and move props around, or getting sent on a wild-goose chase for a prop the director suddenly decided he had to have right then.

"Maybe," I allowed, then figured we should get back on topic. "So, we have a sketch of the woman I think is my biological mother, but I'm not sure how far that's going to get us."

He drank some coffee, expression considering. "I

suppose the first thing to do is try to dig up what we can about any missing-persons cases here in New Mexico around the time you were born, maybe as much as a year later. After all, we don't have any idea when she died, or how much time had passed after she donated her eggs."

No, we didn't know that, just as we had no idea what might have driven her to do such a thing in the first place. Had she needed the money? I didn't know much about the whole process, but I did know that women could get paid a decent chunk of change for donated eggs...in California, at least. Maybe the laws were different here in New Mexico.

There was just so much I didn't know.

Before I could speak, Isaac went on, his tone musing, "It's odd that a witch would have done such a thing in the first place, though. After all, she was taking the risk of having a child with powers born to people who would have no idea what they were getting into."

Put that way, the whole situation seemed much stranger. My shoulders lifted, and I said, "I don't know. Maybe she needed the money?"

"Maybe." He shook his head then. "That doesn't make a lot of sense, though. Witches tend to be...well, not rolling in money or anything, but our power to attract abundance usually means we're comfortable at least."

"Oh," I said, and stopped there. It sounded like a bunch of law of attraction woo-woo to me, but since I'd pretty much accepted woo into my life by this point, I realized I probably shouldn't make a disparaging comment.

Isaac's dark eyes assumed an amused glint. "Don't tell me you weren't wondering how I could afford my house."

"I never—" I began, and stopped, because of course I'd wondered pretty much that exact thing.

To my relief, he didn't look offended at all. "I got a deal on the place because it needed some work, and I spent the first year I lived there making repairs. Even so, I could only afford the house because I'd inherited some money when my mother passed. And then the accident happened."

Isaac stopped there, but I remained silent. I certainly wasn't going to interrupt him when he was clearing up details that had puzzled me. Maybe he thought it was all right to be in a confessional mood because I'd told him all that crap about my mother and the way she'd treated me when I was a child.

"I honestly didn't know whether I'd be able to keep the house," he went on. "My brothers helped me get things set up so I could live on the ground floor, but still, no one knew when—or if—I'd be able to go back to work. The family kept the store open with limited hours, trading off who could work there as best they could, but it still wouldn't have been enough, especially with all my medical bills. I had insurance, but...."

Once again, he paused. I could only imagine what the accident must have cost him.

"I thought maybe you'd gotten a settlement from

the other driver's insurance," I said, and Isaac sent me a grimly amused smile.

"The other driver died in the accident, and he didn't have insurance. It would have been his fourth DUI, if he'd lived. Anyway, it was looking pretty dire there for a while."

I leaned forward in my chair, once again wrapping my hands around my mug of coffee. "So, what happened?"

Something in Isaac's expression lightened, as if recalling all this had brought the experience back to him a little more vividly than he'd planned. "Well, I was showing some improvement, but the doctors still couldn't give me anything close to a firm date when they thought I'd be able to go back to work. I'd just gotten home from my latest appointment with my physical therapist, and there was a letter waiting for me."

"A notification that you'd won the lottery?" I quipped, and his mouth quirked even as he shook his head.

"Not exactly, but close. No, it was a letter from one of my clients."

"'Your clients'?" I repeated. "You mean, one of your customers?"

"No," he said. He lifted his mug of coffee and swallowed some. "That is, I have the store, but I also do readings for people, perform spells. It's nothing you'll find on the store's website or anything I advertise, but word still gets around to the people who need me to intervene with something. Anyway, I had a client who asked me to help her with her fertility issues—she wasn't getting any real assistance from the medical community and was feeling desperate. So, I performed several rituals over the space of a few months, and she ended up getting pregnant and giving birth to a healthy baby boy."

"That could have been coincidence," I said dubiously. Not that I wanted to knock Isaac's magic or the power of the rituals he'd performed, but still, the doctors had all told my mother she'd never be able to conceive, and yet she'd had my brother Cade. Strange shit happened sometimes.

"Possibly," Isaac responded, not looking at all offended by my skepticism. "But I don't think so. And my client didn't think so, either. She said in her letter that it was all due to what I'd done for her, and she'd been so wrapped up in the pregnancy and having the baby that she hadn't heard about what had happened to me until one of her own clients mentioned it to her. But she said she wanted to give back...and sent me a check for fifty thousand dollars to say thank-you."

My eyes widened. "That's a pretty big thank-you."

"Having a child when you thought you'd never be able to have a family of your own is also a big deal. She and her husband are quite successful," Isaac added. "I knew sending me that money wouldn't cause her any hardship. All the same, though, it was a gesture I hadn't expected—and the money she sent was enough to keep me going, keep making the payments on my house—until I was able to get back to the store and get back to performing rituals for people."

"That's pretty amazing," I remarked, and a crinkle of amusement touched the corners of his eyes.

"Or just part of being a witch," he returned. "The universe provides when we need it to. Which is why I'm not sure I can believe your mother donated her eggs out of a need for money and nothing else."

I supposed that made some sense, but at the same time, I couldn't quite figure out what else would drive a woman to give up such an intimate part of herself, especially since she couldn't have known who would be getting those eggs. From what my father had told me about the fertility clinic they'd worked with, the whole setup had been made as anonymous as possible.

"It is strange, though," Isaac said. "I'm just trying to puzzle out why your biological mother would have ever considered doing such a thing."

"Because she wanted to make sure there would be more witches in the world?" I asked—a feeble question, but I honestly couldn't come up with any other explanation.

However, Isaac didn't take my query as a joke, but frowned slightly. "I suppose I could see that happening. It depends on what her family was like."

"Why would that make a difference?"

His fingers tapped against the side of his mug, but he didn't drink any of the coffee inside...probably because, like mine, it had gone lukewarm by that point, and so had lost a lot of its appeal.

"Witch families can vary greatly in their makeup, in how they operate," he replied. "Some are very tight-knit and opposed to intermarrying with outsiders...which can lead to some problems, as you can imagine."

Unfortunately, I could. Inbreeding was never a good look.

"Others are much more open," he went on. "Families like mine view these talents as gifts from God, and so we don't try to control them too much."

Once again, I found myself echoing Isaac's words. "'Gifts from God'?" I said. "I thought witches were pagan."

Someone else might have sent me an indulgent smile at that kind of comment. Because it was Isaac, he looked serious enough as he said, "No, being a witch is all about the power within you, what you were born with. Witches can be Christian, Buddhist, Wiccan, atheist...it's really up to the individual. My family is very Catholic and still goes to mass every Sunday. Or at least, most of us do. I stopped after the accident for obvious reasons, and I haven't really gotten back into the practice of attending. But I still see myself as a member of the Church."

A Catholic witch. Who would've thought? Then again, I had to admit my experience of witches wasn't exactly very broad...although that experience seemed to be widening daily.

So, maybe my bio-mom had been running away

from a restrictive family and had decided that selling her eggs to a fertility clinic was some sort of subversive act. Or maybe she really had needed the money. Just because Isaac had said most witches tended to be prosperous, it didn't mean they all were.

"Do you think my biological mother was from New Mexico?" I asked next, and Isaac tilted his head at me.

"I suppose that's what we'll need to find out," he said.

Chapter 12
Left Turn at Albuquerque

As it turned out, Isaac had a cousin who worked for the Santa Fe police department...because of course he did. I wondered what it would be like to live in a place where you had connections everywhere, but I supposed that was what happened when your family stayed put in the same locale for generations.

Anyway, Isaac took my sketch into the small office adjoining the break room, scanned the image, and then emailed it to his cousin, explaining that he was helping a friend and wanted to know if anyone matching that description had been reported missing some thirty-odd years ago.

"It's still kind of a long shot," he admitted after he sent the email. "I mean, it's not like we're dealing with the dark ages before computers, but still, not everything was computerized in the early '90s. We'll just have to cross our fingers."

"And light a candle?" I suggested with a grin, not really serious.

But Isaac took the comment at face value. "That's a good idea," he said. "Candle magic is a very effective way of focusing our powers. And I think I have just the right one."

Which was why we ended up back in the break room, a candle smelling faintly of vanilla and cardamom burning on the little bistro table as we both concentrated on the intention of discovering my biological mother's true identity and—I hoped— finally bringing her some peace.

And that led me to my next question.

"How is it that I'm even seeing all these things?" I asked as the candle burned away in the background. Isaac had said we should keep it going for at least an hour, hopefully more, and that he would snuff it once he thought it had done its work. Apparently, blowing out a candle was a big no-no, as doing so would blow away all your intentions at the same time.

It seemed I had a lot to learn about all this magic stuff.

Thank God he was willing to teach me.

"I have a couple of theories about that," Isaac replied. He'd told me he should probably re-open the shop, and so we'd headed back to the store proper, leaving the candle burning in the storeroom. But even though he'd unlocked the front door and turned around the sign in the window, it didn't look as though anyone was beating down the door to buy a crystal or a book on tea-leaf reading.

I reassured myself that he had other, less visible means of support, and that the lack of customers probably wasn't a huge problem. Besides, if anyone showed up to shop, we'd have to stop talking, and I certainly didn't want that.

"So, what are your theories?" I asked, after darting a glance at a couple of people passing the shop's front window. It appeared they were intent on a different destination than The Enchanted Circle, however, because their pace didn't slow and they continued along the sidewalk, disappearing a moment later.

Isaac had been headed toward the bookcases at the back of the shop when I asked the question. Now he paused in front of one of them, looking thoughtful. "Well, my main theory is that your mother must have enchanted those glasses to have them keep a record of what was happening around her."

I considered his suggestion, then frowned. "But if that's the case, why wouldn't all these visions be from her point of view? When I see them, it's like I'm watching a movie, like I'm some sort of omniscient spectator and not the person all this stuff actually happened to."

Isaac straightened a book on one of the shelves, crutch propped under his arm, and then shifted back toward me. "Magic doesn't necessarily work that way. For your mother to get an accurate rendering of whatever was happening in her life, she would have wanted the enchantment to step outside her, for lack of a better explanation. And because it's magic, that would have been completely possible...if she was gifted enough."

So, the eyeglasses I'd found at the antique mall had been hers? Those glasses hadn't seemed like the sort of thing a twenty-something would want to wear, but then again, hadn't the early '90s been all about grunge and granny dresses and looking like a throwback to the hippie era? Since I'd been only a toddler at the time, I couldn't really comment, but I supposed it was possible.

"Okay," I said. "What's your other theory?"

"That the glasses belonged to her killer," Isaac replied. "And that's why you're not seeing things from her point of view."

I didn't like that idea very much at all. The mere thought of having a cold-blooded murderer's glasses slipped under my pillow—or tucked into my jacket pocket, as they were now—made an uneasy twinge pluck at the muscles between my shoulder blades.

"You'd think a killer would want to hang on to something like that," I said lightly, doing my best not to show how Isaac's speculation had gotten to me.

"You would," he agreed. "And so I'm not sure that's the right theory. A third one is that they belonged to someone else entirely, someone who was a witness to the whole thing, for whatever reason."

I couldn't help shaking my head. "I get the feeling this particular killer wouldn't have left any witnesses around."

"Probably not," Isaac said. "And so I think that one's probably a long shot. At the same time, we might not want to discount it entirely."

The door to the shop opened, and I immediately

turned toward the display of Tarot and oracle cards behind me, pretending to be perusing the various options on the tabletop. Out of the corner of my eye, I watched as a couple of women around my age, maybe a little younger, went up to Isaac. One of them gave him a frankly appraising look, and I had to do my best to fight back an irrational and utterly pointless flare of jealousy.

"We're looking for some pendulums," the woman said breathlessly. She had one of those baby-high voices that set my teeth on edge, although I had no way of knowing whether that was her natural tone or whether it was something she'd affected because she thought it was appealing to the male half of the species. How she'd come by that particular conclusion, I didn't know, although I assumed it had something to do with watching too many episodes of *Keeping Up With the Kardashians* during her formative years.

"Right," her friend chimed in. This woman's voice wasn't quite as high-pitched, but I recognized the Southern California drawl right away. "We saw some witches on Instagram using them, and they looked totally cool."

Witches on Instagram? I generally stayed off social media because I saw it as a massive time suck, but I supposed I could see how that might be a thing.

However, watching the cool, efficient way Isaac handled the two women—and ignored their not-so-subtle attempts at flirting—I had to guess that most... if not all...of those witches on Instagram weren't the real thing, but only people who thought playing at magic might be an easy way to gain more followers. At least, I couldn't see someone like Isaac, whose powers appeared to be genuine, putting himself out there like that. The website for his store didn't have one of those "follow us on Facebook!" logos on it, or anything else to indicate the shop had any sort of web presence at all beyond the actual site itself, which made sense for someone who most likely wanted to keep a pretty low profile.

It probably only took him about five minutes to handle this unwanted intrusion, but it felt like an hour to me. However, the two women eventually wandered off, clutching their paper bags of pendulums and crystals.

"You think they're actually going to use those?" I asked as he came back over to where I'd been loitering by the bookshelves the entire time.

A wry smile played around the corner of his mouth. "I somehow doubt it. Or at least, I can see them messing around with those pendulums for a couple of days before they get distracted by something else. But hey—a sale is a sale."

I supposed that was one way of looking at it. In retail, you couldn't exactly pick and choose your customers, although my instincts told me Isaac was probably a little more discriminating when it came to who he did rituals and readings for.

And I realized that even if Isaac's wasn't the busiest store in the world, he was still at work and didn't need me constantly distracting him. He'd given me some insights—and, more importantly, had provided a comforting presence when I definitely needed one, but I really couldn't expect him to drop everything and hold my hand every time I hit a bump in the road.

"Well, I should get back to the house," I told him. "But thanks for talking me through all this. It helped a lot."

For a second or two, he only regarded me, face almost expressionless. He must have realized I thought I was intruding, though, because he didn't ask me to stay, but only said, "That's what I'm here for. And if you need anything else, you know where to find me."

I offered him a smile, one I had to pray looked almost genuine. "That I do. Have a good one, Isaac."

And I headed out, hoping I'd struck just the right casual note. No mention of getting together for dinner, or that I'd drop by later that day. The last thing I wanted was for him to think I was clingy, or that I couldn't manage all this on my own.

Whether I actually would be able to was an entirely different question.

It actually felt good to putter around the house a bit, and to head out to the local grocery stores and pick up a few odds and ends. The parking lot at Santa Fe's one and only Trader Joe's was an absolute nightmare, but I managed to return home unscathed and put away my purchases, wondering what I should do next. It felt beyond strange to be idle like this, to realize I didn't have to do anything with my time that I didn't want to do.

All right, then. We were working on the hypothesis that the glasses had belonged to my mother once upon a time, but how had they ended up at that antique mall in Albuquerque? Except for a few minor scratches, they appeared to be in remarkably good condition for a pair of eyeglasses that must have exchanged hands multiple times over the past thirty years.

Well, the day was mine. And I'd just realized what I should do with it.

Since I'd already grabbed a quick bite for lunch, I was pretty much ready to head down to Albuquerque. I brushed my teeth, refreshed my lipstick, and headed out to the garage.

Midday, the traffic was pretty light, and so I made it to the heart of Albuquerque in a little less than an hour. It felt kind of strange to be back here so soon after beating feet to Santa Fe, but I'd figured the only person who could possibly give me any information as to the provenance of the eyeglasses was the man who ran the antique mall, and so that was where I headed.

The place seemed pretty dead on that Thursday afternoon. Just like the fateful day when I'd bought the glasses in the first place, I had to wander around a bit before I found the owner, who was helping an elderly couple with a truly hideous pair of Dresden porcelain lamps.

Once he had set the lamps aside, and they'd wandered off, presumably looking for some knick-knacks to supplement their ugly new lighting décor, he turned toward me. Something about his expression seemed almost startled, as if he hadn't expected to see me again so soon.

"Hi," I said. "I wanted to ask you about these glasses."

And I pulled them out of my jacket pocket.

Almost at once, he seemed to shut down. "No returns," he said, dark eyes narrowing a bit.

I summoned a reassuring smile. "I don't want to return them," I replied. "But I was wondering if you could tell me where they came from."

His little Vincent Price mustache twitched. "I wouldn't know anything about that," he said. "I just sell what the vendors put out in their various stalls."

That possibility probably should have occurred to me. Pushing back my disappointment, I said, "Well, can I talk to the vendor? Do you have their contact information?"

"I can't give you that," he said, his tone almost prim. "But she's supposed to be here on Saturday afternoon to add more things to her stall. You could come back then and ask for yourself."

Great. I really didn't like the idea of having to drive all the way back down here on Saturday.

Then again, what else did I have to do with my

time? It wasn't like I would have earned a deserved day off after putting in a hard week on the set.

Trying not to sound too disheartened, I said, "I'll do that. Thanks for the info."

And I went back out to my SUV, climbed behind the wheel, and then sat there for a moment, wondering what the hell to do next. It seemed beyond ignominious to turn around and head straight back to Santa Fe, and yet, I couldn't come up with any other options. The one and only person I knew in Albuquerque—well, besides Ida Martinez, who I doubted would be too thrilled to hear from me —was Isaac's cousin Joy. And since she was probably busy up at I-25 Studios right now, it wasn't as though I could give her a call and ask her if she wanted to go wine tasting or something.

I tapped my fingers on the steering wheel, a frown pulling at my brows. There had to be something I could do.

Then I realized I was a woman with unlimited free time and money in the bank.

Obviously, I needed to go shopping.

I'd already plotted out the most likely shopping destinations when I first got to Albuquerque, so I knew I wasn't too far from ABQ Uptown, an outdoor mall that had a variety of upscale restaurants and shops...among them, a MAC store.

Well, I had a few lipstick colors that needed replenishing.

That seemed to settle things. I pushed the button for the ignition, then backed out of my parking space and headed toward Lomas Boulevard, since I knew I could take that route to get to my destination.

And even though I'd been stymied in one pursuit, I was able to spend the next few hours happily shopping, picking up items I knew I wouldn't have gotten for myself if I'd still been working full-time on set. That kind of work didn't require anything pretty or even stylish, just functional pieces that could layer and stand up to some hard work.

Since it seemed as though my days as a prop shopper were behind me, I indulged myself in designer jeans and embroidered hoodies and the sort of free-flowing cardigans I'd admired on other women but knew would only have gotten in my way at work. Heeled boots and fun belts and a luscious teal-green wool coat I couldn't resist, since it looked so great with my hair. And, of course, an entirely decadent stop at the MAC store, where I got replacements for my lipsticks that were running low and bought a few shades I thought would be fun to try for the upcoming fall and winter.

Clearly, my subconscious mind had already decided I wasn't going anywhere, even if I had my reservations about remaining in Santa Fe when I was so obviously at loose ends.

The retail therapy did a lot to improve my state of mind, though, and I turned up the radio and sang along once I was on the highway headed home. Maybe I didn't have the most perfect pitch, but so what? No one else was in the car to hear me.

My mood improved even more when my phone *bing*ed as I was passing through Bernalillo just north of Albuquerque, and I allowed myself a quick glance at the screen.

A message from Joy.

Hey, it said, *want to get together Sat. afternoon & go wine tasting? There's a new place that just opened up near the Plaza.*

Albuquerque, I recalled, had its own plaza at the heart of the old downtown, even though it wasn't as big and fancy as the one in Santa Fe. I'd never made it over there, and this sounded like the perfect opportunity to go exploring, to put aside all the drama of the past few days and go out and have fun like a regular human being.

I picked up my phone and dictated a reply. *Sounds great. What time?*

How about 3? I have some errands I need to run first.

OK, I sent back. *Send me the deets & I'll meet you there.*

Will do.

A moment later, a link for the tasting room's website came through. It looked bright and sunny and welcoming, and very new.

See you then! I replied, and I got a thumbs-up icon a few seconds later.

Well, it looked like my Saturday plans were handled. With any luck, Joy and I could extend the wine tasting into an early dinner, and then I really wouldn't have to worry about what Isaac was up to, or whether it would be utterly transparent if I invited him over for takeout or something. I actually could cook if I stuck to a few tried-and-true standards, but I hadn't really tested out the kitchen in my new digs and would prefer to try it myself before I started cooking for anyone else.

If he would even accept such an invitation. I thought it fairly likely he'd consider that crossing a line. So far, he'd been friendly...and nothing more.

Which was as it should be. Both our lives were complicated enough without throwing a relationship into the equation. No, we just needed to be friends and nothing more.

Uh-huh, I thought, but I didn't want to give myself too much grief over that little white lie. At least this attraction to Isaac had proved I was more than ready to move past my failed marriage and look forward instead of dwelling on everything that had gone wrong in my life.

I'd just have to wait and—in Isaac's parlance—see what the universe intended for me.

Chapter 13
Time to Wine Down

It was past five by the time I got home, and everything at the house appeared to be precisely where I'd left it, which was definitely a relief after my experiences at the rented place down in Nob Hill. I put away my new purchases...and did my best not to imagine myself wearing them while going out to dinner with Isaac. We might have shared a few meals, but they'd been strictly business. Expecting anything more was just silly.

However, he did call a little after six. "Everything quiet over there?" he asked.

"Very," I said. For a second or two, I considered telling him about my aborted trip to the antique mall, but since nothing had come of it, I didn't see the point. "I did some shopping, but that's about it."

"Good," he replied. "It sounds like the cloaking spell is doing its job. I just wanted to let you know that I heard back from my cousin with the Santa Fe P.D."

"And?" I asked, although I wasn't holding out a lot of hope.

I caught the faintest hint of a sigh through the phone's speaker. "And...nothing. I knew it was kind of a long shot, but I suppose I was hoping they might have something on file that would provide some sort of a clue."

Honestly, I couldn't even allow myself to be terribly disappointed. After all, we were talking about someone who'd probably died at least thirty years ago. Pretty much anyone who'd been on the force back then would have retired by now...or worse...unless they'd been a rookie fresh from the police academy.

"Well, you tried," I said.

Isaac's reply came back at once. "Oh, I'm not giving up that easily. Roy said he knows someone with the FBI, and so he's going to pass the sketch along to them. They've got much better databases, and if it turns out your biological mother died someplace other than New Mexico, there's a much higher chance of the Bureau having access to information about that case."

While all that made sense, I didn't know how thrilled I was about getting the FBI involved. What if it turned out that she'd died of natural causes, no matter how frightening my visions might have seemed on the surface? I really didn't need the FBI thinking I'd sent them on a wild goose chase.

Almost as soon as that thought passed through my mind, though, I could feel how wrong that particular theory was. I still had no clear idea exactly what had happened to the woman who'd contributed to half my genetic makeup, but I knew for damn sure there had been absolutely nothing "natural" about her death.

"Thank you," I said. Those two words sounded awkward at best, but I didn't know how else I was supposed to respond.

"It's the least I could do," Isaac replied. "But I'm glad everything's been quiet."

I reflected that I could have done with a little less quiet, if it meant having him come over to the house. However, I only made a noncommittal sound.

"Oh," he went on, his tone shifting slightly, becoming brisker, "I don't want you to think it's an imposition or anything, but I was talking to a long-time client today, and he said he might have some work for you."

"'Work'?" I repeated, hoping I didn't sound too dubious. To be perfectly honest, I'd been kind of looking forward to some time off, even though I knew eventually I'd start to get bored out of my mind if I didn't have anything to do with myself.

"Not prop shopping," Isaac said. Although I couldn't see his expression, of course, I got the feeling he was smiling slightly, crinkles showing at the corners of his dark eyes. "No, he produces a lot of independent films, and he's looking for someone to do some storyboarding for him. Totally freelance, obviously—there's no studio to go to or anything like that."

I let myself relax slightly. That sounded as though

it could be a good gig...and hadn't I been fantasizing about doing that very thing just earlier that day?

The skeptical side of my brain tried to tell me this was all too good to be true, but I did my best to ignore it.

"That sounds like fun," I said. But then I realized I wasn't really set up for that kind of work and quickly added, "I don't have a portfolio or anything... and I don't have any art supplies—"

"It's fine," Isaac cut in. "He said he could give you a couple of scenes to sketch out, and you could use those as a sort of audition. As for the art supplies, there's a great place over on Cerrillos. It's called Artisan—you can Google it."

Despite myself, I was getting a little excited. Was it possible I might be able to fall into another career as easily as that?

"Got it," I said, then paused. So many thoughts were passing through my mind, and I wasn't sure which one I should articulate first. I blurted, "This is really so much, Isaac. I mean, first you found me this house, and now you might have found me a job—"

"It's really nothing," he broke in, sounding a bit embarrassed. "That is, I think this is more the universe providing for you than anything else. I told you things usually work out for us witches...if we're willing to take a breath and understand that things come to us when we need them most."

A comforting philosophy, that was for sure. I still didn't know whether I could completely believe him, but I was willing to go along for the ride right now. If nothing else, this would be a welcome distraction from the continuing enigma of my biological mother's death.

"Can I give Peter your email?" Isaac continued. "I wanted to check with you before I started handing out contact information."

"No, that's fine," I said hastily. "And you can give him my phone number, too. Whatever's easiest."

"Perfect. It sounded like he wasn't going to need anyone for a few more weeks, but I'll go ahead and pass your number and email along to him, and that way he can get in touch when he's ready to get started."

Better and better. Maybe by then, I would have figured out exactly what had happened to my mother...and what I wanted to do about it. For all I knew, the person responsible for her death was also long gone. Thirty years was a pretty long time.

Isaac and I said goodbye after that, and I set down my phone. No mention of when he wanted to see me again, although he hadn't rescinded his offer to have me reach out to him if anything strange should happen.

Not that I expected any such need to arise. No, I'd have a quiet evening at home, and would have to figure out what to do with myself the next day. On Saturday, though, I had my wine tasting with Joy to look forward to.

And that should be enough. After the revelations of the past couple of days, I should be happy to have a bit of downtime.

God only knew when I'd have it again.

On Friday, I decided to go to the movies, mostly because I couldn't even remember the last time I'd actually watched a movie in a theater—Dave preferred to stay at home and stream stuff, since that way he could drink as many beers as he wanted and safely fall asleep on the sofa. Maybe he could have been persuaded to go to Violet Crown in Santa Fe, since you could order alcohol and real food there and consume it while watching the movie. Then again, he'd always been kind of a tightwad, and so might have still balked at the cost of such an outing.

But now I didn't have to worry about persuading my ex to stick a crowbar in his wallet, and so I was able to order a glass of malbec and a mini pizza, and consume them both guilt-free while I watched a halfway decent rom-com. I'd decided I wanted to watch something utterly fluffy because I figured if I was going to indulge myself, I might as well go whole hog. And while it was sometimes hard for me to check my brain at the door and not be scrutinizing a film for every little bobble or mistake, I thought I did a pretty good job of allowing myself to relax and enjoy the outing.

That killed a few hours, and afterward, I headed over to Artisan on Cerrillos to get some art supplies. Nothing too crazy—a storyboard artist didn't need pre-stretched canvases or a rainbow of oil paints—

but I bought a variety of pencils and charcoal, and some sketchpads in several different sizes. Maybe nothing would come of Isaac's friend's offer to hire me as a storyboard artist, and yet I still figured it couldn't hurt to have the stuff on hand so I could get some practice in.

The rest of the day I spent playing, getting reacquainted with the feel of a pencil in my hand, the soft, soothing sounds of the graphite tip as I moved it across a fresh piece of paper. I re-created favorite scenes from movies, since I thought that would be good practice. And then dinnertime came, and I put together a quick stir fry and had a glass of white wine.

Nothing else from Isaac. No ghostly visitations or strange visions, and I began to wonder if everything I'd seen had been manufactured in my own mind and nothing else.

But no, I certainly hadn't imagined the wreckage in my rented house in Nob Hill, and I also hadn't hallucinated the way Isaac had made our water glasses rise off the table in his kitchen. Magic existed, even if it might have retreated to the corners for the time being. Just as well, probably. I had the feeling that having it in your face 24/7 could get kind of exhausting.

When I went to bed, however, I put the glasses in the top drawer of the nightstand. Maybe placing them under my pillow had created the desired result of making me see a vision I might otherwise not have witnessed, but at the same time, I didn't have any desire to repeat that experience.

That proved to be a wise move, because I slept soundly and dreamlessly, and woke up a little before eight the next morning feeling like a whole new person. In fact, I was energized enough to put on some yoga pants and a long-sleeved T-shirt, and take a brisk walk around the neighborhood before I even had my morning coffee. Quite a few other people were out and about, walking their dogs or simply getting some exercise as well, and I nodded and smiled at them as they passed. Everything felt cheery and calm and utterly, utterly normal.

Yes, I could definitely get used to this.

And how nice it was to get ready for my return trip to the antique mall and my wine-tasting date with Joy and know that I had fun new clothes to wear, and wouldn't have to put on the same old, same old for the millionth time. The radio silence from Isaac wasn't quite as fun, but I told myself it was the weekend and things were probably busy at his shop. Besides, I doubted his friend-of-a-friend FBI agent would be following up on a decades-old cold case on a Saturday morning.

No, I just had to put all that behind me and allow myself to enjoy the day.

On the drive down to Albuquerque, though, I found myself wondering how much I should tell Joy. Obviously about the house, but did I really want to drag her into all this mess about my long-dead bio-mom? Some of that was pretty heavy stuff, after all.

Then again, I didn't want to lie, since without Joy's help, I would never have met Isaac. What would have happened if he hadn't been there to offer some much-needed advice and very necessary mental clarity?

I really didn't want to know. Nothing good, probably.

Since it was a Saturday, the parking lot at the antique mall was much more crowded than it had been on Thursday afternoon, and I had to park a good ways away from the entrance. No biggie, though—I wasn't here to buy, but to get information.

The stall where I'd bought those fateful eyeglasses had several people browsing in it, which wasn't ideal. However, I was relieved to see a stranger helping them, obviously the owner. She was a tall, thin woman who looked like she might be in her late fifties or early sixties, with gray-streaked brown hair pulled back into a no-nonsense ponytail and wearing a 1950s-style beaded sweater and a pair of rhinestone cat-eye glasses. Clearly, she'd decided to embrace the vintage aesthetic full on.

I loitered off to one side, pretending to be perusing a rack of similarly embellished sweaters. The stall was a treasure trove of them, if you were into that sort of thing.

But eventually the browsers moved on, and I knew I had to seize my opening before someone else showed up.

The stall owner was turned away from me, adjusting a vintage leopard-print fur coat that hung from the door of an antique armoire. Not the best setup for my approach, but I'd have to make do.

"Excuse me," I said.

The woman turned around, expression faintly inquiring. "Can I help you with something?"

"I hope so," I replied, and reached into the pocket of my leather jacket so I could pull out the enchanted eyeglasses. "I bought these here about a week ago."

"I don't do returns," she said quickly.

Man, they were really sensitive about that sort of thing around here, weren't they? Then again, I had to imagine that the margins for this sort of stuff couldn't be all that huge, and accepting returns after someone had second thoughts about buying a '70s-vintage polyester pantsuit could really eat into your bottom line.

"Oh, I don't want to return them," I assured her. "I was just wondering if you'd put the plain lenses in to replace a prescription."

Her brows—penciled a few shades darker than her gray-streaked hair—pulled together. "No, I don't have the budget to do that sort of thing. I sell vintage eyewear as I get it—I figure it's up to the buyer to decide whether or not to replace the lenses."

Interesting. So, my bio-mom had gone walking around with glasses that were purely props and nothing more?

The more I thought about it, though, the more that sort of strategy made sense. If she really had been on the run from someone, then wearing prop glasses was a cheap and easy form of disguise. People would tend to look at the glasses rather than the color of her eyes or the shape of her nose, and so she'd be a little more difficult to describe accurately to anyone who was trying to track her down.

"Okay," I said. "Can you tell me where you got them?"

The stall owner shrugged, the iridescent sequins on her cream-colored sweater glittering under the fluorescent lights overhead. "Not really. I mean, I work with several different suppliers from all over the state. They pick through the local thrift stores and then send me the stuff they think I can sell here. Most of the time, I get things in fairly large batches, and they're not itemized. I just pay what they're asking— or not—and then I put the items in my stall here."

Great. If the woman had "pickers" working all over the state, that meant the eyeglasses could have come from Las Cruces down south, or Taos...or Truth or Consequences, for all I knew.

Even though I'd known this was something of a long shot...after all, we were talking about thirty years' worth of getting passed around from thrift store to thrift store here...I couldn't quite push back the wave of disappointment that passed over me at this new development. If the vendor didn't even know where the glasses had come from, how in the world would I ever be able to track down who'd found them in the first place?

She must have noticed the dismay on my face, because the stall owner said, "I'm really sorry. I just don't know anything more than that."

"It's okay," I said quickly. "I figured I'd ask. Thanks for your time."

And I turned around and headed out, the glasses tucked back in my pocket. I tried to reassure myself that this wasn't the end of things, that Isaac still had his friend-of-a-friend working on the case inside the FBI, but I wasn't feeling terribly hopeful. The glasses could've been found by a hiker or a rock hound or even a prospector years after my mother had died alone in the desert, although I had to admit they looked in pretty good shape to have suffered that kind of abuse.

Yet another mystery I doubted I'd be able to solve any time soon.

Old Town Albuquerque was pretty packed, since the weather was beautiful, and literally hundreds of thousands of tourists had descended on the city to attend the Balloon Fiesta, which had just started this weekend. Most of the activity was taking place much farther north, since the balloon field was located somewhere near the next-to-last exit before you were out of the city sprawl entirely, but still, the event created plenty of spillover.

After some hunting, though, I found a space in a pay lot, and made my way toward the wine tasting room. Luckily, it seemed as though most of the tourists were more interested in visiting the shops and the restaurants than getting a glass of wine...probably because there seemed to be more families with small children than anything else.

And, even more to my relief, Joy had gotten there

ahead of me and snagged a table at the tasting room's small outside seating area, so we could sit there and sip wine and watch the world—or at least, this small corner of it—pass us by.

"Hey," she said as I came up to the table. "Did you have any trouble finding the place?"

"Not at all," I replied, and pulled out a chair and sat down.

"What's wrong?" she asked after taking a good look at my face. "You look way too gloomy for such a gorgeous day."

At once, I made an effort to assume a more pleasant expression. "Oh, it's nothing. I was trying to follow up on something, and it turned out to be a dead end. I'm probably just feeling a little frustrated."

Joy looked sympathetic, but then she brightened and said, "Well, a glass or two of wine should fix that."

"I hope so."

A server came out then and asked if we wanted to do a tasting or have glasses, and since neither of us had had the winery's offerings before, we both opted to do a tasting.

"With maybe a glass to follow up," Joy told me, dark eyes laughing.

That sounded like a good idea—especially since the menu offered a charcuterie board, and that would help provide some ballast for all the wine.

"Count on it," I said with a grin.

We exchanged some chitchat about the production while waiting for our wine flights to come out—

apparently, my replacement wasn't doing so well, but Jake steadfastly refused to eat crow and ask me to come back.

"That's fine," I said. "I wouldn't come back even if he asked me."

"Oh?" Joy responded, her perfectly arched brows lifting slightly.

I had to wait to reply, since the server came back with our wine flights and gave us a little spiel about the various samples, but eventually the two of us were left alone again.

"I'm thinking about exploring a different career path," I said, once I'd sampled the first wine, a light, just barely sweet viognier. "I don't think prop shopping is going to do it for me in the long run."

Joy sipped some of her own wine before saying, "Really? Spill."

So, I told her about my idea of storyboarding, and how Isaac had already made a connection for me.

"Nothing's totally firm yet," I said. "But still, things are looking up." I paused there to finish my taste of viognier before continuing. "Is it weird, though? I mean, Isaac found the house in Santa Fe for me, and now he's getting me in touch with a producer who might get me some work. I just feel like he's done an awful lot for someone he barely knows."

Those words of concern only made Joy smile slightly. She reached over to finish her own little sample of viognier, then replied, "That's Isaac. He's always helping people. He's not so good about accepting help for himself, but...."

So, I was another of Isaac's charity cases? I told myself I shouldn't look at the situation that way, but it definitely seemed to me as though I was just another project in a long line of people to whom he'd extended a helping hand, rather than someone he'd taken a personal interest in.

"No, it's not like that," Joy said, as though she'd read my mind. Or rather, my distinct lack of a poker face had probably told her exactly what I'd been thinking. "He's just a very giving person, and he saw you were in a jam and could use a little assistance. Besides, you're a...."

The words trailed off there, and I guessed she'd been about to say "witch" and then had decided uttering that word out loud on a crowded patio in downtown Albuquerque probably wasn't the greatest idea in the world.

"That makes a difference?" I asked, and she nodded.

"Definitely. There aren't that many of us, you know." She paused there, a deprecating grin pulling at her red-glossed lips. "Of course, I'm probably being a little generous in including myself in that 'us.' I'm not like Isaac...or you, I'm guessing."

"Do you use it all?" I asked, deliberately avoiding the M-word.

"Not really," she replied, then took a sip of rosé, the next wine in our flight. "I mean, just sort of law of attraction kind of stuff. People are a little surprised to see how young I am, considering my IMDB credits, but I just attracted the shit out of those jobs. I'm planning to be Hollywood's premier hair artist by the time I'm done."

Well, judging by the work I'd seen her do during my brief time on set, I'd say she was well on her way. Re-creating hairstyles of the 1880s was no picnic.

"But that's pretty much the extent of what I can do," she went on. "I'm not like Isaac. Honestly, no one in our family is really like Isaac. It's almost like everything got concentrated in him."

I absorbed that statement as I tried the rosé. It was very dry and light, just the way I liked it. I might have to pick up a bottle to take with me.

"Does it work like that?" I asked. "Kind of hit or miss, I mean."

Joy tapped a French-manicured finger against the side of one of her tasting glasses. "It can. I think it depends on the family, though. The Zamoras haven't worked super hard to cultivate it or anything...we're just really happy when someone like Isaac pops up."

"Especially since it sounds like it's rare for a guy," I remarked.

"Exactly," Joy said. She swallowed the rest of her rosé and gave me a considering glance. "Speaking of Isaac...any developments there?"

"You playing matchmaker?" I asked, letting myself be amused rather than offended.

She pushed her perfectly waved hair back off her shoulders and tilted her head at me. "No," she said. "I mean, I'd be glad to see my cousin getting a personal life again, but that's his decision. It just sounded as though you two were spending some time together, and so I suppose I was just hoping...."

No need to say anything else; it was pretty obvious what Joy had been hoping, since it was the same thing I'd been wishing for, too.

"Well, I guess you can keep hoping," I told her. "He's pretty much all business."

Her shoulders drooped a little, but she reached for the glass of sangiovese, the next wine on our tasting cruise, and sipped some. "I wouldn't give up hope yet," she said. "You have to remember how hard things have been for him—you know, with the accident and Lena taking off and everything. She made him think he'd be a burden to anyone he was with."

What a crock of....

"That's ridiculous," I said indignantly. "Isaac is one of the most self-sufficient people I've ever met."

"You know that, and I know that...." Joy released a breath and reached for her little taster of sangio. "I keep hoping one day he'll figure it out. It's been almost three years since the accident, after all. Time to move on. But he's always been kind of oblivious to that sort of thing."

"What sort of thing?"

She grinned then, brown eyes sparkling with amusement. "I've seen girls chasing my cousin since junior high, and he never seemed to notice. I think the only reason he and Lena got engaged was because he actively chased her."

"Oh?" I said, doing my best to ignore the flare of

jealousy that awoke, green-eyed, somewhere deep inside. "Is she very attractive?"

"Very," Joy replied. "That's the problem—she could always wrap anyone she wanted around her little finger."

Great. So, not only was Isaac's ex apparently a major wench, she was also drop-dead gorgeous.

"But you have absolutely nothing to worry about," Joy went on. "That relationship is dead as a doornail. Besides, you're just as pretty as she is, only in a different way."

I could feel myself flushing, and reached for my own glass of sangiovese. Compliments and I didn't get along very well. "Oh?" I said.

"Yeah. We don't get too many redheads around here. You stand out in a crowd."

Which could be good or bad. Sometimes it was better to fly under the radar.

I finished the sangio and returned the glass to the holder it had been transported in, and then paused to get my bearings. Right—the next one was a red blend. "So, you don't think the situation is hopeless?" I asked, and Joy shook her head.

"Not at all," she replied and lifted her glass to clink it against mine. "You just have to give it time."

Time was the one commodity I had plenty of.

I could only hope that would turn out to be a good thing.

Chapter 14
Sigil Making

As it turned out, Joy had also thought it would be fun to grab an early dinner after our wine tasting, so we had some awesome Indian food before we went our separate ways. I only had one glass of wine with the meal, since I had to drive all the way back to Santa Fe, and although I heard my cell phone ping as I was passing the exit for Madrid and the Turquoise Trail, I didn't actually pull out my phone to look at the screen until I was safely parked inside the garage.

The text was from Isaac.

I'm not working tomorrow, it said. *Do you want to come over for lunch? There are some things I'd like to show you.*

Coming from anyone else, a message like that would've been loaded with *double entendre.* In this case, however, I guessed he just wanted to go over some more magic stuff with me.

No invite for a dinner date, but lunch was better

than nothing. As Joy had said, I just needed to be patient.

Sure, I replied. *What time?*

One o'clock? We'll eat first and then get to work.

That sounded a little ominous, but I reminded myself I was still feeling my way through all this witchy stuff, and so I needed to seize whatever opportunity I could to learn new skills.

Sounds like a plan, I sent back. *See you at 1.*

He replied with a standard thumbs-up, which I assumed meant we'd sealed the deal.

Grinning, I tossed my phone back into my purse. I'd been sort of dreading figuring out what to do the next day, guessing that almost anything would feel like a letdown after my outing with Joy, but now I didn't have to worry about it.

Just as Isaac had told me, sometimes the universe really did come to your rescue.

When I walked into his house the next afternoon, the most delectable aroma met me.

"What is that?" I asked.

"Homemade enchiladas and beans and rice," he replied. "Come on in."

I followed him into the kitchen, where the heavenly scent was even stronger. "You didn't have to go to all that effort—" I began, but he shook his head.

"I invited you over for lunch. My late mother

would spin in her grave if I didn't offer you proper hospitality."

A mental image of him standing on those crutches while chopping onions flashed through my head, but then I noticed several bowls sitting on the kitchen table, and a chair pulled up to them. Most likely, he sat down for as much of the slicing and dicing as possible, and only got back on his crutches when he absolutely had to.

"Well, I wouldn't want that," I said, deadpan, and Isaac grinned.

"Everything's pretty much ready. Would you mind carrying the enchiladas into the dining room, though? The casserole dish is kind of awkward to manage when you're on crutches."

He spoke naturally, as if asking for assistance was no big deal, but I thought I detected something almost tight in his smile. Deep down, he probably disliked needing the help, even if he knew it was necessary.

"I don't mind at all," I told him. "Pot holders?"

He pointed to a drawer near the oven, and I reached in and got out a mismatched pair, one red, one blue, and opened the oven door so I could extract the enchiladas. The dish was pretty heavy—not to mention blazing hot—and so I was glad I was there to lend a helping hand.

While I took it into the dining room, where a trivet awaited the casserole dish, Isaac emptied the rice in a bowl and brought that out as well. A covered bean pot and a pitcher of water with lemon slices floating in it already sat on the table, so it looked like we were good to go.

We both sat down, and I picked up my napkin and placed it in my lap. Cloth, too; apparently Isaac wasn't one to half-ass things.

"How was your Saturday?" he asked.

"Good," I replied. "I met your cousin Joy to go wine tasting, and I also swung by the antique mall to see if I could find out anything more about my bio-mom's eyeglasses."

Isaac lifted the lid from the bean pot and put a healthy helping of delectable-smelling beans on my plate, then helped himself to some as well. After that, we dished up enchiladas and rice, and he said, "Any luck?"

"No," I said, trying not to sound too disheartened. "The gal who owns the stall where I bought them didn't know where they'd come from. But she did tell me they had regular glass in them when she got them, so maybe they were never prescription. I was thinking maybe my mother was using them as a disguise in addition to a magical recording device."

"Couldn't someone else have put plain glass in them along the way?"

"I suppose so," I said. "But I don't see what would have been the point." I paused there to take a bite of chicken enchiladas. Wow. Those were probably the best enchiladas I'd ever eaten.

I said as much to Isaac, and he looked faintly embarrassed, telling me, "Well, it's my mother's recipe. She left me her cookbooks, too, along with her grimoire. We used to cook together all the time—my brothers weren't interested in that kind of thing, but I thought it was fascinating."

"She was obviously a good teacher," I replied, thinking again what a contrast Isaac was to my ex. Dave barely even wanted to do something as simple as nuke a frozen dinner. No, he'd been the king of takeout and DoorDash.

My compliments must have embarrassed Isaac a little, because he only hitched his shoulders and took a bite of beans. Since I could tell he didn't really want to pursue the subject, I figured I should circle back to the glasses.

"Anyway," I said. "I didn't learn much in Albuquerque, but at least I had fun with Joy. The Old Town section down there is really cute."

"It is," he replied, but there was something almost guarded in his tone, as though he thought it might be a betrayal of his hometown of Santa Fe if he praised another city.

I didn't think Santa Fe had much to worry about. No, I hadn't explored it thoroughly, but what I'd seen was definitely far more picturesque than Albuquerque could ever hope to be, with all the pueblo-style buildings and the tall old trees and the fascinating little side streets that truly felt as though they might whisk you off into a hidden corner of the Land of Enchantment.

"So," I said next. "What did you want to teach me today?"

"A few techniques," Isaac replied. "Just some

things to add an extra layer of protection to what you already have in place."

That didn't sound too scary. But....

"What about the cloaking spell?" I asked. "I thought you said it was working just fine."

"It is," he said after swallowing a mouthful of enchiladas. "But it never hurts to be as careful as you can."

Since I couldn't really argue with that remark, I nodded, and the conversation shifted to Santa Fe, and certain points of interest he thought I might like to visit. No mention of accompanying me on any of these expeditions, and I allowed myself an inner sigh. Joy had told me to be patient, but I honestly hadn't been able to detect even a single hint that Isaac was interested in anything more than making me the most capable witch possible.

After lunch—and after I'd cleared the table, over-riding Isaac's protests that he could do it himself—we went to his lair.

All right, his basement. I didn't know if base-ments were a thing in New Mexico or whether Isaac's house was a special case, but this California girl was impressed, particularly because we descended by means of an elevator that was hidden around the backside of the staircase.

"If you had an elevator put in, why not have it go upstairs, too?" I inquired as we descended to the lower level.

"Because that would have cost more," Isaac replied. "Also, I could survive okay just living on the ground floor of the house. Not being able to come down to my workshop would have been a much bigger hardship."

The elevator stopped, and the doors opened. He flicked the light switch on the wall next to us, and my eyes widened as I took in our surroundings.

The space was huge, probably the same size as the home's footprint. All around us were shelves filled with books and jars containing all sorts of ingredients I couldn't quite identify. In the center of the basement were several long wooden tables, cluttered with more mason jars and baskets of dried herbs and what looked like a fairly elaborate candle-making setup.

"I can see why you'd need to get down here to work," I said after an amazed look around. "I didn't realize you made all your own stuff for your rituals."

Again, Isaac looked faintly embarrassed. "I try to," he replied. "There are a few things I farm out, but yes, I make spell oils and ritual candles, and spell jars—little jars filled with herbs and crystals designed to concentrate a spell's power—as well. Not having access to all my supplies would have been a real trial."

"So, you're going to teach me to make candles?" I asked with a grin. While I liked to sketch, I couldn't have been remotely referred to as artsy-crafty.

A corner of his mouth lifted. "No, the candle is already made. What you're going to do is carve a sigil into it and charge it with an intention of protection."

"What's a sigil?" I asked. Maybe I'd heard the word before, but it wasn't the sort of term that generally popped up in casual conversation.

"A magical symbol," Isaac said. "A representation of a spell, something that carries its own power with it."

Okay, that didn't sound too crazy. Or at least, since it appeared I'd pretty much given up the fight and acknowledged that magic was real, making sigils didn't seem like too huge a leap.

"How do I make one?" I asked.

"Easy enough." He indicated for me to follow him over to one of the tables, where a tall white candle waited next to several sheets of blank paper and an ordinary-looking No. 2 pencil. "The simplest way to do it is to think of the word whose power you want to invoke for your spell. In this case, that's 'protection.' Take out all the vowels and see which letters are left, and then create a design using those letters."

I thought I was starting to get the picture. "Kind of like a monogram?"

"Close enough. Start sketching it out, and then when you have a design you're happy with, you'll etch it into the candle wax."

Those instructions seemed pretty straightforward. I picked up one of the pencils and moved one of the pieces of paper closer to me, then began quickly sketching out the beginnings of a couple of designs. I could tell right away that one of them wasn't going to work, so I focused my attention on the design remaining, adjusting the curve of one letter here, pulling the tail of the "P" over there so it entwined with one of the "N"s. The whole time, I was acutely aware of Isaac standing a few feet away, watching me in silence. No, it wasn't as though I could smell his aftershave or anything like that—I didn't think he wore any—but more that it felt strangely intimate to be here with him in his sanctum, even if we weren't doing anything remotely romantic.

I did my best to focus my intention on the design, although I didn't know how successful I was being. Then again, maybe intention wasn't as important right now, and wouldn't really matter until I began to actually carve the design into a candle.

After about ten minutes of trial and error, I thought I had a design that would work. I stepped away from the table so Isaac could get a better look at the paper.

"How's that?" I asked.

He moved closer so he could pick up the sketch. "It looks perfect. Elegant, but strong. It should be very effective. Now for the next step."

That next step involved tracing the design onto the large white candle he'd already provided. I didn't find that too difficult, but actually carving it into the candle using the small, sharp pick Isaac provided was a lot more work. I had to cut deeply enough into the wax that the design would be clearly visible, and yet at the same time keep the strokes delicate so the pattern wouldn't be muddied and lose its efficacy.

And through all of that, I also had to do my best to think of why I was tracing this sigil into the candle, what I wanted it to accomplish.

Someone had killed my mother, and I still didn't

know why. Someone had broken into my house in Albuquerque and trashed the place, even though I'd escaped unscathed.

Still, it seemed pretty clear that I couldn't pretend danger didn't still lurk out there somewhere, even if I had absolutely no idea who it was or what form it might take.

So, I needed some protection. The cloaking spell seemed to be doing a pretty good job of making me escape any unwanted notice, but I needed an extra layer of protection just in case that spell failed me.

How a candle could accomplish that, I didn't know, but if I was going to believe in magic at all, then I also had to believe it could do things that didn't make sense on the surface.

As I painstakingly carved my sigil into the wax, I thought of the light of the candle expanding and creating a sort of protective dome around my new home in Santa Fe, of how nothing that meant me any harm could get through that barrier of glowing golden light. That light would burn all night while I slept, and protect me once I awoke and got started on my day.

I didn't know how much time passed. My whole world had shrunk down to the candle in my hands, warmed slightly now from my touch, and the intricate pattern that had taken shape on its surface.

Eventually, I blinked and looked up, and saw Isaac watching me, an approving expression on his face.

"Very well done," he said. "It will do a good job of protecting you."

"You're sure?" I asked. For some reason, my brain felt a little fuzzy, as if I'd awakened from an unexpected nap.

"Absolutely." He reached out and touched the candle briefly, then nodded, as if it had assured him of its power. "Light it when you get home, and leave it burning."

"What if I have to go out?" I asked. "You're not supposed to leave a burning candle unattended."

A corner of his mouth lifted, but his tone was serious enough as he replied, "This candle has been built to protect you. It can't cause you any harm. Just make sure it's sitting on a plate or something that'll protect the surface underneath, and try to keep it out of any drafts." He paused there, that little lift at the edges of his mouth shifting into an outright smile. "Unless you have a cat that might knock it over, I think you're safe."

"No cats," I told him. "I'm massively allergic."

Something I'd found out as a child after visiting a friend whose family had two enormously fluffy Persians. I went into a sneezing fit that took hours to subside.

Some witch I was.

Isaac leaned against the table, shifting one of his crutches out of the way. The tight look to his mouth told me he'd probably been standing for too long, but I knew better than to say anything. He was his own best judge of what his body could manage and what it couldn't.

"Well, then your candle should be fine," he said. "And when it burns down to its last few inches, let me know, and we'll get together and make another one."

"So, I'm going to have to keep burning these candles for the rest of my life?" I inquired then, realizing I sounded just a little cranky.

This time, he didn't smile. Dark eyes serious under those sexy hooded lids, he said, "No. Just until we figure out who broke into your house in Albuquerque. With any luck, it'll be a police matter after that, and you'll be able to focus on other things."

That sounded hopeful. But I remembered how Isaac had said someone had definitely used magic to get past the deadbolt on the Nob Hill house. If it really had been a witch—of either gender—who'd gotten into my rental home, would they be clumsy enough to have left enough incriminating evidence behind to give the police a solid case?

Somehow, I doubted it. But I didn't bother to contradict him, and only said, "That would be nice."

His manner seemed to shift then, and he looked almost diffident. "But it's probably better to have a little extra insurance, just in case."

"'Insurance'?" I repeated.

Isaac didn't reply right away, but instead headed over to one of the shelves behind us, which held a variety of minerals, most of which I didn't recognize.

Once I got past clear quartz and amethyst, I was pretty much lost.

Clearly, he knew exactly what he was looking for, because he reached for a smooth, shiny gray stone that appeared almost metallic, then picked it up and brought it over to me.

"For you," he said.

"It's beautiful," I replied. "What is it?"

"Hematite," he said. "It's been charged with a very special spell only you can activate. If something happens—if something comes up you're not sure how to handle—then all you have to do is hold the stone and say, 'Isaac, I need you.'"

"Oh, is that all?" I quipped, but the serious expression he wore didn't shift a bit.

"Yes." He paused, then went on, "I know it might sound melodramatic, but sometimes you get in situations where it's not safe to make a phone call...or you're unable to do so, for whatever reason. I'll feel the vibration from the stone and come to provide whatever assistance you might need."

What was I supposed to say to that? I'd never had anyone offer me such unconditional help—not the friends who always said they'd be there to talk, but who usually managed to be MIA when some shit really went down in my life, and definitely not my mother, who always seemed able to manufacture an excuse to be busy elsewhere whenever I needed a shoulder to cry on.

"Thank you," I said quietly, staring down at the stone as I turned it over in my hand. It felt cool against my skin and yet somehow almost alive, as if those vibrations Isaac had mentioned were already activated and just sitting there, waiting for me to ask for its help.

Help I sincerely hoped I would never need.

Then I looked up. "Do you really think I'm going to run into that sort of situation?"

His shoulders lifted a fraction of an inch. "I don't know. I've been feeling sort of off today, heavy, like there's a storm coming but it hasn't risen above the horizon yet. And honestly, it could be nothing. Usually my instincts are pretty good, but I'd be lying if I said I didn't misread those sorts of signals from time to time."

That disclaimer didn't make me feel much better about the troubling words he'd just uttered. A storm coming, but he didn't know from where...or even what sort of storm it might be.

"I'm being really careful," I said, and he nodded.

"I know you are. And having this candle burning at your place will definitely help. All the same—keep your eyes open."

What could I do except promise I'd do exactly that? I murmured, "Sure," and soon afterward, I was on my way home, the precious protection candle riding shotgun on the passenger seat of my Palisade.

I had to hope the candle would be enough to protect me from whatever dark force seemed to have invaded my world.

Chapter 15
Connections

Despite my galloping heebie-jeebies, the rest of my Sunday was quiet. I went home and lit the candle—luckily, I'd found a little black metal plate in one of the cupboards that apparently was designed for that purpose, since it already had some wax drippings on its surface—then made a few more sketches and watched TV. The whole time, though, I found myself looking over my shoulder, wondering if something was going to get past the magical defenses I'd set up and pounce when I wasn't looking.

Obviously, nothing did. If something really was lurking out there, it was taking its sweet time to make a move.

Monday was similarly quiet. I did laundry, tidied up, sat in the backyard and read while enjoying the mild weather. Might as well take advantage of it while I could, since I'd heard winters in Santa Fe could be pretty rough, thanks to an average elevation of more than seven thousand feet.

And then on Tuesday morning, I heard from Peter Nielsen, the producer who was looking for a storyboard artist. He said he was in town for a few days and was hoping to meet for coffee so we could discuss the project.

Since I'd been starting to feel a little stir-crazy, I leapt at the chance to get out for an hour or so. And because I'd been spending so much time sketching over the past few days, I'd built up a fairly decent portfolio of pieces I could show him.

For just a moment or so, the thought passed through my mind that maybe I was being a little impetuous. After all, I didn't know the guy. I could be walking to a meeting with the person who'd trashed the Nob Hill house, his suggestion of a chat over coffee actually a ruse intended to lure me out of my sanctuary with all its various warding spells.

But almost as soon as that thought passed through my mind, I realized I was being silly. This wasn't a stranger, but someone Isaac knew, a man who had to have already passed whatever vetting process he used to screen his clients and make sure he was working with people who wanted to use his magic for worthy ends. There was absolutely nothing to worry about.

If I wanted this job, I needed to go to this meeting.

So, I spiffed myself up in some of my new clothes, tucked the sketchpad under my arm, and headed out —first making sure the protection candle was still burning. It looked cheerful and bright, and utterly safe on its iron plate carefully placed in the center of the peninsula in the kitchen so there was no chance of it being anywhere near something flammable.

It would have to do.

The coffee shop where Peter wanted to meet me was only a couple of blocks away, so I decided to walk. It really was a beautiful day, the sky that clear, bright blue you never saw in Los Angeles, with faint, lacy tracings of high cirrus clouds to give it a little definition. Some of the leaves on the trees had already begun to turn, however, and although the sun was warm enough, I thought I sensed just the faintest bite at the back of the breeze that ruffled my hair, letting me know summer was gone and winter would be on its way soon enough.

Peter Nielsen turned out to be around ten years or so older than me, with bright blue eyes and a head shaved to hide his early pattern baldness. He gave my hand a hearty shake, and thanked me for coming on such short notice.

"Oh, no worries," I said as I sat down at the little bistro table in the center of the coffee shop. The place was packed, even though one would have thought that most people should be at work at ten in the morning, rather than out sipping coffee. Then again, this was Santa Fe. I had a feeling it would continue to surprise me for a good long while.

Peter looked approving. "Well, let's get our orders in, and then I can take a look at your sketchbook."

Since this was purely for fun, I went ahead and got a mocha latte, while he ordered an espresso. I could see why that might be his drink of choice; he was one of those tall, thin, intense types who always seemed full of nervous energy.

Such a contrast to Isaac, who exuded the kind of calm strength that had been sorely missing from my life.

But I wasn't here to meet Peter as a possible dating prospect, but hopefully as a future boss. After we'd drunk a few sips of our respective beverages and traded brief anecdotes about how we'd met Isaac—apparently, they'd known each other for years, since Isaac's shop had been a sponsor of an indie film festival in Santa Fe—Peter nodded toward my sketchbook.

"Let's take a look at that, shall we?"

A tremor of nervousness fluttered in my stomach, but I told myself I had nothing to worry about. It wasn't as though my entire existence was riding on getting this gig. If it didn't work out, something else would come along.

Still, I knew my fingers shook just a little as I opened the sketchbook to the first of the series of practice storyboards I'd drawn over the weekend. It was a depiction of a scene from *Blade Runner,* a movie I absolutely adored for its moody cinematography and lush scene setting. I wanted this to work. I wanted to prove to the world—and to myself—that I could seamlessly switch careers and continue to forge the life I wanted.

Peter didn't say anything, only studied the sketch for a moment before flipping over to the next one, and the one after that. For all his edgy energy, he obviously could maintain a great poker face when he needed to, and so I really had no idea what he thought of my work.

He went through all the sketches, backtracked to a couple he seemed to want to study a bit longer, and then closed the pad and handed it back to me.

"That's very good work," he said, and although I didn't exactly let out my breath, I did allow myself to relax against the back of the chair. "And you're available for a project that would need to be done by the end of October?"

I nodded, doing my best to avoid beaming like a crazy woman. "Yes, that will fit in my schedule."

What a joke. I didn't have anything remotely resembling a schedule, but Peter didn't need to know that.

"Great." He drank down the rest of his espresso before continuing. "I can offer $4K for the project. Does that work for you?"

Because I'd done some research on what I could reasonably expect to earn as a storyboard artist, I knew he was coming in at the low end of the pay scale, but that was all right. This would be my first project, after all, and I couldn't expect to demand top dollar. Besides, the project's fee would definitely be enough to cover my expenses without having to dip into my savings, and that was the most important thing right now.

"Yes," I said, trying to sound neutral and professional. "That's doable."

The laugh lines around his blue eyes—eyes almost the same shade as the sky outside—deepened a bit as he smiled. "Excellent. I'll get the contract put together and email it to you along with an NDA when I get back to my hotel room. Once I have the signed paperwork from you, I'll go ahead and send you what I have, and you can get started."

I smiled in return. So much for my worries that this meeting was going to turn into some kind of supernatural ambush.

"Sounds great," I said.

He thanked me then and left, promising as he went that he'd get the contract over to me in the next couple of hours. I still had most of my mocha latte left to drink, and so I sat at my table and savored the coffee, letting myself relax into the sights and sounds and smells around me. Even though I'd spent nearly a week here in Santa Fe, it was in that moment when I truly felt as if it had become a real home.

I had an awesome place to live, and a job. Yes, there were still about fifty million unanswered questions hanging over my head, but at the same time, I couldn't help thinking that things were definitely looking up.

That sensation of well-being only increased after I got the contract from Peter as promised. Although I knew my father would have told me to get a lawyer to look it over, I didn't know anyone in Santa Fe and didn't want to hold things up while I tried to find an attorney. Yes, I knew I could have probably called Isaac and requested a recommendation, but I couldn't help thinking I'd asked enough of him already.

Besides, the contract was pretty boilerplate. It specified that I needed to produce no fewer than sixty storyboards based on the provided script and the director's notes, and that they had to be delivered by October thirty-first. I'd get half my fee up front, and the second half on delivery.

Easy-peasy.

I did the whole Docu-Sign thing, signing online and saving a copy to my laptop's hard drive. A few minutes later, I got an email from Peter welcoming me aboard and letting me know I should be getting the script and its accompanying notes in the next forty-eight hours.

Well, that had been pretty painless.

I wanted to celebrate, but how? Joy was hard at work down in Albuquerque, and Isaac was also working. However, his store closed at six.

Would it be too much if I invited him over to dinner to thank him for introducing me to Peter Nielsen?

No, of course it wouldn't. That would just be the friendly thing to do. There didn't have to be any other motivations involved.

Right.

However, I went ahead and picked up the phone anyway, figuring I might as well strike while I was still riding the high of signing that contract. Isaac's phone rang a couple of times—I'd called his private cell rather than the phone at the shop—but then he picked up.

"Penny?" he said, voice taut. "Is everything all right?"

Funny how he just assumed something had to be wrong for me to call him...or maybe not so funny, considering everything that had happened during the past week. I shook my head, even though he couldn't see me, and said, "Yes, everything's great. I met with your friend Peter, and I got the job! I just signed the contract."

I could practically feel Isaac's relief vibrating through the phone's speaker. "Oh, that's great news!"

"It is," I said. "And I really want to thank you for introducing me to him."

"Oh, it was nothing—" he began.

I cut him off. "No, it's not nothing. It's a whole lot of something. I'll have this job on my resume now, which means I'll be able to get more jobs storyboarding in the future and hopefully make a career out of it. And I wanted to say thanks by having you over for dinner tonight."

No reply right away, and I bit my lip. Maybe I'd just made a huge miscalculation.

Or maybe Isaac already had plans and was trying to come up with a polite way to turn down my invitation.

"You don't have to go to all that trouble," he said at last.

"I want to," I said firmly. "And it's not like I'm going to be making beef bourguignon...or homemade enchiladas," I added, my tone now a bit sly. "But I can whip up a pretty decent plate of spaghetti and meatballs, if you're into that sort of thing."

"A spaghetti dinner sounds great."

I didn't quite sag with relief, but I was definitely glad that he'd decided not to argue with me any further. "Then...seven o'clock?"

"I'll be there—and congratulations on the job."

We hung up then, and I stared down at my phone, a goofy smile on my face.

He hadn't said no.

And that meant I needed to get moving. I might have promised Isaac a spaghetti dinner, but I didn't have a single one of the necessary ingredients in the house.

Time to go grocery shopping.

———

When Isaac showed up at seven that evening, the house was filled with good smells, the table was set, and some carefully neutral acoustic guitar music was playing in the background. I'd gone back and forth with myself as to whether I should light the trio of pillar candles at the center of the dining room table, and had finally compromised by lighting all of them but also turning on the chandelier overhead, albeit slightly dimmed so we wouldn't get blasted.

Maybe it was all still a little too romantic, but I thought I hadn't gone over the top.

Much.

Isaac had a bottle of chianti in one hand, no mean feat while also managing a pair of crutches. "An offering," he said, and I immediately took the wine from him.

"Perfect," I replied. "Come on in."

"It smells wonderful."

"I hope so," I said. "My cooking skills are a little rusty, and I'm still getting used to this kitchen."

More like, I was getting used to how vastly superior it was to any other kitchen I'd ever used, since it had all nearly new Viking appliances and a tall wine fridge tucked between the pantry and the peninsula. I'd never been a huge cook, but I thought I could take it up as a hobby with a kitchen like that.

Isaac's eyes crinkled slightly in amusement. "I'm sure it will all be wonderful."

I decided to go with the vote of confidence and not argue. "Everything's almost ready," I told him. "So, you can go ahead and sit down, and I'll bring everything out to the table."

Just a brief pause, as if he'd intended to offer to help and then realized I'd probably shoot him down. Instead, he said, "Thanks," and headed into the dining room.

Since I'd already set out the salad, all I really had to do was get the bowls of pasta and the rich sauce with meatballs swimming in it, and then hurry back for the garlic bread and little bowl of parmesan I'd grated while the spaghetti was boiling. Soon enough, I was sitting down at the dining room table, glad to see that Isaac had already opened the bottle of chianti and had poured some into each of our glasses.

"Congratulations," he said, and lifted his wine glass so he could gently clink it against mine.

"Thank you," I replied after I'd taken a sip of the chianti. It was very good—I didn't recognize the label, and wondered if he'd bought it at a wine shop downtown. I'd gotten a bottle myself, but it was just TJ's stuff, not on the same level as what we were drinking now. "I really do appreciate you passing my info on to Peter. He seems like a stand-up guy."

Isaac also drank some chianti. Then he said, "Yes, I've known him for almost seven years now. He really loves producing independent films and doesn't see any need to go on to the bigger Hollywood stuff. But he's very good at what he does—his films are always getting nominated for awards at Sundance and Cannes, festivals like that."

Better and better. Not that being a movie's story-board artist was the most visible position in the world, but still, being associated with critically acclaimed films would only look that much better on my resume.

"I'm really looking forward to getting started," I said. "I should be getting the script and notes soon, and that will give me something to focus on."

For just a second, Isaac's gaze slid toward the protection candle, still burning on the peninsula that separated the dining room from the kitchen. I wondered how many days it would last; so far, it had been burning for more than twenty-four hours and had only used up maybe half an inch of wax. "Yes, I can understand wanting to move on."

An awkward little silence fell. Then I ventured, "I mean, I still want to find out what happened to my biological mother. I *need* to, actually. But getting this job seems like a signal that a new chapter is beginning for me."

"I can see that," Isaac said. He took a bite of spaghetti and half a meatball, and sent me an approving glance. "This is really good."

"I'd like to say it's an old family recipe," I returned with a grin. "But my mother doesn't really cook. This is something I got off a Food Network YouTube video."

"Well, it's delicious," he said. Then he tilted his head, his expression considering. "If your mom doesn't cook, what did your family do for meals?"

"We went out," I replied. "Or rather, my parents went out a lot. I had a lot of babysitters and takeout."

Because I'd been raised that way, I hadn't thought much about spending the majority of my evenings as a child being watched by some high school girl while we ate pizza or Chinese takeout or whatever. True, the families on TV didn't seem to operate the same way mine did, but TV wasn't reality. It wasn't until I got a little older and started comparing notes with friends that I realized my situation was anything but normal.

Isaac broke off a corner from his garlic bread and

put it in his mouth, his expression thoughtful. "That must have been hard."

He looked sympathetic, but I didn't want his sympathy. Or rather, while it was nice to see that he cared about what had happened to me as a child, those days were long behind me, and I didn't want to dwell on them now.

So, I shrugged and took a sip of chianti, and said, "It really wasn't that big a deal. I mean, most kids probably would love to eat pizza and burgers and Chinese food all the time instead of having to force down their mom's crappy meatloaf or whatever."

That comment made him chuckle. "I suppose so. My mother was a great cook, a real kitchen witch. We were spoiled."

"How did she have time to do all the cooking while running a store?"

Obviously, that wasn't a sensitive question, because Isaac was still smiling slightly as he reached for his own glass of wine. "Well, she closed at four-thirty every day so she'd be home in plenty of time to make a proper meal. And of course, the store wasn't open on Sundays at all, because we needed to go to Mass, and then she went home and put together a big Sunday dinner for the family."

"And your father?" I asked. I'd noticed that Isaac hadn't really mentioned him so far, and wondered what the deal was with that. Had he bailed out on his family and kids?

Isaac's smile faded a bit. "He died when I was seven. Brain tumor."

Damn. I'd really put my foot in it with that one. "I'm so sorry."

"It's okay," he said, albeit a little too quickly. "It was a long time ago."

Maybe so, but I still had to think losing a parent when you were that young had to leave scars that would never really go away. "And your mother never remarried?"

"No." He sipped some chianti and then set his glass back down. "She said she was too busy with us kids and the store to worry about anything like that, but honestly, I always believed it was because she knew she'd never find anyone like him again and so didn't even bother to try."

A real love match, then. I thought of my own parents, still together after almost forty years. Considering how difficult my mother could be to deal with, I had to wonder why my father hadn't walked out long ago. If they lived separate lives, I'd guess that he was simply trying to avoid what would be some insanely hefty spousal support, but that wasn't it. They went on vacations together all the time—weekends in Palm Springs, a week in Hawaii here, a month spent in Tuscany there. My father seemed to genuinely enjoy her company, which led me to conclude that the real issue with my family was me... not through anything I'd done, but simply because she still couldn't look on me as her true child.

"Your mother sounds like an amazing person," I said.

"She was," Isaac said softly. "We all miss her every

day. And I suppose that's why I wouldn't give up the store, even after the accident. She worked so hard to make it successful that it would have felt like a betrayal."

A wash of guilt went over me. If I'd been a truly loyal child, like Isaac, wouldn't I have tried harder to learn more about my father's business, to maybe take over once he was gone?

But I'd never had any interest in real estate, and, to his credit, my father had never pushed me to get involved with the business beyond having me visit him at his office a few times and taking me on some tours of job sites. He was still working hard and showed no signs of wanting to retire. I'd always sort of assumed that he kept going because he loved what he did and didn't want to spend his days playing golf or whatever, but now I wondered if his workaholic nature was partly because he knew he didn't have anyone to hand the business off to. True, there was my little brother Cade, but since his main focus in life these days seemed to be partying and doing the bare minimum to skate through his classes at USC, I kind of doubted my father viewed him as a viable successor.

"Well, it's a wonderful store," I said. "It's the kind of place where you could browse for hours."

"And hopefully buy something," Isaac returned, mouth quirking a bit.

I shot him a mock-severe look. "You know what I mean."

Apparently relenting, he said, "I do. And I sell a

lot to people who would claim they wouldn't have anything to do with all that woo-woo stuff."

I thought of the woman who was leaving the store the first time I went there. She definitely didn't look like the type who would be swinging a pendulum to help her divine the future, or laying out a Tarot spread every time she had a big decision to make. And yet she'd gone in there and bought a chunk of amethyst for more than two grand.

"How many people really do believe the 'woo-woo stuff'?" I asked.

Isaac settled back in his chair, his gaze thoughtful. "A lot more than you might think. Of course, the problem is that if they don't have any witch blood, then none of these things are really going to work for them."

"At all?" That was kind of sad, wasn't it? All those people thinking that the cards would give them guidance, or that if they bought a book of spells, they'd be able to hex their nasty neighbor or brew the perfect love potion, but in reality, all of it was just a huge waste of their time?

"If they have a little bit of witch heritage hidden somewhere in their ancestors, then they might get some kind of a result," he replied. "Not enough to do the sort of things you or I could do, but enough to influence a pendulum or the turn of a Tarot card. And if someone's using oracle cards, there isn't any real magic involved in those, just a different means of getting some insight into a problem."

Because the metaphysical really hadn't been in my

wheelhouse until a week or so earlier, I barely knew what an oracle card was. Putting that aside, I decided to focus on a more pertinent part of Isaac's statement.

"And just exactly what *can* I do?" I said. "I mean, I haven't noticed a lot of magical fireworks going on, if you know what I mean."

Once again, he glanced toward the protection candle where it sat on the tiled kitchen peninsula a few feet away. "Magic doesn't have to be loud to be effective," he said, then picked up his fork and helped himself to a bite of spaghetti and meatballs. "That candle there proves how strong you are."

I really couldn't see what he was driving at. "Why would you say that?"

"Because I've never seen a spell candle burn that slowly," he replied. "The slower the burn, the stronger the magic behind it."

"You're the one who made that candle," I pointed out, and he shook his head.

"I poured the wax. You're the one who carved the sigil into it and set the intention to have it protect you. A candle that was all my magic and none of yours would have burned at least a few more inches down."

If he said so. Since I was so new to all this magical stuff—and basically bumbling my way around—I supposed I had to take Isaac's comment at face value.

"But," he went on, "I do think you should work more with your magic, get in touch with it. I've been helping you as best I can, but we only get true control over our abilities by going within and understanding what we can and can't do."

"'Go within'?" I echoed. "How?"

"Well, meditation is usually the best way to get a connection with our inner selves."

With some difficulty, I stifled a snort of laughter. More than once over the years, I'd done my best to try meditating, mostly because I had friends who swore by it and said it really helped them maintain an even keel. And because my life tended to be pretty chaotic, thanks to my weird work hours and not always knowing from month to month whether I even had a gig or not, I'd given meditation the old college try.

Only to fail dismally. Possibly there was a circuit in my brain that was just missing, but I'd never had the ability to turn off my racing thoughts and just be. About the most I'd ever been able to manage was a few sessions of some rhythmic breathing.

"Not much into meditation, right?" Isaac asked then, dark eyes glinting with amusement.

Or maybe the little gleam I'd glimpsed was just a reflection from the candles at the center of the table.

"Not really," I admitted. "I can never seem to focus."

"I'll send you links to some videos on YouTube that can help," he said. "And you also have to remember that you're not trying to achieve some sort of exalted state. You're just trying to get to a mental space where you can tune into the magic inside you."

"Okay," I said, doing my best not to sound completely dubious. I'd tried this sort of thing so many times before that my chances of success now seemed pretty low, and yet I knew I'd make the attempt.

I didn't want to disappoint Isaac.

"What do these powers even feel like?" I asked next. "You can really sense them, just by reaching within?"

"It's not as hard as it sounds," Isaac said. "For me, it always feels like a sort of light and warmth here." He brushed the hand that wasn't holding a fork against his solar plexus.

"You're sure it's not just heartburn?" I joked, and he gave me a rueful shake of his head.

"Pretty sure," he replied with a curl of his lip. "And you'll be able to feel it soon enough, too. You just have to try."

"I'll do my best," I said.

After that, we talked some more about our respective families before the conversation moved on to the enigma of my biological mother. Isaac hadn't heard anything from the friend-of-a-friend FBI agent, but that was to be expected.

"I'll let you know as soon as he contacts me," he assured me. "Even if it's only to tell you he didn't find anything. We should be prepared for that, just because this is a very old crime we're dealing with."

I'd just eaten the last bite of pasta and meatballs on my plate, so I set down my fork and said, "I know. I keep telling myself that. And I suppose I can always try a private detective if the FBI databases pull up a big fat zero."

"True. That's another option."

He didn't sound overly enthusiastic, probably because he was thinking the same thing I'd been thinking even as I brought up the possibility of hiring a P.I. If the FBI couldn't provide any useful information, with all their vast resources, then how would a private detective be able to do any better?

Well, that was a worry for another day. In the meantime, we'd just have to wait...and I'd have to work on my magic, even if I had only a very foggy idea of how I was supposed to go about doing such a thing.

I hadn't bothered with getting anything for dessert, mostly because the spaghetti and meatballs were a big enough meal on their own, and also because I didn't want Isaac to think I was going overboard. The lack of a dessert meant our meal ended a few minutes after that, with him offering to help with clean-up and me politely shooting him down.

"It's fine," I assured him. "You have to get up and go to work in the morning, and I don't. From the way Peter was talking, I probably won't have much to do until Thursday at the earliest."

Isaac didn't bother to argue with me, probably because he could tell from my expression that my mind was made up. Instead, he picked up his crutches from where they'd been leaning against one of the unoccupied chairs and got to his feet, again with the grace of long practice. "Well, thank you for dinner. It was great."

"I'm glad you could come over," I responded, rising from my own chair as I spoke.

We were now standing almost face to face, a lot closer than we'd been during any of our other encounters. His eyes caught mine, and my heart seemed to skip a beat in my chest.

The moment lasted longer than I'd thought it would. I didn't look away, barely dared to breathe.

Then he said, "I didn't intend to do this."

"Do what?" I asked, since he really hadn't done anything...yet.

"You know what I mean."

I stared up at him, at the taut set of his mouth and the glitter in his deep brown eyes. "Is it so wrong?"

He didn't reply right away, although he broke our eye contact and glanced down, as if looking at the crutches that propped him up, the legs that still wouldn't obey his commands. They didn't look particularly slender, unlike the lower limbs of other people I'd known who were in wheelchairs full-time. Was that magic, or just a hell of an effective physical therapist?

Because he didn't seem as though he was going to reply any time soon, I said, "What Lena told you about being a burden—that was bullshit. She walked out because she was weak. Do you think I'm weak like her?"

That question prompted a smile. "No."

"Well, then," I said. "There shouldn't be anything

holding us back. Unless I'm misreading the situation? If I am, just tell me to back off now."

When he spoke, his voice sounded almost strangled, as if he was forcing out the words despite his better judgment. "You're not misreading anything."

"Good," I said firmly. "Then go ahead and kiss me, Isaac."

And in the next moment, he bent and pressed his mouth against mine. He tasted like chianti and a bit like spaghetti sauce, and his lips were just as savory and delicious. Because of the crutches, he couldn't pull me into an embrace, but I was okay with taking the lead, with wrapping my arms around his waist and feeling how strong and slender he was, like a tree that had weathered all sorts of storms but could still stand proud and firm.

The kiss lasted a long time. Eventually, however, he straightened, lifting his head, although he didn't try to slip away from my embrace. No, he just stood there staring down at me, as if I were some sort of unicorn that had wandered across his path.

In his mind, maybe I was.

"There," I said, trying to keep my tone light. "That wasn't so bad, was it?"

He grinned then, laugh lines crinkling around his eyes and that delicious mouth of his curving up in amusement. "No, I'd say that was the very opposite of bad."

Another kiss followed those words, just as yummy as the first. Eventually, though, we pulled apart, with him stumbling just a little as he dealt with his crutches.

"I should probably go," he said quietly.

I didn't want him to leave. No, I wanted to go over to the couch and make out like a couple of teenagers...and see what happened next. But I knew what a big step he'd just taken, and realized I'd have to let this go a whole lot slower than I probably would have liked.

That was all right, though.

I knew he'd be worth the wait.

We went to the door, and he bent and kissed me on the cheek, promising to call me the next day. I smiled at him and said that would be great, and waited there as I watched him make his way down to the front path and over to where his van was parked in the driveway. A few minutes later, he started to back out, and I judged it safe to finally close the door.

I might have had a pile of dishes waiting for me, but right then I thought I might be the happiest woman in the world.

Chapter 16
Getting Framed

The next morning, I woke up energized and ready to start my day, my mind replaying those kisses with Isaac as extra fuel to get me up and moving. My body craved him in a way I hadn't craved anyone for a very long time. Honestly, I might have married Dave and been with him for almost seven years, but I had a feeling he'd never gotten my motor going the way Isaac had with just a couple of kisses.

Pent-up sexual energy, I told myself, and yet I didn't think that explained all of it. More than anything else, this seemed like crazy physical chemistry, a chemistry I'd sensed almost as soon as I'd met him, even if he had to take a lot longer to unbend and acknowledge its existence.

Well, it was acknowledged now, that was for sure. Where it would all go next, I had no idea. However, what I did know was that I needed to take my cues from him and not rush things. Isaac was coming off a very long dry spell...a dry spell during which he'd apparently done his best to convince himself that no woman would want someone in his condition.

I had a feeling our interactions last night had done a pretty good job of disabusing him of that notion.

My good mood only increased when I got a text from him a little before ten.

Dinner tonight? it asked. *I know a place here downtown that has a flamenco show. It'll be fun.*

What a uniquely Santa Fe way to spend an evening. *Sounds great,* I sent back. *Is it dressy?*

Moderately. No need to break out an evening gown, though.

I sent back a tongue-sticking-out emoji and added, *I can handle that. What time?*

Pick you up at 7?

It's a date.

After I typed those words, I hoped that wasn't pushing things too much. But no, we'd kissed last night. Our relationship had progressed to a very different place from where it had been this same time the day before.

And apparently Isaac didn't have any problem with my comment, because he replied with, *See you at 7.*

That seemed to be that. I was now very glad about my somewhat extravagant shopping trip at ABQ Uptown a few days earlier, because otherwise I wouldn't have had anything to wear.

Then again, I was now living in the heart of Santa Fe. I probably could have scared up something here if necessary.

But it wasn't necessary, which was a good thing, since I'd planned to do some stuff around the house and then work on my sketches for most of the day.

A little before noon, though, I got an email from Peter. He said there would be a small delay because he and the director were hashing out a few last-minute details, but he still anticipated that work would begin on Monday. I wrote back and said that was fine and to keep me posted, but after that exchange, I realized I didn't have to spend the day sketching if I didn't want to, since now I'd have a little more time to practice before I really needed to start worrying about my drawing skills.

Or rather, there was an entirely different set of skills I needed to work on.

As promised, Isaac sent me an email with the links to the meditation videos he'd told me about. I had to admit, they did seem a lot more approachable than the techniques I'd tried in the past, and after lunch, I sat down on the living room floor and practiced my breathing, practiced letting everything float so I could find the stillness within, the stillness that would lead me to the heart of my magic.

For just the barest moment, I thought I did feel something, so fleeting I wasn't sure whether it might not have been my imagination and nothing more. A warmth, as Isaac had said, a sort of glowing strength that maybe had been there all along, only I hadn't possessed the skill or focus or whatever you wanted to call it to recognize that spark of magic for what it truly was.

Feeling a lot more hopeful than I'd been earlier that day, I climbed to my feet and went into the kitchen to get some water from the pitcher in the fridge. A gorgeous day beckoned outside the window, all bright skies and fresh breezes and the first golden leaves of autumn showing on the trees.

Since I'd mostly done my chores for the day, why not get out and explore? Since moving here, I'd run to the grocery store and to Trader Joe's, had ventured down Cerrillos Road to go to the art supply store, but I hadn't spent a huge amount of time downtown beyond going to and from Isaac's store.

And there was the Georgia O'Keeffe Museum only a few blocks away from the house. I could go spend a couple of hours there, and then wander around the Plaza and downtown until it was time to go home and get ready for my date with Isaac.

That sounded like the perfect plan. As had become my routine over the last thirty-six hours or so, I glanced over at the candle where it sat on the countertop, but it continued to burn serenely on its little iron dish, the flame straight and unwavering, apparently unaffected by any passing drafts. Just like the day before, it had burned down less than an inch, and obviously had a long way to go before it would need to be replaced.

Heartened that the protection spell was doing so well, I fetched my purse and locked up, then headed out on foot. After so many years of having to drive pretty much anywhere I needed to go in Southern California, there was something almost empowering about knowing I could visit so many places nearby without having to get behind the wheel of my SUV.

On that weekday afternoon, the museum was busy but not packed—a good thing, since I liked to have some space to experience art without having to bump shoulders with a bunch of tourists. I could move from painting to painting at my leisure, had enough time to pause in front of each photograph in the gallery of works by Georgia O'Keeffe's husband, Alfred Stieglitz, who'd obviously spent a lot of time cataloguing their life together. So used to seeing her as she was in the later years of her life, weathered and austere like one of the rock formations on her beloved Ghost Ranch near Abiquiu, it was almost jarring to see a much younger woman laughing on the back of a vintage motorcycle or wearing a party frock that seemed far too frilly for her.

After I was done at the museum, I wandered in and out of various stores and galleries near the Plaza, locating the wine shop where Isaac had probably bought the chianti for our dinner the night before, looking at some art that truly spoke to my soul, especially one huge painting, taller than I was, of a summer monsoon storm over a golden field.

But since my current living situation was a

temporary one, and the house already had a very fine complement of local art, I couldn't exactly justify dropping more than ten grand on a painting that wouldn't even have a permanent home. I took a card from the gallery, telling myself that if I got my own place here in Santa Fe, then I'd think about buying the piece...assuming it hadn't been snapped up in the meantime.

Of course, that thought led me to wonder if maybe someday I'd get to share Isaac's spacious, welcoming house on Del Norte Lane. It was probably stupid to be speculating about living together after we'd only shared a couple of kisses, but on the other hand, human beings were inherently hopeful. We always wanted the best possible outcome, even if it might not seem very likely at the moment.

Go slow, go slow, I told myself. *Just because you've got a mad crush on the guy doesn't mean you're meant to be together forever.*

Wise words, I supposed. But I'd never been too good about putting the brakes on things—Dave and I had gotten engaged only three months following our first meeting, after a fast courtship that had left me convinced he was the only one for me.

Yeah, and look how that turned out, I thought then, shaking my head at myself. Luckily, no one passing by on the sidewalk seemed to notice or care, even though I tried to disguise the head shake by reaching up to touch my hair, as if rearranging some curls that had gotten tangled by the wind.

Of course, Isaac and Dave were polar opposites,

and so I couldn't exactly base any speculation on them behaving the same way in a given situation. And some people probably would say I shouldn't be jumping into a relationship when my divorce had only become final a few months earlier, but I wasn't going to worry about that. The marriage had been dead long before then, even if I hadn't known it at the time.

A shop filled with inviting housewares beckoned from across the street, and I waited for a break in traffic to hurry over and take a closer look. Maybe I didn't have any need for new clothes—although I'd seen a few pieces that made me want to whip out my credit card—but getting some new table linens or a few other homey odds and ends sounded like fun. That sort of thing would be easily transportable, after all, and then I wouldn't have to worry about staining any of the placemats or tablecloths that had come with the house.

Besides, I loved to browse kitchen gadgets, and could happily spend hours looking at stuff even if I didn't have any intention of bringing it home. By that point, it was a little after four, and so I still had plenty of time to shop to my heart's content without worrying about whether I was eating into prep time for my date with Isaac.

A lot of the table linens were a little too Southwest kitsch for my taste, but I found a lovely table runner and matching placemats in sort of a kilim pattern in brown and blue and rust that I thought would work great with the decor in the house, and so

I had one of the clerks hold those pieces at the cash register while I shopped around a bit more.

Toward the back of the store was a section devoted to smaller decor items—vases and small figurines, little mirrors, and an assortment of picture frames.

I'd actually never been that into putting up family pictures around the house, maybe because Dave's parents' home was cluttered with the things, including some really godawful large-scale ones hanging on the walls that looked as though they'd come out of the world's most cut-rate JC Penney photo studio. That was in direct contrast to my parents' style of decorating...and what had probably started me down the road of avoiding most family paraphernalia.

But on a shelf off to one side I spotted a frame that I felt drawn to. It was antiqued tin set with opaque tumbled stones, probably types of quartz and onyx and jasper, although I didn't know enough about minerals to be absolutely sure. I liked how it was intricate without being ornate, and how it had a handmade feel that seemed to fit with the whole Santa Fe vibe.

My hand reached out to lift it from the shelf. It was heavier than it looked, sturdy, solid. And while I didn't have anything to put in it right now, on my phone I had a good photo of my father and me taken last Christmas, one I'd sent to him and knew he'd had framed and was now sitting in his office.

It would be kind of fun for us to have matching

pictures. All I'd have to do was send the .jpeg file to Walgreens or something, and have the photo lab there make me a print. That way, I'd have something personal at the house, something that was uniquely mine.

I took the frame over to the cash register and added it to the other items they were keeping there for me. The total was a bit more than I'd expected, but I probably should have realized that any store right on the Plaza wasn't going to have prices like my local Kohl's.

That was all right, though. Peter had already Venmo'd me the deposit for the storyboarding gig, and it wasn't as if I didn't have plenty of funds of my own even if I hadn't gotten the money yet.

After picking up my bag of goodies and thanking the salesclerk, I headed out, walking across the square so I could make a beeline for the house. There were still tons of shops I hadn't explored yet, but that was all right. I could save them for another day—maybe Sunday, if Isaac and I wanted to make a day of it.

I had to admit it felt a little strange to be thinking of us as doing things together. No, I couldn't say we were officially a couple yet, but I wanted to believe we were at least on our way.

The protection candle was still burning steadily when I got home. I put away my goodies, checked my email, and then got out my selection for that night's date, a dead-simple sheath dress in a gorgeous dark brick shade that worked well with my red hair. Some knee-high boots with slender heels, top it with my leather jacket, and I thought I had an outfit that was dressy but not over the top...and just sexy enough to —I hoped—make Isaac very glad he'd decided to take me someplace a little special that night.

I went into the bathroom and futzed with my makeup a bit, going for more of an evening look just for fun. Since I'd been wearing my hair partially pulled back the first time I met Isaac, I decided to replicate the look and see whether he would notice.

All the primping and prep took me about forty minutes. By the time I was done, it was about six-thirty, still way too early for him to show up.

So much for trying to time this all perfectly.

But rather than get involved in something else, I decided to go to the living room and wait there, maybe turn on the TV and watch something mind-less until he showed up. That way, we could head out almost as soon as he got here.

Purse slung over my shoulder, I left the master suite and walked down the hallway. When I emerged into the living room, however, I came to a dead stop, adrenaline surging, heart pounding.

A man I'd never seen before was sitting on the sofa. He looked as though he was around my age, with sandy brown hair and hazel eyes. Even through my shock, my brain registered that he was almost ridiculously good-looking, with the sort of chiseled features and pouty lips you might find on a male model, or on this year's latest TV heartthrob.

As soon as our eyes met, he rose from the couch

and sent me a smile that was probably meant to be charming but only made a shiver run down my back.

"Hi, Penny," he said, casual as though we were long-time friends who'd just bumped into one another on the street. "I've been waiting for you."

Chapter 17
Speak of the Devil

Somehow, I managed to push out some words past the shock that sent my heart pounding and a shiver of unease over my entire body. "Who the hell are you?" I demanded. "How did you get in here?"

My rude tone didn't appear to faze the stranger at all. "Oh, I'm afraid I can't tell you who I am," he replied as he uncrossed his legs and sat up a little straighter. "Let's just say I'm an old friend of the family...your mother's family."

For a second, I just blinked at him. What in the world was going on here? How could he have known anything about the woman whose face I'd seen only in a dream?

Because as shocked as I was, I somehow knew he'd referred to my biological mother, and not the woman who'd raised me.

"'My mother's family'?" I repeated. "Who are they? Who was she? What was her name?"

The apparition smiled slightly, then held a finger

in front of his lips, although I wasn't sure whether he was telling me to shush or seeming to signal that he couldn't...or wouldn't... answer my frenzied questions. "Like I said, I can't tell you that."

"Okay," I said, planting my hands on my hips. Once I'd realized he wasn't going to lunge at me right away, my pulse had eased up a little, but I wasn't about to let my guard down. "We can start with something a little simpler. How did you get inside my house?"

His smile broadened. "The same way I got into your house in Albuquerque."

Ice shivered its way down my spine. This model-pretty man was my intruder, the person who'd trashed Ida Martinez's house?

Realization flared next. Isaac had told me that whoever had broken in had used magic to do so, which meant the stranger must be a witch of some kind. But how the hell could he have even gotten in here? I'd left the protection candle lit all day....

Inadvertently, I glanced toward the spot where the candle sat on the kitchen peninsula, its flame burning steadily without a single flicker. Still smiling, the intruder looked in the same direction, and his grin only broadened.

Voice jeering now, he said, "Oh, you didn't think your little arts and crafts project would be enough to keep me out, did you? I suppose against an ordinary witch, it might have worked, but...."

"So, you're not an ordinary witch?" I asked then. I had to admit that I was a little proud of myself for sounding so unruffled, even though uneasiness churned away in the pit of my stomach and adrenaline kept singing its shrill song along all my nerve endings.

The intruder brushed an invisible piece of lint off the sleeve of his dark gray dress shirt, then rose from the couch. Standing, he looked much taller than I'd thought he would be, and I had to prevent myself from taking a step backward. "Of course not," he replied, sounding almost offended. "I'm a demon."

"A demon," I said flatly. Once again, I took in his model-perfect appearance, the expensive shirt and lightweight wool slacks, the shiny lace-ups he wore. He looked like one of the eager young men who'd wanted to apprentice with my father and learn how to make their own millions by squeezing a little more blood out of L.A.'s overheated real estate market. "If you're really a demon, where are your horns and tail?"

For just a second, I thought I caught a flicker of red in the stranger's—the demon's —dark eyes. "Left behind in Hell," he said cheerfully. "We find we get a lot more done if we present a less threatening appearance when working on this plane."

My brain honestly didn't want to process any of this. However, I had to accept the unwelcome fact that he'd gotten in here, had gotten past the protection candle I'd so painstakingly crafted, and so I wasn't dealing with your regular garden-variety home invader here...or even a run-of-the-mill witch.

"And actually," the demon went on, "you did

make things a little difficult for me. After I trashed your house in Albuquerque, I thought for sure you'd go running back to California and I'd be able to grab you easily. But no, you had to come to Santa Fe and start learning to be a witch." With what sounded like some extremely grudging respect, he added, "That cloaking spell you cast was pretty effective."

Was I supposed to feel honored by his praise? Frowning, I said, "But you still found me anyway."

So much for Isaac's assurance that the combination of the cloaking spell and the protection candle would be enough to shield me from harm. If I somehow managed to survive this encounter, we'd have to have a little conversation about that.

"Oh, sure," the demon said cheerfully. "The cloaking spell only hid you when you were here in town. I sensed your trail from those two trips you made to Albuquerque recently, but each time I tried to trace it back here, it disappeared. I could tell you must be hiding somewhere in the heart of Santa Fe, but I didn't know exactly where."

I crossed my arms, a little intrigued despite myself. "So, how did you find me?"

"That," the demon replied, and pointed at the tin and stone frame I'd bought at the kitchen shop and set on the mantel, although it still contained only the stock photo it had come with. "I made a honey pot."

"'A honey pot'?" I repeated.

"A lure," he said. "I knew you were a lodestone, just like your mother. And—"

"Wait," I broke in. "You knew my mother?"

The unpleasant smile returned to his lips. It was almost disconcerting to see such an ugly grin on the mouth of someone who was so conventionally attractive.

His demon nature asserting itself, I supposed.

"Of course," he said casually. "I killed her."

The rage boiled up out of nowhere. Or at least, right then it felt like my fury had come from nowhere, and yet I knew it was merely the end product of all the uncertainty, all the revelations of the past few weeks, all the worry and wonder about what had really happened to my biological mother.

I flew at the demon, not thinking, maybe driven by the impulse to drive the heel of my pointy dress boot right into his crotch. However, I got within a foot of him...and slammed into something invisible, something hard enough to knock me right on my ass.

The wind didn't exactly get smacked out of me, probably because I landed on the oriental rug that covered the living room floor and not bare Saltillo tile, but I still gasped.

"Not so fast," the demon said as he wagged a finger at me. "You think I don't have my own defenses?"

Painfully, I pushed myself up to my feet. I supposed it was a good thing I was wearing tights under my dress and not actual pantyhose, or they probably would have been shredded by that friendly little encounter.

"I guess I just found out," I said, wishing I didn't sound so out of breath.

"There are a lot of things you need to find out," the demon replied, although once again, his tone was almost cheerful, as if our whole exchange had amused him more than anything else.

I ground down my anger and pushed it into the background. Despite knocking me on my butt, so far, he hadn't done anything overtly threatening, and I wanted answers.

"Why did you kill my mother?"

He cocked his head to one side, considering the question. "Because her mother told me to."

My eyes widened. And I thought *I* had mother issues.

"What?"

A shrug. "Your mother broke the rules. Disobedience on that level needed to be punished. So, I was summoned to take care of the problem."

The earth felt as though it was tilting beneath my feet. What kind of monster would have her own daughter killed, simply because she hadn't done as she was told?

A monster who apparently was my biological grandmother...and a witch who summoned demons to do her dirty work.

Lovely.

The rage was still simmering beneath the surface, but I knew I couldn't let it come back up to a boil. Not when I was dealing with a demon who had defenses I couldn't seem to get past. And the Witchery 101 stuff Isaac had shown me so far certainly wasn't enough to help me with my current situation.

"All right," I said, forcing my voice to return to a calm I certainly wasn't feeling at the moment. "So, you set up a honey pot. I assume that frame must have some kind of spell on it to act like a beacon or whatever?"

"You learn fast," the demon said with a smirk. "Because you're a lodestone, you attract magical objects to you—like your mother's glasses. But you also can detect magic around you, and that's what happened with the frame. There's a reason why you chose it out of all the other frames in that shop."

I looked over at the frame in question. Sitting there on the mantel, it did look out of place. Not that it was unattractive, but more that it just didn't fit with the overall decor of the house. I would have done better to buy one of the hand-painted ceramic frames that had also been on display at the shop, but I'd gone straight to this one like, well, iron filings getting pulled toward a magnet.

Clearly, I'd been played. Big time.

But I didn't want to waste my energy on self-recriminations. Maybe later on...if I survived all this... I could see if there was some way to safeguard myself against getting sucked in by a similar spell. Right now, though, I had much bigger matters to worry about.

"All right, you found me," I said. "Now what? I end up in a shallow grave, just like my mother?"

The bravado in those words was mostly for my

own benefit. I didn't think the demon would believe it for a second.

He smiled. Now that I looked closely, there did seem to be something a bit off about his teeth, as if they were just a little too big for his mouth. The incisors were definitely more pointed than the average human's. Still, it wasn't the sort of thing you'd probably notice unless you were really trying to find evidence of his inhuman identity, as I was.

"Yeah, I should've buried her a little deeper," he said. "I forgot about those frigging vultures, or how they might pick up those glasses and drop them miles from where I'd buried her."

So, that was how the glasses had gotten into circulation despite there not being a whisper about a Jane Doe being found in a forgotten canyon somewhere. I hadn't been able to figure out that piece of the puzzle.

Not that it mattered now.

"But," the demon went on, "that's not why I'm here. No, now that it's clear you've developed your mother's talents and are worth something, your family wants you with them."

The same people who'd cold-bloodedly ordered my biological mother's death? I didn't think so.

"I have a family," I said as I stared the demon down. Now I could really see the reddish tinge to his dark eyes, like a flame hidden somewhere deep within his pupils. "And, last I checked, they didn't go around hiring demonic hitmen just because one of their kids did something they didn't like."

The demon chuckled. It was a horrible scraping sound, like rusty hinges protesting a graveyard gate being wrenched open in the middle of the night.

"That's not your family, Penny," he replied, his tone almost kindly, as if he'd decided to take pity on my ignorance and explain the ways of the world to me. "That is, they raised you, but magic passes through the mother's line, as do family connections. Your true family is your mother's family, and no one else. And now you'll be going to them."

I wanted to say, *Over my dead body,* but since this particular demon obviously had a taste for mayhem, I didn't think flinging that kind of a retort at him was such a good idea.

However, I had no idea how to stall him, prevent him from doing pretty much whatever he wanted. Isaac certainly hadn't taught me to hurl lightning bolts—if that kind of an attack would even work against a demon. I had to admit I was woefully unprepared for this sort of confrontation. All along, I'd been regarding my supposed magic with skepticism, hadn't really believed in it despite the evidence that it actually existed...and that it could possibly help me out of a jam exactly like this one.

At the edge of my peripheral vision, the candle I'd inscribed still burned steadily. And okay, it hadn't done such a great job of keeping this demon out of my house, but the protection spell I'd visualized had been all about keeping out any witches who might mean me harm. Neither Isaac nor I had known we weren't dealing with a witch at all, but a being not of this world.

Isaac had told me the candle was strong, and I'd responded that was because he'd poured the pillar in the first place. Now, though, a realization began to struggle its way to the front of my mind, like a tiny seedling doing its best to burst through a patch of parched earth.

That candle was strong because we'd made it together. Our combined magic had created something far greater than anything we could have done on our own.

I couldn't beat this demon by myself. I didn't even know how. But maybe...just maybe...Isaac and I could do it together.

Eyes locked on the demon, I said, "I don't think so," even as my hand plunged into my purse, scrabbling for the side pocket where I'd placed the hematite stone Isaac had given me a few days earlier.

My fingers closed around the stone, cool and smooth against my frantic fingers. The demon frowned, as though he could tell I was up to something but couldn't tell what.

Voice clear, I said, "Isaac, I need you now."

And...nothing happened.

Well, unless you wanted to count the demon throwing back his head and howling with laughter.

"You honestly think that crippled *brujo* is going to help you out of this?" he asked once he'd recovered himself. "The man can't even stand up on his own."

"So what?" I flung back. "At least he's a man, and

not some creature from hell who has to come running whenever a witch snaps her fingers."

At once, the scowl was back. "I did not come *running*," he growled...and it truly did sound like a growl. For just a second, his eyes glowed pure red and his features began to distort, before he seemed to get control over his human appearance and go back to being the model-slick man I'd first spotted sitting on my sofa.

I wasn't fooled, though. I'd now had a glimpse of what lurked beneath that façade...and I didn't like it very much.

"Oh, well, maybe you can explain the process to me, then," I said sweetly, willing to goad him a little more. The important thing was to keep stretching this out until Isaac got here.

Yeah, and how long is that going to take? the practical side of my mind inquired. *Even if he headed out the door the second he got that mental signal, it's still going to take him time to get into that van, and even more time to drive over here.*

Well, that was true. Even so, I refused to give up hope. For all I knew, the candle was still doing its best to protect me, even if it couldn't prevent the demon from breaking and entering and taking up residence on my sofa.

His eyes narrowed, and for a second or two, he only stared at me, gaze speculative. Then he said, "Oh, I get it. You're trying to stall for time. Well, that's not going to work. We're going.

Now."

Chapter 18
Call the Cavalry

The demon stepped toward me, and I took a step back. "I'm not going anywhere with you," I told him. "I thought I made that clear the first time."

A blink, and he was standing next to me, hand wrapped around my bicep in a grip of steel. I winced and tried to tear my arm from his grasp, but a second of tugging told me I wasn't getting away. How exactly he'd been able to close up five or six feet of space between us in the blink of an eye, I had no idea. Some kind of special demon power, I supposed.

"And I thought I made it clear you didn't have any choice in the matter," he replied. Now that he had the upper hand—for real—he was back to being his usual smug self. "I need to deliver you to your grandmother, and then I'll be done with this whole mess. She promised she wouldn't summon me again if I brought you to her, and that I could stay on this plane for a while and enjoy myself once I handed you over. So, if you think you're getting in the way of my trip to the Bahamas, you're sorely mistaken."

Well, then. If I'd only known my stubbornness was keeping my demon friend from enjoying his Caribbean vacation, I would have surrendered long ago.

Before I could reply, though, the front door was flung open, and Isaac walked in.

Yes...*walked.*

My eyes widened, and I almost blurted out a *what the fuck?*, but the warning look in his dark eyes stopped me. The strain was obvious in the taut cords of his neck and the way he moved stiffly, as if he had to tell his usually uncooperative limbs to make every movement, and yet I could tell he didn't plan to back down until I was safe.

The demon's grip on my arm only increased. "You're too late, *brujo*," he sneered. "I got her, fair and square."

"You got nothing," Isaac returned. His gaze shifted to me for a second. "Are you all right, Penny?"

"Just peachy," I said. No way in the world was I going to let this...thing...that was holding me know just how scared I was that we wouldn't be able to get out of this, that the spell which obviously was holding Isaac up might collapse at any second, taking him down with it. Exactly why he'd cast such a spell, I wasn't sure, since he seemed to safeguard his energy so carefully, but then it hit me.

The demon had already made a derogatory comment about Isaac's disability, had made it clear he didn't see the *brujo* as a worthy adversary. By walking into the confrontation under his own power, he was throwing the demon off balance, making the creature wonder if his human opponent might be stronger than he thought. And while I couldn't claim to be an expert at this sort of thing, I had to think that any time you made your enemy question whether his own abilities were up to snuff, that had to be a positive thing.

"Good." Isaac looked back at the demon. "I assume someone summoned you to do their dirty work?"

The demon's nostrils flared, but he actually gave a fairly direct reply...for him.

"That's how it works, isn't it?"

Once again, Isaac looked in my direction. His head inclined just the slightest bit toward the candle, as if he, too, understood that we would have to do this together if we wanted to succeed.

Fine by me...except for the part where I had absolutely no idea how we were supposed to proceed.

Luckily, Isaac didn't have that problem. From inside his pocket, he pulled out a pretty rosary, silver and with what looked like faceted garnet beads making up the chain.

"You will leave this place, foul demon," he intoned, his voice seeming to deepen with authority.

In response, the creature only snickered. "You're going to have to do better than that."

Well, in the movies, the exorcist never cast out the demon on the first try, either, and so I supposed I shouldn't be too disappointed that nothing much seemed to have happened after Isaac made his demand.

Undeterred, he took another of those miraculous steps forward. "You have no business here, demon."

The creature's grip tightened on my arm. "I have plenty of business. *She's* my business. You're the one who's butting in where he doesn't belong."

Okay, that was enough. "I am *not* your business!" I snapped, even as I drove the heel of my boot straight down onto his foot.

"Ow!" he yowled, and loosened his grip on my bicep just long enough that I was able to tear my arm from his grasp and go running over to Isaac.

"Good work," he said, eyes glowing with approval. "Take my hand."

No worries. I grabbed hold of Isaac's free hand and hung on like he was a life raft and I'd just survived the sinking of the *Titanic*. "Now what?" I murmured. The demon had taken a step toward us and then paused, as if he didn't know for sure whether he was ready to tangle with us as a combined force.

Or maybe he was trying to decide what to do next. It seemed clear enough to me that my biological grandmother—whoever she was—wanted me brought to her in one piece. If I got caught in the crossfire and harmed in some way, I had a feeling she wouldn't be too gentle with her demon lackey. She must have been hideously powerful, or she wouldn't have been able to order around a supernatural being like he was someone she'd hired to paint her house.

"Give me your strength," Isaac said. "Follow my lead."

I gave a cautious nod. Right then, I wasn't really sure what "giving my strength" even meant, but I'd do my best.

Once again, Isaac lifted the rosary. "I cast you out, foul beast! I send you back to the depths of hell from whence you came. You come from nothing, you are nothing. Leave this plane, worm!"

And even though I couldn't explain how it was happening or what Isaac was doing, I felt the oddest tingle in my fingers, looked down to see our clasped hands surrounded by a warm golden glow. That glow grew until it enveloped him completely—and me as well, my entire body shimmering with a light that looked like the sun coming up over the horizon on a clear summer morning.

The demon snarled. For a second time, his visage shifted, only on this go-'round, it didn't look as though he intended to return to his human shape. No, that was an honest-to-God demon standing there in an expensive dress shirt and lace-ups, his dark red skin slick with some kind of unholy sweat and malevolence gleaming in his blood-colored eyes.

But then he lifted his own hands, and glowing green light erupted from his fingertips, shooting outward at Isaac and me.

"Oh, hell no!" I cried out. I didn't even know what I was doing, but I imagined clear white light surrounding the two of us, sort of the way Isaac had told me to visualize the spell of protection settling around the little house in Nob Hill.

The demon's green fire exploded outward in all directions, knocking pictures off the walls and sending the throw pillows on the sofa into midair. To my relief, though, that seemed to be the only real damage the back-blow had caused.

Thank God. The security deposit on this place had been pretty hefty.

"Good work," Isaac murmured. "Let's keep it up."

He moved forward, and I went with him. Unfortunately, the demon didn't back away, but stood his ground, baring pointy yellow teeth at us.

"Cute trick," he said. "But you'll have to do better than that."

Before I could even blink, lightning lanced out from his fingertips. Isaac's fingers tightened on mine, and together we threw up a barrier, an invisible shield to protect us from the rogue bolts. Unlike the green fire, those bolts disappeared as soon as they hit the barrier, which was a good thing. I didn't want to think what might have happened if they'd continued to arc around the room.

"We *will* do better," Isaac said. "You have no place here, demon. I think it's time to cut your losses."

"He won't do that," I put in. "My grandmother hired him to fetch me. I think he's more scared of her than he is of us."

The demon's fangs bared again at the word "scared," but he didn't move.

"Is that it?" Isaac said. His tone had shifted, now sounded almost conversational, rather than those *Exorcist*-inspired commands he'd been tossing out a few minutes earlier. "Penny's family sent you?"

"Yes," the demon replied. "And a job's a job."

Isaac tilted his head. "True, but you don't have any personal interest in this, right?"

For a second, the demon's hairless brows drew together, as if he couldn't quite figure out what his adversary was driving at. Then he said in grudging tones, "Maybe."

"Well, then," Isaac continued reasonably. "Maybe we can work all this out. What if we could hide you from Penny's family, make sure they can't retaliate for you not bringing her to them?"

That suggestion didn't seem to go over very well, because the demon's nostrils flared as his thin lips lifted in a sneer. "You're not powerful enough to go up against them. They'll figure it out and come after me anyway, and grind you into dust along the way."

"Maybe, maybe not," Isaac responded. He still looked calm, assured, and not at all like someone trying to bargain a demon out of his new girlfriend's life. "It's hard for me to say, because I don't even know who they are."

That comment made the demon chuckle. "Ah, you think you're so clever, don't you? I can't tell you who they are. My body will literally explode into a million pieces if I say anything."

Ouch. That sounded like a hell of a curse—or one of the worst contracts I'd ever heard of. And I thought entertainment industry lawyers were tough.

Isaac, however, didn't seem too affected by these revelations. Voice still calm, he said, "Well, then maybe you don't need to say anything at all. Maybe I could cast a spell to hide you from them, and then you could go off and do whatever you want. Don't you demons usually jump at a chance to get to stay on this plane and have a little fun?"

The demon sent him a suspicious look...while I forced myself to stand there and bite my tongue. Honestly, I couldn't believe Isaac was seriously offering this creature any kind of deal that would allow him to escape punishment for what he'd done.

But then, he hadn't been around to hear the demon confess to murdering my mother. I supposed it was possible he thought the safest thing to do was to just make our unholy friend go away somehow without causing any more drama or fuss.

"We do," the demon said after a pause that went on for way longer than I would have liked. "Problem is, I don't think you're strong enough to cast that kind of spell on your own. You don't have any idea of who you're dealing with here."

"Because you won't tell us, jackass," I cut in.

Although Isaac didn't exactly shoot me a warning look, I got the impression he wasn't overly thrilled by my interruption. "No," he said easily. "On my own, I'm not. But I can work with Penny to cast the kind of spell that will ensure her family will never be able to find you or summon you again. Don't you think that's a reasonable solution to all our problems?"

He sounded awfully confident, especially since I had absolutely no idea how to cast such a spell, or even what shape it should take. But maybe he was just counting on using my strength as a sort of boost, so to speak, while he did most of the heavy lifting.

At the same time, though, I had to wonder if Isaac even had the magical reserves to do such a thing, considering he must also be expending a lot of energy to maintain the spell that kept him standing on two feet. If he collapsed, what would the demon do to him...to the both of us?

I really didn't want to think about that.

The demon scratched his hairless head. I couldn't claim to be an expert on demon expressions or anything, but he seemed to be both skeptical and hopeful at the same time. The deal Isaac had offered him was probably sounding pretty sweet, and yet I got the feeling that demons weren't exactly the most trusting people in the world.

"So...." the demon began, then paused. "You really think you can hide me from them?"

"On my own, no," Isaac replied. "But with Penny's magic in the mix, absolutely. You can kind of think of it like getting an inoculation. Since she'll be helping, using her own family's brand of magic to shield you, it'll be like getting a tiny bit of live virus to protect you from a far worse disease."

Once again, the demon went silent, considering.

Then he looked over at me and said, "Your grand-mother really is a pain in the ass to deal with."

"I'll bet," I replied. I doubted I could see eye to eye with a demon on all that much, but on that one particular topic, we were definitely in agreement.

And while I hated the idea of letting this creature get off scot-free—especially since he hadn't given me a single bit of useful information as to who this nefar-ious witch family of mine actually was—I also had to admit that the idea of pissing off my unknown grand-mother by sending her demon lackey to live in permanent bliss in the Bahamas was also pretty appealing.

"All right," he said at last. "I want this monkey off my back—so to speak. What do I have to do?"

Something about the tense set of Isaac's shoul-ders relaxed slightly. "Nothing at all," he said easily. "Just stand there while we cast the spell."

The demon nodded. "Okay."

Once again, Isaac tightened his fingers on mine. I held on to his hand, hoping to hell he knew what he was doing. What if the spell backfired, and instead of sending the demon off to some kind of permanent vacation, it brought my grandmother and the rest of my unholy biological family right down on our heads?

Isaac might have been a heck of a *brujo*, but I didn't see how he could possibly prevail in such a confrontation.

But because I had to believe he knew what he was doing, I just clung to his fingers and hoped for the best. And weirdly, I could almost feel the power passing from me into him, the glowing center of magic at the core of my being lending him the strength he needed to cast the spell that would remove this pesky demon from both our lives. Maybe one day I'd be able to do such a thing on my own, but I was so new to all this, I thought it better to just help with the assist rather than trying to fly solo...to mix a couple of metaphors.

Again, that thought passed through my mind, as if it came from someplace utterly outside me, the universe letting me know I needed to trust its guidance on this one.

You are stronger together.

I didn't know whether Isaac had picked up on that inner guidance, or whether it was telling me something he already knew, or at least had guessed. In the next moment, though, he lifted his head and stared straight at the demon, one of those faint smiles I'd come to appreciate so much tugging at the corners of his lips.

When he spoke, his voice seemed to reverberate through the room like thunder.

"I cast you out, demon! I consign you to the abyss, to eternal torture!"

The demon's eyes blazed red. "Fucking liar!" he spat.

But even as he hurled that insult at Isaac, the demon began to writhe, twisting in torment, although I couldn't see any reason for his current agony.

Well, except the words that continued to spill from Isaac's lips, words given extra power because of the magical strength I was lending him.

"Begone, and trouble this woman no more! You are banished from this plane, from the world of light! You may never be summoned again, but reside eternally in Hell!"

By that point, the demon had fallen to his knees, an unearthly keening issuing from his throat. However, at Isaac's last pronouncement, he went still, unearthly features almost hopeful.

"You mean that?" he asked, his voice barely a gasp. "I don't have to worry about ever being summoned again?"

"Yes, I mean it," Isaac replied in his normal voice. "I'm laying a geas on you that will keep you trapped in Hell forever."

"Then carry on," the demon said.

"I banish you!" Isaac cried out next.

Two things happened almost at once. First, the demon blinked out of existence, presumably on his way back to Hell. Second, whatever force of will that had been holding Isaac up seemed to desert him, because he sagged suddenly, crumpling on the oriental rug. And since I was holding his hand when he went down, I fell with him, sprawling across his torso as I barely managed to avoid face-planting in the middle of his chest.

"Oof," he grunted, and I immediately pushed myself up so I wouldn't be cutting off his airflow. While I had to admit that I'd sort of enjoyed lying on top of him, I definitely didn't want to prevent him from breathing properly.

"Are you okay?" I asked worriedly as I settled into a kneeling position.

He put a hand to his head. "I'm not sure."

"Where does it hurt?" What a stupid question. Considering the way he'd crashed to the floor, I had to assume it hurt everywhere...especially since he wasn't exactly of sound body at the best of times.

For a moment, he didn't reply, and I wondered if I should get up and grab my cell phone, call an ambulance. But then he said, "Nowhere. That is, I think the rug broke most of my fall." He glanced up at me, almost apologetic. "I think my walking spell is done for now, though. Can you help me over to the couch?"

"Sure," I replied.

It wasn't too easy to maneuver all six feet plus of him to the sofa, but luckily, it wasn't too far away, and all my years of schlepping props around definitely came in handy now as I somehow managed to leverage him onto the couch. He sort of flopped back against the cushions, then pulled in a breath.

"Much better. Thanks."

I got to my feet, then went over and sat down next to him. The house seemed almost preternaturally silent, the only sounds I could detect the ticking of a wall clock on the opposite side of the room and the faint hum of the refrigerator from the kitchen.

"Did we really get rid of him?"

Isaac glanced around, then nodded. "Yes, he's

gone. And he's going to stay gone, thanks to the way you lent your magic to mine, so it would be strong enough to lay a permanent geas on the demon to ensure he can never again leave Hell."

Because I still wasn't sure exactly what a geas was —some sort of magical command, I assumed—I knew I'd have to take Isaac's word for it. "My bio-grandmother is going to be pissed."

"Probably." A weary smile played around his lips. "But first she's going to have to figure out what happened to her pet demon, and since he won't be responding to her summons anymore, that could take her a while."

Isaac's reply relieved me a little. I had no reason to think this unknown grandmother of mine would give up so easily, but I wanted to believe the two of us had earned some breathing space.

"So...what now?" I asked.

Isaac glanced over at the clock on the mantel, then shifted so he faced me more directly. "If we hurry, we can still make our dinner reservation."

I stared back at him. Was he joking?

"You're seriously thinking about going to dinner after all this?"

"Of course," he said with a smile. "Banishing demons works up a hell of an appetite. Besides, do you know how hard it is to get reservations at El Farol?"

Not being a native Santa Fean, I couldn't hazard a guess.

And you know, I realized I was pretty hungry, too.

"Let me get my coat," I said.

———————

Penny's adventures will continue in *Finders, Keepers,* releasing in July 2022.

Also by Christine Pope

LATTES AND LEVITATION

(Cozy mystery/Paranormal romance)

Caffeine Before Curses (August 2022)

Magic After Muffins (October 2022)

Pastries and Prophecies (February 2023)

———

UNEXPECTED MAGIC

(Urban fantasy/Paranormal romance)

Found Objects (April 2022)

Finders, Keepers (July 2022)

Lost and Found (September 2022)

Finding Destiny (January 2023)

———

HEDGEWITCH FOR HIRE

(Mystery/Paranormal romance)

Grave Mistake

Social Medium

Household Demons

Perpetual Potion

Jingle Spells

Wandering Monsters

Uninvited Ghosts (July 2022)

THE WITCHES OF WHEELER PARK*

(Paranormal romance)

Storm Born

Thunder Road

Winds of Change

Mind Games

A Wheeler Park Christmas

Blood Ties

Healing Hands

Wishful Thinking

Smoke and Mirrors

MISS PRIMM'S ACADEMY FOR WAYWARD
WITCHES*

(Fantasy/Academy Romance)

Misspelled

Dispelled

Expelled

PROJECT DEMON HUNTERS*

(Paranormal Romance)

Unquiet Souls

Unbound Spirits

Unholy Ground

Unseen Voices

Unmarked Graves

Unbroken Vows

THE DEVIL YOU KNOW*

(Paranormal Romance)

Sympathy for the Devil

Charmed, I'm Sure

A Wing and a Prayer

THE WITCHES OF CANYON ROAD*

(Paranormal Romance)

Hidden Gifts

Darker Paths

Mysterious Ways

A Canyon Road Christmas

Demon Born

An Ill Wind

Higher Ground

Haunted Hearts

THE WITCHES OF CLEOPATRA HILL*

(Paranormal Romance)

Darkangel

Darknight

Darkmoon

Sympathetic Magic

Protector

Spellbound

A Cleopatra Hill Christmas

Impractical Magic

Strange Magic

The Arrangement

Defender

Bad Blood

Deep Magic

Darktide

THE DJINN WARS*

(Paranormal Romance)

Chosen

Taken

Fallen

Broken

Forsaken

Forbidden

Awoken

Illuminated

Stolen

Forgotten

Driven

Unspoken

THE WATCHERS TRILOGY*

(Paranormal Romance)

Falling Dark

Dead of Night

Rising Dawn

THE SEDONA FILES*

(Paranormal Romance)

Bad Vibrations

Desert Hearts

Angel Fire

Star Crossed

Falling Angels

Enemy Mine

TALES OF THE LATTER KINGDOMS*

(Fantasy Romance)

All Fall Down

Dragon Rose

Binding Spell

Ashes of Roses

One Thousand Nights

Threads of Gold

The Wolf of Harrow Hall

Moon Dance

The Song of the Thrush

THE GAIAN CONSORTIUM SERIES*

(Science Fiction Romance)

Beast (free prequel novella)

Blood Will Tell

Breath of Life

The Gaia Gambit

The Mandala Maneuver

The Titan Trap

The Zhore Deception

The Refugee Ruse

STANDALONE TITLES

Hearts on Fire

Taking Dictation

Golden Heart

Night Music: A Modern Reimagining of The Phantom of
the Opera

Ghost Dance: A Sequel to Gaston Leroux's The Phantom
of the Opera

Flight Before Christmas

* Indicates a completed series

About the Author

USA Today bestselling author Christine Pope has been writing stories ever since she commandeered her family's Smith-Corona typewriter back in grade school. Her work includes paranormal romance, cozy paranormal mystery, and urban fantasy, among others. She makes her home in New Mexico.

Christine Pope on the Web:
www.christinepope.com

 facebook.com/ChristinePopeAuthor

 twitter.com/ChristineJPope

pinterest.com/ChristineJPope

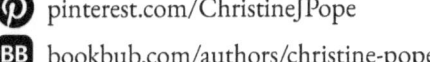 bookbub.com/authors/christine-pope